BREAKING OUT OF PINEWOOD

- - - - - - - - - - - - -

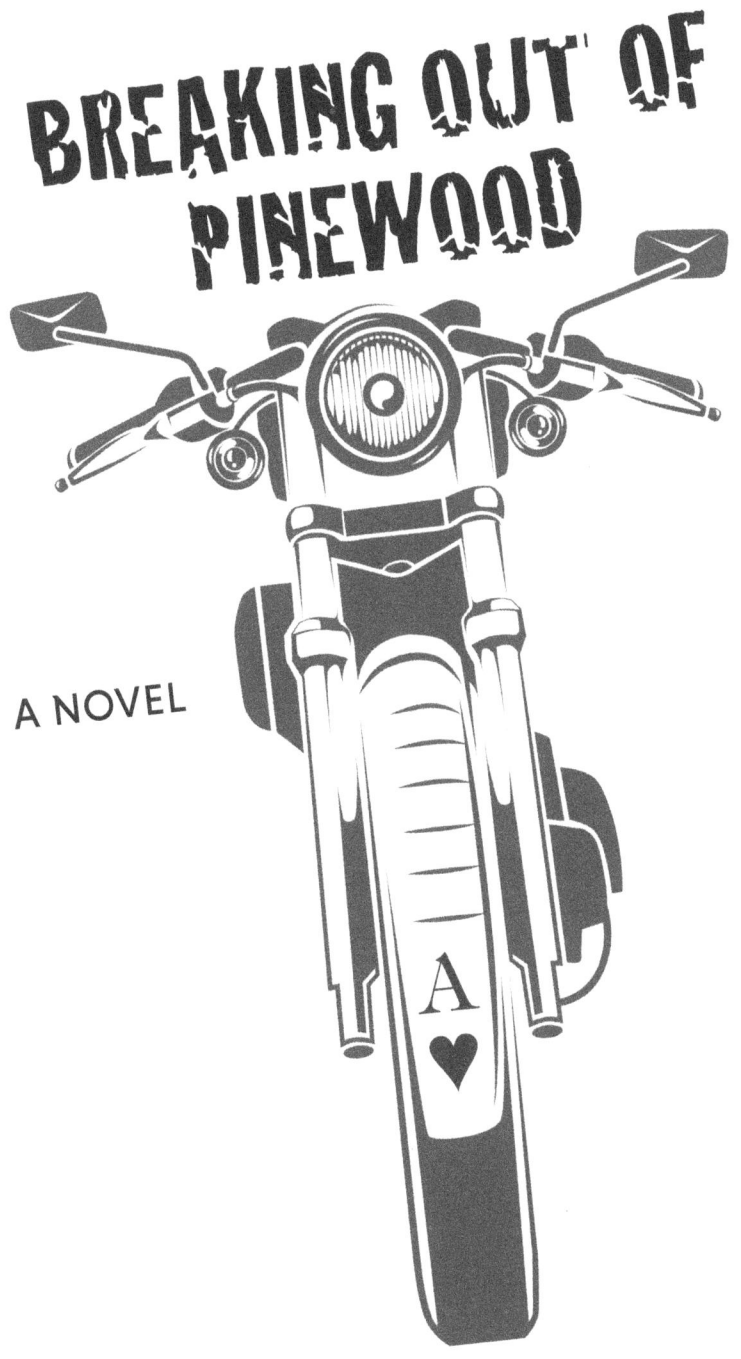

BREAKING OUT OF PINEWOOD

A NOVEL

LINDA K. GOLDMAN

Copyright © 2024 by Linda K. Goldman

All rights reserved. This book may not be reproduced in whole or in part without written permission from the publisher, except by a reviewer who may quote brief passages in a review; nor may any part of this book be reproduced, stored in a retrieval system, or transmitted in any form or by any means electronic, mechanical, photocopying, recording, or other without the express written permission from the publisher.

This is a work of fiction. Names, characters, businesses, places, events, locales, and incidents are either the products of the author's imagination or used in a fictitious manner. Any resemblance to actual persons, living or dead, or actual events is purely coincidental.

Edited by Martha Fuller
Layout and design by Sharon E Rawlins

PLENTIFUL PRESS
plentifulpress@gmail.com

ISBN 979-8-218-33600-4 Print
ISBN 979-8-218-37473-0 eBook

Printed in the United States of America

To Jack

FOR ALWAYS BELIEVING IN ME

CHAPTER 1

1963

WHEN FOLKS ASK WHAT I WANT TO DO WHEN I GROW UP, I don't have to think twice. "That's easy," I say, "break out of smalltown Pinewood."

Everyone knows the other guy's business in our tiny mountain town. Some of the old biddies can't wait to jump on the phone to gossip about who's getting up to what, especially me. "Angela's been fighting again," or "I saw her hitchhiking," and anything else that's no big deal.

Funny thing is, my own Mama and Pops don't pay me much mind.

You could say I'm growing up fast. Been doin' my own laundry since I'm eight. I'm used to it, now I'm thirteen. Anyhow, I can't mess up the clothes since nothing is new. It's all from thrift shops. Only my underwear is new, straight out of the Sears catalog.

My friend, Dede's mama, keeps telling me, "With your light-red hair and dark-brown eyes, you should wear green, Angela, green pants, green sweaters, green dresses."

"Dresses?" I say, "No way, no how I'm wearing a dress. Like I'm pretending to be some fancy girl from Denver?"

We already have enough green around here. No need to wear it.

Besides, clothes don't matter to me, not one bit. Maybe it would be different if I had a big sister. That would be nice.

I would like it even more if I had a real big brother. But I don't. So, I made up a secret big brother for myself a while back. No one knows about Eddie. Yep, Angela and Eddie, the O'Reilly kids. I see him as clear as can be in my mind. Like me, he has strawberry blonde hair, way more freckles, and stands five foot ten. When Mama and Pops go out at night to tie one on, I talk out loud to Eddie. Other times when they get into it, screaming and fighting, I think the roof might fly off the house. I thank God for Eddie.

I have a deep chill in my bones half the time up here in the mountains. If we had the money to do fun winter sports, maybe I wouldn't mind so much. I've heard about Aspen, a fancy ski town about an hour drive from here. Never been there. It might as well be 500 miles away. But Pinewood is no ski town, that's for sure. We're as basic as it gets around here. If you see a lady with lipstick, it's a small miracle. Or a big deal event, like today.

Mama sits me in front of the mirror. She wants me in red lipstick for our neighbor's Annual Summer Party. Not pink lipstick, *but red*.

"Why do I have to wear lipstick?" I ask. Mama frowns as she concentrates. Her left hand squeezes my face, so my lips pouch out. Such a roughneck. I heard that a roughneck is someone tough, crude, and ready to fight. . . .

"Owww!" I say.

"Oh, hush up," she says, and goes way over my lip line.

"Mama, I look like Bozo the Clown!" I wipe it on my sleeve. She throws up her hands and glares at me. I'm a thirteen-year-old kid. What could she be thinking? I've known these folks here on Beaver Drive my whole life. They would laugh if they saw me like this.

BREAKING OUT OF PINEWOOD

Most streets in Pinewood have names like Antelope Lane and Wildflower Road. But you heard it right. We live on Beaver Drive.

Been here since the day Mama brought me into this world. Pops said I came in kicking and fighting and squalling. Maybe I knew right then and there I shouldn't be stuck in this godforsaken town. When I can get a real job, I'll save every single penny so I can bust out of here.

Sandy and I sit in a couple of shaky old lawn chairs behind her house on Sunday afternoon. We don't have those nice green lawns like you see on TV. Nothin' but dirt and dried up pine needles.

"You know what, Angela," says Sandy, "you're like this pineapple." She takes another messy bite.

"A pineapple," I question, "and why do you say that?"

"Because," she says, juice dripping down her chin, "you're tough on the outside but sweet and soft on the inside."

"You think I'm tough?"

"Sometimes," she says. "Like the time you stole those roller skates at Skater Heaven."

I nod.

"And the old man caught you?"

"That's right. I *almost* got away with it."

"Whew!" she says, and brushes her hand across her forehead like it just happened. "I cried like a newborn baby, so scared he would call your folks."

"If they knew . . . ." I shudder.

"You asked him not to make the call," says Sandy. "And he listened. You stayed calm and cool and tough."

Sandy must see the hurt in my eyes. I don't think of myself as tough.

"But don't get me wrong," she says, "you are the best, sweetest friend *ever*."

The first week of August drags by. At 10 on Saturday morning, it's already 90 degrees outside. Sweat rolls down my neck. Mama and Pops yell their heads off, as usual, about the bills, the messy house, or who drank up the last of the booze. I push out the front door once I can't take it anymore. I make a beeline to the General Store. Sure enough, Dusty Britches sits in his usual spot on the front porch. He's been rocking there for as long as I can remember. He rocked when little Buddy Vespers fell off the roof and died helping his dad replace some shingles. He rocked when his wife ran out on him. He even rocked when Aunt Millie's Pies and Burgers closed their doors. The town folk had a Memorial Service in Pinewood Park for Millie. After years of hard work, she was all tuckered out. But Dusty Britches stayed put. He rocked through it all.

He must have the world's longest, whitest beard. Looks like Father Time. And now he's half blind. Can't see a thing unless you're right up in his face.

"Hey, Dusty," I say as the screen door slams behind me.

"That must be Angela," he says. He became a voice expert once his eyes started to fail.

"How are those folks of yours?" he asks.

"They're still like a couple of coyotes," I say, "howling at the moon." He chuckles. Everyone in Pinewood knows about Gerry and Grace, The Fighting O'Reilly's.

I creep past the work gloves, pliers, whiskey, wine, and beer and try to decide which candy bar to buy. I hand the new owner five cents for a Milky Way. She walks over to help another customer. When the time is right, I slide a couple packs of Juicy Fruit gum and an Abba Zabba in my jeans. Energy zips through my body. *I deserve it.*

When I do get sticky fingers, I only take small things, maybe an ashtray or a small toy, anything I can stash in my pocket. Once I get the stuff home, I may not even know what to do with it. Sometimes I throw it away. But not candy. No, I never throw candy away. I hide it in the bottom dresser drawer, under my PJs. Mama never looks in there. At least I don't think so. I bought a diary and hid that under my PJs, too, but changed my mind and tossed it out. If Mama ever saw what I wrote about her and Pops, she would throw a hissy fit.

I leave the General Store and know I need to kill more time before going home. I cross Pinewood Boulevard to the Go Get 'Em Café.

"Hey there, Angel," says Faye, the owner. She places a fresh baked apple pie in the glass display case. Those will sell out in no time. Everyone says it reminds them of their grandma's apple pie. Never met my own grandparents so I'll have to take their word on that one.

It cheers me up to see Faye Vespers' smiling face when she sees me. Makes me feel special. Her hair is tied up in one of those nets. I've never seen her without one. The hardest working woman in this town.

"Can I cut you a slice of pie?" asks Faye, wiping her hands on her apron. "My treat."

"Sure thing," I say. Would anybody in their right mind turn down an offer like that? She seems to know when I have trouble at home.

I settle in at the counter next to a burly truck driver. He's hunched over his Trucker's Delight Special of eggs, bacon, ham, hashed browns, baked beans, and toast. He never looks up once and plows through it in record time. I mind my own business, taking it slow and easy with the pie. Maybe things will settle down at the O'Reilly Funny Farm by the time I get there.

No such luck. When I open the front door, they're still going at it.

I hightail it out of there and head into the garage. I dig around until I find my stash of sketching pencils and big pad of white paper and tuck it under my arm. Once I make my way to Highway 133, I jam my thumb in the air for a ride. An old man with a veiny red nose from Pinewood recognizes me. He pulls off to the side of the road in his old jalopy pick-up truck. He tips his cowboy hat at me.

"Where you headed, young lady?"

"Can you drop me down the road at Fisherman's Bend?" I ask.

"Sure thing," he says, in his raspy voice. "Jump in." He doesn't say another word as he squints straight ahead at the winding highway. Only sound is the crunch of gravel under the tires. I'm glad we don't talk, that he leaves me be.

The old man drops me off where I asked. The Crystal River weaves back and forth with a family of cottonwoods at one bend. I find a favorite hideaway. The one between some bushes where me and my friends like to smoke cigarettes. Two fishermen cast their lines into the water. As their lines arch over, it looks like dreamy music. A shaggy dog, like the one from *Dennis the Menace*, stands by. He doesn't make a sound, like he knows not to bother the fish.

I pick up my pad of paper and get to work on sketching the pup. But I leave the grown-ups out of the picture.

CHAPTER 2

YOU MIGHT SAY I'M THE LEADER OF MY PINEWOOD FRIENDS, Sandy, Dede, and Sue. We're all the same age and take the same classes. We can do homework together. I should say, *they* do homework together. I'm not too interested in school. Even though Sue is the best student, and I may be the worst, they like my ideas. They all listen to me.

One time I talked Pops into taking us camping. We laughed, setting up our tents. That took about five times as long as it should have. Pops sat back in his camp chair and watched us struggle. When you're laughing, you don't care. We roasted hot dogs on long sticks over the campfire and sloppy, yummy S'mores. We laid on old Army blankets and looked up at the stars. We felt proud sleeping in those tents we set up all by ourselves.

Pinewood kids are bored to tears living here a big chunk of the time. And the grown-ups are too, most of 'em with dead-end jobs. That's sure true for my folks. Pops finished high school by the skin of his teeth. He's been a carpenter ever since. Too bad he's kind of clumsy. I stopped counting after he broke his thumb for the fourth time, not to mention three cracked ribs, a sprained arm, neck, and ankle. Mama spends most of her time at the Poker Palace. She can beat the pants off most of the men in town. When we walk down the street together, other card players call out to her. "Hey, it's Poker Face Grace." I want to hide.

When not playing poker, Mama doesn't get around to cleaning the house. So, who gets handed the job?

"Angela, get on into the kitchen," she says, looking up from *Photoplay* magazine. "Those dishes from last night need washing."

Besides that, I vacuum the rugs, sweep the deck, and scrub the sink so clean you could eat your lunch in there. I sing "Walk Right In" and "It's My Party" to make time pass.

Mama doesn't bother much with the neighbors or other ladies in town. Most afternoons, she hunkers down into the couch with her Camel cigarettes in front of the TV, watching *Queen for a Day*, her favorite show, where some poor lady may win a sewing machine or refrigerator because of her sad life. Mama can hardly tear herself away from that show. I'll watch it when I'm trapped inside from hard rain or heavy snowfall.

I wouldn't be surprised to see fish coming from the sky, it's raining so hard today. I settle in next to Mama, wearing her latest find from Miser's Mercantile thrift shop. It's faded jeans and a navy blue sweater with three deer parading across the front. Jack Bailey, host of *Queen*, reminds me of the guy on the Monopoly board, but without the top hat. He wraps a fur-trimmed cloak around a tiny haggard woman. Poor thing has five kids and a sick husband. Mr. Bailey hands her a bouquet of red roses and sets a crown on her head. She cries when they roll out a new Singer sewing machine like that's the best present she ever wished for. Mama, eyes glued to the screen, blows a few fat smoke rings.

"You've gotta watch out for most women. Never trusted them, myself." She exhales a thick line of smoke through her nose. "At your age, it don't matter much. When they're older, they talk behind your back."

My friends would never talk behind each other's backs. Not now, not ever. They're better than most grownups. I can tell Sandy anything about my folks, my dreams, anything at all, and she will never tell a soul. We love to sneak out of the house late on a summer night when a full moon lights the way. She brings just enough whiskey, so her Pops won't notice it missing. We talk about making our own money. We talk about escaping Pinewood one day. We talk about everything under the sun.

"Mark my words, Angela," says Mama, "you gotta be careful with women."

"What about these ladies on *Queen for a Day*?" I ask. "I bet they don't talk behind somebody's back." Mama, cigarette between her stained fingers, aims it at me, like a teacher pointing at the blackboard, ready to teach a lesson.

"It's different with those ladies," she says. I wait to hear why those ladies are different, but Mama tunes me out as *I Love Lucy* starts. I escape to my room and draw a picture of the lady on *Queen for a Day*, robe, crown, and all. It's still one crazy bad downpour. I hope it clears up soon.

CHAPTER 3

POPS LUMBERS IN FROM WORK AT 5:30 MOST NIGHTS, LATER in the summertime when it stays light out. Sawdust and dirt coat his overalls. Constant grime lives under his fingernails. As usual, he bangs his dented black lunch pail onto the kitchen counter. He and Mama don't even look at each other.

"What's for dinner, Grace?" Pops hollers.

Mama says nothing at first, but it already sounds like an argument.

"You'll see, *Gerry*," says Mama, her voice annoyed and flat. When she's not looking, he flips her the bird. He knows I see him making fun of her. She can be such a grouch. I don't blame him too much. Still, it makes my stomach hurt. Does he want me to laugh at her, to be on his team? This goes on *every single night*. I don't know what to do, so I do nothing. That seems like the best idea.

Mama's dinners are mostly out of a box, a can or somethin' thrown together. Tonight, we have Tuna à la King. I thought we would have a special dinner fit for a king. Turns out to be canned tuna, cream of mushroom soup, and canned peas heated together. She pours the mess over toast.

Pops frowns at the goop on his plate. "Canned spaghetti is better than this crap. What'd it take to get real food around here?"

"This is real food." Mama shovels in a forkful to prove her point.

Pops stands up, crashes the chair against the dining room table, and grabs a couple Coors from the fridge to escape outside to the deck. I eat a few bites and spit what's left of it into my napkin when Mama isn't looking. She finishes her tuna thing and lights up a cigarette while I bundle up to join Pops outside. He guzzles down the first can in one go. He holds it up to me.

"Love me a good Colorado Kool-Aid," he says, smacking his lips. "Not as much as you liked that Hershey's bar, though. Remember that?"

How can I forget the time I got a thrashing for stealing a couple of Hershey bars. Pops flipped me over his knee right there on the front porch of the General Store. All Main Street could see. I ran to Sandy's house and hid under her bed. It took less than an hour for Pops to figure out where to find me and drag me home.

"Course I remember," I say.

I love the cold night air on my face, relieved we got out of the house. But I sure wish my folks wouldn't argue so much. They loved each other when they were young. Do they still? I can't tell. It's hard to know.

"After a nice day," says Pops, "it's already cooled off fast." He leans on the deck railing and takes a deep breath, like he's on a ship looking out to sea, even though it's pitch-black out. "Must be in the high 40s. But that's September for you."

"I like this time of year," I say. I zip my jacket to my chin and jam my hands in my pockets to stay warm. I'll do anything to spend time out here alone with my Pops.

"How come you like it, Angela?" he says. No one calls me Angie. Not anymore. A long time ago, most everyone tried calling me by that dumb nickname. I threw a crazy fit. No one in their right mind would ever call me Angie again. I huddle into my jacket and explain.

"I like when the Aspens turn orange and red and gold." Still, I bet the warm Hawaiian sun would win out over the chill in Pinewood. Pops takes a noisy swallow of his second beer and plops in an old wooden chair. He pulls a pair of work gloves from his pocket, slips them on, and straightens up in his chair.

"I remembered somethin' I haven't thought about in a long while."

"What Pops?" I love his stories. Spending time with him always cheers me up.

". . . about a pet rooster I had when I was a little kid."

"You never said anything about a pet rooster?" I hang on to every word.

"Yup. A funny little guy. Followed me everywhere." He drifts off for a second like he sees the rooster in his mind. "His name was Raymondo," says Pops.

"Raymondo?"

"That's right. We got him from a Mexican family. They moved to an apartment in Rifle, so they gave him to us. He didn't understand English, only Spanish."

"What? How could you talk to him?"

"I couldn't. He had to learn English." I see a little smile creeping around Pops's mouth.

"What a smart rooster," I say. This is big news to me. I heard about the other animals but never this one. "What happened to Raymondo?"

"He fell in love," he says, chuckling, "with the chicken who crossed the road!"

"C'mon, Pops."

"Hah," he exclaims, "gotcha!"

I roll my eyes and say, "That's too dumb."

"But Raymondo was for real," he says. "I'd carry him around in my arms and sit with him on my lap." Pops's eyes go all soft and lovey. "We had him for the rest of his life."

"That's a crazy good story," I say. "I never heard about a rooster before. I sure hope you didn't end up eating him."

"No, we wouldn't do that. He was part of the family. We gave him a proper funeral out back where we buried all our dogs."

I've been begging him for a pup for as long as I can remember. He always puts me off. Maybe he'll make good on his promise to go down to the shelter and look for the right dog for my fourteenth birthday.

He looks sad thinking about Raymondo. I place my hand on his arm.

"Hey, Pops, who's all coming to your birthday party next week?"

He tears the cellophane off a new pack of Lucky Strikes, pulls the lighter out of his jacket pocket, and lights up the first one of the night. Most likely, he'll smoke half the pack by bedtime.

"Just us and some guys I work with," he says. "The years are rolling by fast." He shakes his head like he wants to shake off time. He flashes his devilish smile—the one Mama couldn't resist back then. Even with that scar down his right cheek, he's still handsome at thirty-one, almost thirty-two, with his thick black hair and flashing Irish eyes.

"But I'm still a kid," he says. That's true, in a way. Most of the time, I feel like the grown-up around here. I guess Mama and Pops didn't think about a baby when they were having all that fun. And then it was too late. Pops polishes off the beer and stuffs his Lucky Strike into the second empty beer can. He smacks me ever so soft on the arm. "C'mon Angela, let's go inside."

CHAPTER 4

*T*HE WEEK SLUGS BY WITH SCHOOL AND OTHER BORING STUFF. Mama and I head down the mountain to the A & P for groceries. The General Store in Pinewood only has the basics. We make a rare stop at Luigi's Pizzeria for a slice of pepperoni. Mama and I tear away at the pizza and wash it down with a bottle of Coke. She lights up a cigarette as soon as she's finished, but I'm still hungry.

"Can I have a second piece, Mama?"

"Don't be a greedy little pig. One is enough. Besides, you want to look good for your Pops's birthday party." Sure enough, she smacked me down like I thought she would. I steal a Snickers bar from the market and stash it in my pocket for later.

After waiting a week, it's time to celebrate my Pops's birthday. Mama said she'll do my hair for the party. I knock at her bedroom door. I can't remember the last time she allowed me in. It could be three years or more. She must be hiding some booze.

She opens up and motions for me to come in. I stay planted, unsure if she means it.

"What're you waiting for?" She grins like I'm an old friend. "Come on in."

She pulls a folding chair smack in front of the bedroom mirror.

"Don't just stand there." She pats the seat of the chair. "Sit down," she says, handing me a little woven basket filled with bobby pins. "Go ahead and hold it in your lap."

I remember she bought that basket at Miser's Mercantile for ten cents. That's the same day I wanted to bring home a skinny gray and white kitten crying outside of the store. Mama said no way.

"I'll tell you when to hand me a pin," says Mama. She sweeps a brush through my hair. I close my eyes. Her other hand clamps down on my shoulder like a stiff little parakeet foot, but I guess it's better than nothing. She stopped giving hugs when I was about five.

"I wonder if that hair of yours will stay strawberry blonde," she says. "Time will tell." She pulls and tugs at my crazy knots and curls to get it under control.

"Ouch! Can't you leave it be?" I say and hold the top of my head to protect it.

"Don't be so touchy," she says, "let me finish." She yanks extra hard.

"Oww!" I didn't want to sound like a baby, but it hurt.

"C'mon now, stop all your complaining." Her voice softens as she looks at me in the mirror. "Anyway, it's gonna look good." She keeps fussing over my hair for a long while, teasing and flipping it this way and that. At last, she lifts my hair off my neck and smooths it.

"Pin, please," she says. I dig into the basket and hand one to her. Six or so pins later, I have a perfect French roll.

"That's more like it," she says. "You look good with all that hair pulled back. You know you got that strawberry blonde color from your Grandma O'Reilly on your Pops's side." She claps her hands together. "So far, so good. Let's see how your friend Sandy's dress looks on you." She pulls out a peach-colored shift from the closet. Sandy's mama sewed it, not mine. She makes all of Sandy's clothes. They don't have much money either, but Sandy always looks nice.

"Turn around, and I'll button you up," says Mama. "All these little buttons are playin' games with my fingers." She stops for a minute to examine them. "Sure wish we had the money for a new dress."

"That's alright, Mama," I say. "You know I'm not much for dresses."

"Our little tomboy." She spins me around to the mirror again. "Take a look at yourself, Angela." It surprises me when her eyes water up. "You look downright pretty for your Pops's birthday."

I check myself out in the full-length mirror for another minute. "You know what, Mama, I like it. And look, I have legs."

She studies me like I'm a dead frog to be dissected in science class.

"Always wished I had long legs like you," says Mama. "How about some mascara to fancy up your big brown eyes?"

"No," I say, "I don't want it."

"How about some powder?"

"Mama, I said I don't care. Who wears all that stuff at thirteen anyway? I already told you when you made me look like a clown." She shoots me an annoyed look, sets the make-up aside, and breathes a long sigh like I'm the most impossible kid in the world.

"I just gotta say somethin' to you now." Her voice is dead serious, so quiet it scares me. "I don't think you realize how boys look at you, Angela." She lights a cigarette. "Men, too."

She looks at me hard to make sure I get the message. I plug my ears with my fingers and stretch my mouth all wide and goofy. "Mama, who cares? Boys are so stupid."

"Listen to me." She shakes a finger at me. "You can't be too careful. You don't want to end up like me." Her mouth locks down. She frowns into the mirror, pats her hair, and hikes up her blue dress. It's way too short since she gained all that weight. Like a tired old lady, she plunks down on the bed and sighs.

"I wanted to go to beauty school," she says. She catches a glimpse of herself in the mirror and takes a deep drag off her cigarette. "Too bad your father knocked me up. We had to get married. That wrecked my chances." My stomach tightens up every time she tells me this same old story. Like it's my fault. I didn't ask to be born.

"There I was, a mother at eighteen," she says. She stares at me as if I need to apologize to her. What do I have to apologize for?

"That really is crazy young," I tell her.

"That's what I'm sayin'. Way too young to get hitched and have a baby," says Mama. She yanks at her dress like that will make her feel better. "At least your Pops didn't run out on me," she says. "That's what happened to Mary Lou McCracken. And you know my own mama flew the coop when I was four."

Here we go again. *Stop!* I think. *Just stop it*. I want to run out of the room.

"Yeah, I know," I say.

"Only eighteen years old. I had no clue how to take care of a baby." Mama takes another deep drag from her Camel and plucks a few strands of tobacco from her tongue.

"Let's get a move on, girl," she says. "Your Pops is waitin' on us."

I follow as Mama clomps downstairs in high heels. I only saw her wear them at her and Pops's tenth-anniversary party in our backyard. Her two-inch heels kept sinking into the pine needles. Then she slipped and almost fell flat on her face. Good thing Pops caught her in time. As we walk over to get Pops, he perches on the edge of his rocker in a blue suit that's way too big for him, with his left leg set in a cast. This time he stumbled and landed on a pile of torn-up concrete.

"My two ladies are lookin' *fine*. Got to be there in ten minutes. Better shake a leg."

"We can shake a leg, but you better not," Mama grins at her joke.

"Very funny," he says, hoisting himself on his crutches. With his thick hair combed straight back, he looks handsome tonight in a fresh white shirt and paisley tie. "Come on, speed it up," he says. "Don't want folks to get there before we do."

Walking into the party, a couple of his pals, still in overalls from their workday, are holding up the bar and sucking back booze. Pops hops over to them on his crutches to shake hands and share a joke or two. Looks like the party started before we even got there. Someone decorated the back room at the Pinewood Inn. Everything is always at the Pinewood Inn. There is nowhere else to go. Red streamers and blue and yellow balloons hang from the ceiling. Pops grins and lights up like I've never seen before. He never had much.

Mama downs a couple of drinks in no time. She flirts with some curly-haired guy with bad skin who found his way into the party. I stand back from it all, glad Pops is having a good time on his birthday. Since I don't have any cousins, I'm the only kid in the room. I watch all this from a corner and sip on my Shirley Temple. Knowing Pops, he would slip some bourbon in there if he wasn't yakking it up with his friends, his tie already loosened up.

"Angela," he calls out and motions to me, "come on over and meet some of my pals."

Pops's voice booms too loud. One fat old guy in overalls looks me up and down.

"Whataya know, Gerry," he says. "Who'd have guessed an ugly cuss like you would have a good-lookin' daughter." His cronies crack up, including Pops.

"She looks like that movie star," says the fat guy. He snaps his fingers, trying for an answer. "You must know who I mean . . . the redhead with Elvis in *Viva Las Vegas*."

"Ann-Margret," Mama shouts from across the room.

"That's it," he agrees, "a young Ann-Margret."

He eyeballs me again, and I move closer to Pops.

"Yep, she's no movie star, but she's a looker," says Pops, and smacks me on the butt. I sneak out the side door as soon as I can. I don't need to stick around with these dirty old men getting more plastered by the minute. I spot a crumbled five-dollar bill on a table near the counter. I slide my hand across it, smooth as can be, and stuff it in my pocket. I don't know who left it behind. It's only five dollars.

I try my luck getting a ride. A truck driver with a cigar jammed in his mouth pulls up in a semi. "Jump in," he says. The gruff voice fits his sharp wolfy face.

BREAKING OUT OF PINEWOOD

"Never mind," I say, "I think I'll walk."
"Was it my good looks?"
He guns it. I walk the mile home in the dark.

CHAPTER 5

*T*HIS WINTER, LIKE EVERY OTHER ONE, MEANS HARD WORK. Pops and I borrow a neighbor's truck and load it up with axes and saws for the big job ahead. Everyone else gets their firewood in the summertime. Not us. Most folks can throw a few logs in the fireplace when cold weather hits. Meantime, Pops and I freeze our butts off deep in the forest.

"Come on, Bob, let's do this thing." That's what he calls me when he wishes he had a son. It used to hurt my feelings when I was little, but I'm used to it now. It mainly happens when we spend time outdoors in the forest or on the river. I wish he had a son, too, so I didn't have to do so much hard work.

I stand alongside Pops as we chop and saw, wearing thick warm jackets, heavy-duty gloves, and boots. The cold wind swirls around us. The pine trees reach high and so close together that no sun shines through.

Once home, we have more hard work to do. We unload the truck, strip off our wet clothes, and drop them on the floor in the mud room. I'm always pooped after a day or two of this, but at least I'm developing some serious muscles. Pops gives me a hefty pat on the back.

"Good work, Bob," he says, handing me a shot glass filled to the top. "Have some whiskey. You deserve it." We click glasses and drink up. He likes to treat me like a grownup every so often. Mama couldn't care less that he gives me booze.

Living far away from all the boozing and fighting is my dream. Someplace calm and quiet with white sand beaches and ocean so clear you can see the fish way below. My fifth-grade teacher brought a map of the world to class one day. For a teacher, he was a nice guy. He pointed out Europe, Asia, South America, and Africa. It was islands so small and far away that grabbed my attention. I wanted to know more. For the first time ever, I spent time in the school library browsing through books, getting lost in the photos. If there could be a heaven on earth, it must be Oahu. That's when the idea to bust out of this town took hold for the first time. For my next birthday, I asked Pops for a globe. It surprised him, but he got it for me. Now, I can point to the Hawaiian Islands with my eyes closed.

Pops slipped on some black ice and jacked his shoulder. He's out of work again, and Mama's in a snit. The three of us are trapped in the house with a storm raging outside. Mama skewers a ball of red and black yarn with her knitting needles. Her usual tense look softens as the needles click clack, click clack. It's the only sound in the house except for Pops snoring in his easy chair, feet wrapped up in his favorite brown Muk Luks.

"That man is getting on my last nerve," says Mama. He sits up in his chair.

"What is your problem, now?" He rolls his eyes, all dramatic-like. Mama ignores him.

"Most of the time," she says, giving Pops the evil eye, "knitting calms me down. Why don't you give it a try, Angela?" I like the clicking of the needles, but that doesn't mean I want to do it myself.

"Do I have to?" I ask.

"Just do it." Mama starts me off with thick yellow yarn and gives me a quick lesson.

"See this here?" she says. "Just watch me." She moves her hands fast, weaving the yarn over and under the needles. "That's it, and you're done. See? Easy."

My hands don't understand what to do. My neck tightens, and my shoulders are up high under my ears. I'd rather be outside riding a horse, shoveling snow, or swinging an ax with Pops. At least we joke around, and we're outside moving around. Mama's eyes are two hard marbles. Thirty minutes feel like five hours. The few rows I finish come out all crooked and tight.

"Is someone torturing you?" asks Mama in her meanest voice. I set the trainwreck down on my lap. Pops wants no part of it and scoots out of the room.

"I'm doing the best I can," I say. "It's just not for me."

"Keep going," she says, her mouth as crooked and tight as my knitting.

"*I hate this.*" I slam the thing down on the floor. Mama drops a half-made sweater in her lap, her face all squinched up like she just bit into a lemon.

"What the hell is wrong with you?" she says. She picks up my mess of yarn. "This looks worse than a mule stuck in shit." She never misses the chance to tell me how bad I've screwed up. Now she wants me to be an awesome knitter. She examines the rows like she's about to perform surgery.

"You did a lousy job." She clucks her tongue. "What could be easier than knitting?"

"I'd rather chew glass," I say, shooting to my feet. "I got a crick in my neck."

No way will I ever pick up knitting needles again.

"Why can't you be like other girls?" says Mama for the zillionth time.

"I don't know, I'm just not." I race up the stairs and plop on my bed. My forehead stretches to the top of my brain, setting off a blasting headache. I call Sandy.

"Hey," I say, "can you talk?"

"Only a few minutes," says Sandy. "Dumb math homework." I walk the phone over to the window and keep my voice low.

"Mama is such a mean shithead."

"Uh oh," she says. "What happened this time?"

"She wants me to learn to knit," I say. "But I hate it and—"

"Get off that god dang phone and do your homework," yells Pops from downstairs.

I yell back, *"In a minute."*

"What did you say to me? Who do you think you're talking to?" He pounds up the stairs and yanks open my bedroom door but a little too hard, wrenching his bad shoulder.

"Ow," he yowls, "fuckin' door!" He kicks a hole in it to teach it a lesson.

"Gotta go," I say.

I take a warm shower to wind down but take a minute to stand naked in front of the mirror. Can't believe I'm up two sizes since I started wearing a bra at twelve. Mama's right about one thing: boys do stare at me 'specially the ones at school. That's why I keep my boobies covered up as much as I can.

I move closer to the mirror and flash a big dumb smile to check the gap between my teeth. It makes me look like Howdy Doody. At least it's not getting bigger. I run a brush through the knots in my hair. I do kind of like my hair. No one else at school has strawberry-blonde hair. Come to think of it, I can't think of one other person in Pinewood. Does it make me special? I don't know.

CHAPTER 6

1965

Saturday nights in the summertime, folks pour into Pinewood Park for a blues, rock, or country band. We toss off our shoes, feet happy and free as we dance on the soft grass. Everyone around us dances to their own style. It could be the only time they don't gossip about each other. Parents order their kids to stay close by as they sway to the band drinking their wine or beer. When the sun disappears behind the mountain, everyone bundles up in blankets or jackets. Some ladies leave the park and check out the latest at Ollie's Antique Shop, a tin-roofed store loaded with junk. They stay open late on Saturday nights in summer because of the crowds. There's old garden furniture you might have seen at your friend's house a week ago. If you're lucky, you may find a baby doll or Elvis Presley ashtray.

Sometimes guys on motorcycles roar into town and drown out the band. They rev their engines to show off. Mama sees me looking at them, maybe a little too long for her liking. She comes over, grabs my arm, bourbon heavy on her breath.

"Stop it, Angela," she says, frowning and giving me a piece of her mind. "Bikers are nothin' but bad news." She pinches me.

"Ouch," I complain, "why'd you do that?"

"I mean it, girl," she says. "You listenin' to me?"

I rub the sore spot on my arm.

"I *hear* you."

With the sky turning dark, it leaves a chill in the air. I wrap myself in the rose-colored shawl Sandy knitted for my fifteenth birthday.

"Just mind what I say," says Mama, "it can only lead to no good."

I try to be good, oh how I really do.

CHAPTER 7

1966

A SUMMER NIGHT IN PINEWOOD PARK IS THE BEST, cheapest Saturday night in town. Tonight, we have a new bluegrass band from Gunnison called Livin' It Up.

Mama and Pops get up from their picnic blanket and dance that funny way they do, their first six-pack of beer long gone. Lots of other codgers join in while Sandy, Dede, Sue, and I sit right in front of the stage. Sandy flirts with the guitar player, who throws it around like a wild man, more like a rocker than a bluegrass guy. Sandy squeals with excitement when he winks at her. Once the band takes a break, Sandy's musician crush doesn't even talk to her, and her smile disappears.

Now that we're sixteen, we talk more about boys. I wish I could talk to Danny Doyle, but he's glued onto Wendy the Snob. She's bragging about her trip to Hawaii, of all places. Hawaii!!

"The water at Lanikai Beach is so clear," Wendy says, "you can stand and see coral reefs."

Sandy shoots me a look. *What a show-off.*

Jealous to the gills, I don't want Wendy to know how long I've dreamt of Hawaii.

The bandstand lights up with multi-colored bulbs as the sun drops behind the mountain. The mood shifts into nighttime mode. I stand up and brush some dried leaves off my jeans.

"Guys, I'm going to get some ice cream from the General Store. Anyone want to come with me?" No takers, so I cross the street for a mile-high rocky road cone. I pass Danny Doyle, who now has his arm around Wendy's waist. When he sees me, he nods, and that's it. So far, Danny is the only boy I've ever kissed. It happened at Sandy's Sweet Sixteen birthday party in January.

When Sandy put that crazy good song, "At Last" on the record player, Danny asked me to dance. He held me closer and closer as we danced the rest of the night, swaying to the music. Then he kissed me as natural as can be. We spent our time together listening to music at his house. We held hands wherever we went. Then Wendy got her hooks into him. I don't know how it all happened. He made some dumb excuse and broke it off with me after two months. It hurts my heart that he doesn't even say hi.

As I cross the street with my ice cream cone, the sky gradually turns darker. A guy sits on his Harley under the soft light of a streetlamp. I notice him checking me out. He must be twenty-three or so. My ice cream melts down the side of the cone. I'm licking as fast as I can.

"Hey, pretty girl, I sure do envy that ice cream cone of yours." His sun-streaked hair is long, with a red bandana tied across his forehead. I smile to myself and keep licking away at the cone. Looks like he takes good care of his motorcycle. It's so shiny he could have bought it yesterday. He smiles at me, admiring his bike.

"I must admit," he says, "she's a beauty. Why don't you jump on? I'll take you for a ride." I shrug and keep walking but slow down a bit. I glance back at him. His black motorcycle jacket reads *Open Road* in yellow block letters. He shifts his body on the seat of his bike, kind of slow and easy like.

"Ever been on a Harley before?" His rough growl softens to warm syrup. That voice of his and those turquoise eyes get me all stirred up. I've never met anyone like him before. I want to keep walking, but I don't move. I bet he knows what I'm thinking. He can see right inside my head. I just know it.

"We'll go for a few minutes," he says, "and I'll bring you right back." He revs the motorcycle again. "It'll be fun, you'll see." I finish off the ice cream cone with a few bites. I wonder if any of it stayed on my face.

"My Mama would kill me," I say, "and I'm not kidding." I jam my hands, nice and safe, into my jeans. He gives me a sideways grin and pats the seat behind him.

"You're okay, darlin'. I don't see no mama 'round here."

Off in the distance, Mama and Pops are still on the grass, getting plastered. They won't notice if I'm gone for a short while.

"That's true," I say. I don't know what to do next, so I do nothing but stand there like a stone statue.

"Come on, darlin'," he says. I can't get over that voice of his. "We'll just go for a quick ride." The smell of fuel triggers more excitement. Those eyes, the same color as the wise old Crystal River in summer, look like they've seen it all. He's as handsome as a movie star, and he's talking to me?

"I don't know," I say. "Maybe." My blood races.

"You'll be okay," he says. I would love to jump on that bike and follow him anywhere. All jumbled up inside, I look down at my feet. His eyes are all over me. I squeeze out a few words.

"Promise to bring me right back?" I say. He crisscrosses over his heart.

"Promise."

"What's your name?" he asks.

"Angela."

"Angela with the face of an angel. That name suits you to a tee." He has an easy laugh.

"I guess we're both on the A-team. My name is Ace." I like his deep tan and the creases in his forehead. All man. He pats behind him again on the leather seat.

"Just throw your right leg over, Angel, and scoot behind me." His Harley is a big machine. I've seen them many times as they pass through Pinewood. They're always on their way to somewhere else. I do as he says and swing my right leg over the bike, the same way I mount a horse.

"Hold on to me," he says. I wrap my arms around his strong body and hang on tight. He smells of leather and sweat and living free.

"Okay, ready?" he says. "Here we go." As he moves onto the highway and picks up speed, my shirt flies up and ripples like a flag, the cool wind against my bare back. The road stretches and curves as we speed up to Marble. The stars are reaching out, like we're on our way to heaven. This is way different than looking through the windshield of Pops's truck. The smell of the fuel, me close against Ace, arms wrapped around him, and the roar of his motorcycle gets me all springy inside like I'm going to pop wide open. I can't hear what he says with all the noise and him talking into the wind, but it doesn't matter. I'm having the time of my life.

When Ace sees a turnoff and circles the Harley down the mountain to Pinewood, it's way too fast for me. We only got started, and now he's turning around. I want to keep going; for this to last forever. But he's keeping his promise like he said he would.

We land in the same exact spot where we started.

"That was crazy fun," I say.

"Yeah," he says, "and this is just a short ride. You've got to see what it's like on the open road." His smile is so big I want to smile right back, but I don't smile much. I jump off, and he grasps my wrist, not hard but warm and firm. His touch sends tingles all through my body. I can't look into his eyes, so I study my boots instead.

"Maybe I can take you for a longer ride one day soon," he says. "Would you like that?"

"It beats pokin' my eye out with a stick," I say.

"What?" he laughs. I better calm down my smart-ass attitude.

"I mean, sure," I say, "that sounds okay." What am I saying? I must be loco. This good-looking hunk wants to see me again. What is going on? I've only had one real boyfriend.

"Want to meet on Monday, say 4?"

"Well, yeah, alright." I sound like such a dumb cluck. The words come rolling out my mouth like I can't help it. I have no control. My heart pounds so hard I'm afraid he might hear it.

"I'll meet you right over there," he says, pointing to a cluster of pine trees. "Sound good?"

"Uh huh." The words almost stick in my throat.

"See you then." He guns the bike and looks over his shoulder. "Don't forget, darlin'."

CHAPTER 8

*E*VEN WITH ALL THE BUSYBODIES IN TOWN, WE KEEP OUR meetings a secret. After school, I ride my bike near the 50-mile marker on the 133, then hide it in the bushes. Ace swoops in on his Harley in that black leather jacket and worn jeans.

First few times we get together, he takes me for rides over McClure Pass, the roar of the bike on the road, me with my cheek pressed against his back, escaping Pinewood for a short while. He gives me a soft little kiss on the cheek. Next time we stop at a roadside stand and buy some apples straight out of the orchard. We chomp on them, watching the world go by as we sit in tall grass and wildflowers scattered on the hillside.

Everything we do together seems special to me. This is living, I think to myself. I'm not sure what he sees in sixteen-year-old me. But we have conversations that are much bigger than my own small life. He tells me of his travels through Montana, Oklahoma, New Mexico, and Utah, stoking the fire inside me to see the big world outside of Pinewood, beyond the Colorado state line.

On our third outing, he kisses me in a way that never happened with Danny Doyle, that's for sure. I feel my temperature rise, and I want more kisses. I want more of him. He lays me down in the grass, a kind of deep kiss that I never knew existed. My breath comes heavy when he kisses my neck and smooths my hair away from my face.

"I think we should go," he says without explaining. *Wait*, I think, *why?*

I follow him back to his Harley without a word, wondering why he decided to leave, wondering what he must be thinking, but too shy to ask. We stop at our usual meeting place with one more long deep kiss that leaves me weak in the knees. Ace climbs back on his bike. He rubs his jaw as if he has something to say. He looks over my shoulder a minute, concentrating on something or another, and comes back to me, fixing on my eyes.

"I'll see you here on Thursday, same time," he says. "Okay?"

"Okay," I say, hungering for him.

On our fourth get-together, I jump on behind him, and we race up the mountain to his friend's house. It's some guy named Gus, who owns the Phillips 66 gas station down in Copperville. We walk across the yard, chickens scattering here and there as he shows me around. He points out the one-eyed horse standing alone in the corral.

"I hear he lost his girlfriend a few months ago," says Ace, "so he's still getting over it." Hearing that he knows animals have feelings opens my heart. He smiles down at me, takes my hand into his, and leads me into the empty barn, except for an old tractor and a few hay bales. He wraps his arm around me and pulls me in for a hug.

"I want to make love to you, Angel," he says. "I want you, but I need to know—do you want me, too?" I nod, unable to squeeze out the words at first.

"Are you sure?" he says. "Can you tell me?"

"Yes," I whisper. "I'm sure. I am scared, but I am sure."

He smooths out a blanket, lays me down with his big strong hands, and strokes my hair. I squeeze my eyes shut.

"Angel," says Ace, "I want you to look at me." He kisses me long and deep, like he wants to swallow me up inside him. He kisses my neck. I tremble as he moves slow and easy, making sure I'm okay, as he unbuttons my shirt and slides off my bra.

"It's going to be okay, baby." He slips out of his jeans and takes mine off. His hands move gently over my shoulders and arms. He takes his time and teases me, scattering little butterfly kisses over my tummy, then my breasts. The only time anyone ever touched me there before was on a dare. Not even Danny got that far. Some dumb kid slammed me against a tree and grabbed my boobies hard. Now I know the difference. I open my eyes and tremble some more.

"You okay?" he asks.

"Uh huh." I don't know what else to say. This is all so new, scary, and exciting. He reaches between my legs and caresses me. His hands wrap around me, holding me. Once his finger slides inside, my brain shuts down, and my body takes over.

"Ready for me, baby?"

"I think so," I murmur. "Never did this before." He cradles my head in both hands and kisses me softly on my lips.

"I'll take good care of you." He slips on a condom, his voice calm and soothing as he talks me through it. It hurts, but not as bad as I thought it would. I've heard awful stories from girls at school. That's what made me so scared. I can tell this is different. Very different. Ace holds me close through it all, kissing my neck, looking into my eyes, whispering in my ear. This has nothing in common with all the bad stories from those girls at school. Ace knows how to treat me. Their first time was with high school boys. His hands cupping my head relaxes me.

"That's it, baby," he says, "I want to make you happy."

It doesn't take long before we find a rhythm together. And I thought riding on his motorcycle was like heaven. My fingertips fly off my hands, my toes leave my feet. Afterward, Ace wraps me up in his arms like he wants to keep me safe. He kisses my eyelids.

"Not so bad?" Those turquoise eyes lock onto mine.

"No, not so bad," I whisper, my shyness returning. "Not bad at all." Ace pretends like he's wiping sweat from his forehead.

"Whew, that's a relief. I hoped it would be good for you. Well, anyway, as good as possible."

"Can I ask you somethin'?" I sit up and touch his arm, wondering what I will say.

"Sure you can," he says.

"I'm a woman now, right?" A soft summer rain pitter-patters on the roof of the barn. His eyes crinkle up, and he pulls me in close to him.

"Yeah, you are a woman now." He strokes my hair, and I purr like a contented pussycat.

Within no time, he's hard inside me again. We can't get enough of each other. We start out tender and sweet, lovin' each other, and then we're like wild bucking broncos. Even with the rain, now a downpour, we fall asleep, arms and legs wrapped around each other. Once my eyes pop open, I grab my jeans and slide them on quickly. It's almost 5:30. I better get home quick.

"You know what, baby?" Ace runs his hand through his long thick hair.

"What?"

A month ago, he rolled into town, a stranger on his motorcycle, and now we're here together. He made me a woman. I don't know what will happen next. If they knew about this, Mama and Pops would shoot me, or him, deader than dead. Ace throws a kiss like he's a French chef that is happy with his meal. Only saw it on TV, but that's what it looks like.

"That was awesome," he says.

"Really, it was awesome?" I pull my shirt over my head, waiting to hear more.

"And you know what else?" A little smile dances around his lips.

"What?" I ask, moving in close, curious to hear what he will say.

"You are one fast learner." He pets my hair.

"What?" I smack him with both hands on his arms and chest, pretending to be mad.

"Kidding on the square," he says and grips my wrist. I freeze at first, but he pulls me up against his strong chest and hugs me for a long time. Now I know everything will be all right.

CHAPTER 9

*E*VERY TIME I SEE ACE, HE TELLS ME HOW I SHOULD BUCKLE down in school and study. He listens to me like no one has ever done before. He seems to care what I have to say. He wants me to have a good life. I tell him that I like to draw.

"Keep going," he says. "Keep practicing. I would love to see what you can do." Next time we meet, I bring him a pencil drawing of Star, my neighbor's gray mare. He raises his eyebrows like he's surprised.

"You know what," he says, "this is really good." He sets the paper down on Gus's kitchen table and studies it. "I would love to see more." He continues to look for a while and scratches his head. "Maybe your folks would sign you up for art classes." My heart fills up from the thought but empties out as fast as it floods in. For sure, he doesn't know Mama and Pops.

"Naw, they wouldn't do that," I tell Ace. "They think it's a waste of time."

"It doesn't matter," he says. "You are good. Keep on going. You hear me? You have talent."

Ace likes to tell me stories about his adventures but doesn't say much about his childhood. Back in Gus's kitchen one Thursday afternoon, we put together a couple of bologna sandwiches on Weber's bread. Ace sits across from me at the yellow Formica table as we eat.

"You know," I say, "I've lived in Pinewood my whole life, right?"

"Sure, I do," says Ace. He nods at me as if to say, go on. The late afternoon sun streams through the window, landing on Gus's lazy gray cat, stretched out on the kitchen counter.

"It's kinda funny," I say, "but you never said where you grew up. I'm kind of wondering."

"Oh," says Ace, busy with his sandwich, "it's not important, you know, lots of different places . . . here and there."

The clock ticks overhead. It's the only sound in the room. He looks over my shoulder instead of at me. I want to know more about him, but he doesn't explain or say another word. I don't know much more about him than the day we met. I want to know *everything* about him. When he's lovin' me, he says how beautiful and sweet I am, how he loves being with me. The rest of the time, he doesn't talk like that.

Each time we meet, we make tender love, the crazy wild kind, or both. We even do it with me straddling him on his motorcycle. He makes me laugh with his jokes. When we're not together, I think of him all the time. It's funny, but I never tell anyone about him. Not even Sandy.

One afternoon in September, Ace and I lounge on Gus's brown plaid couch in the living room, our feet propped on his pine coffee table. In the middle sits an old ashtray from the Pinewood Inn overflowing with cigarette butts. Scattered all over the room are *Hot Rod* magazines. Ace reaches behind him.

"I have a little present for you," he says. He hands over a 33 1/3 record, *Hard Travelin'*, by Ramblin' Jack Elliot.

"Should I open it?" I say. Funny when my shyness takes over and when it doesn't.

"Sure thing," he says, "let's put it on the stereo." We settle into the couch nice and easy like the best of friends. Ramblin'

Jack rolls out the words like he's rolling down the highway. Ace leans back and closes his eyes with the nicest little smile on his face.

"I bet you sound just like him when you sing," I say. Ace goes pink, laughs, and slaps his knee.

"You're way off base on that one, Angel. I love music but can't carry a tune worth a damn. Wish I could, but I can't." He pets my arm. "Thanks anyway, sweetheart."

I always think of Ace when I play the record at home on our old Phillips record player. It's real down-home Colorado kind of music. Even my folks like it. Good thing they never ask where I got it, but I'd come up with some kind of answer. A week later, Ace gives me *The Free Wheelin' Bob Dylan*. I listen to "Blowin' in the Wind" over and over again.

"Is that supposed to be music?" says Pops. "People pay good money for that crap?"

"Turn it off," yells Mama. "He gives me a headache."

Ace doesn't stay anywhere for more than two or three months. He takes odd jobs for a while, and then he moves on. He loves to tell me stories, like when he rode his Harley across Mexico. He met the Ramos family in a small town near Guadalajara.

"Kindest folks I ever met," he says, "inviting me to eat with them when they didn't have much for themselves. I can't speak Spanish, and they couldn't speak much English, so we could hardly talk to each other. But we laughed. We ate *pozole*, a kind of stew. We drank tequila."

He gazes off somewhere like he's seeing a movie in his mind. I want to see it and share it with him, too.

"Somehow, those folks and I understood each other," he says, staring straight at me, "like we were family, you know?

I'll never forget it. Best part for me, though, is when it's just me, my bike, and the road."

My stomach takes a deep dive.

"Please, *puh-lease* take me with you when you go." He kisses me, his lips soft on mine.

"I'm sorry, Angel. When I'm on the road, it's just me, solo, all the way. That's how I like it. Right now, I'm here with you. Let's enjoy it."

He kisses me again, and I sink into him.

Mama doesn't notice all the afternoons I'm gone with Ace. Doesn't ask where I've been or what I've been doing. One time I come home as the couch flames up from her cigarette. There she was, stone drunk, her mouth hanging open, snoring up a storm.

First, I grabbed the dog's dish and threw water on the fire. Then I ran to the sink and filled up a pitcher. Mama tried to hide the burned-out spot with a doily, but any fool could see that a doily didn't belong there.

I always wished for a mother like Mrs. Nelson on TV with her handsome sons David and Ricky, always pretty in her dresses and high heel shoes. Mama is nothing like Mrs. Nelson, in her thrift store clothes and a cigarette hanging from her mouth.

I live for the afternoons. I can escape from my boring life and sneak off with Ace. Whenever I'm not with him, he's on my mind. I think about him when I'm at home in my room or doing chores, but especially when I'm in class, and my teachers catch me daydreaming.

After a few months, Ace talks about Montana and Wyoming. I know in my heart he wants to hit the road again.

"Can't you stay awhile longer?" I ask. He smooths the hair away from my face and kisses my forehead. We're sitting on a blanket, a slight September chill in the air.

"I can't, baby, not much longer." He stands up and walks in circles, looking down at his big, strong hands that know every inch of my body.

"I told you from the start," he says, cracking his knuckles, "remember?" I nod. It's true, he did tell me, but it doesn't matter. What will I do when he goes? He gets to travel, having new adventures, and I'm stuck here in Pinewood.

"I've got to keep moving," he says. Does he care that he'll be leaving me behind? Moving means more to him than I do. When he sees fat tears roll down my cheeks, he scoops me up and kisses me. Our tongues dance until I'm dizzy. He flips me onto my back, pins me down on the blanket, and rips off my jeans. We go for a long time, panting like two wildcats. He looks into my eyes and then buries his face in my neck.

"I love you, Angel." His words are muffled as he nuzzles me, but I hear what he says as clear as can be.

He loves me! I can't get his words out of my head. No way can I sleep tonight. I stare at the ceiling. In the morning, I drag myself to school and daydream all through class. I've wanted to tell him I love him so many times but was too scared to say it. I ride my bike to the usual spot and wait, hidden in the bushes. Time crawls by. It seems like an hour or so. My stomach starts to cramp up. He's never late.

I wonder if he had an accident. I open my canteen for a long cool drink of water. Maybe that will settle my jumpiness. A deer family comes up close to me. I hold my breath. The mom leads her two fawns across the highway. Their golden coats glow against the black macadam road, but they cross in a tricky spot, where it bends into a blind curve. The doe and one of her babies make it across. A second later, a Walmart truck almost hits the other fawn by a few inches. The creep doesn't even slow down to make sure she's okay.

I breathe deep once the three deer take off together, soon out of sight.

CHAPTER 10

WEEKS LATER, I CAN STILL IMAGINE ACE'S SEXY GROWLY voice, his scent of leather and sweat. One day he says he loves me, then *poof*, he's gone. I begin to call myself Angel, just like he did. If anyone calls me Angela, I ignore them. Sadness drags me down and takes over my life.

My stomach aches, my body aches, I can't stand it when the stupid boys at school talk to me. I miss his tough, tender love and our special talks. I miss his encouragement to keep drawing and do well in school. But nothing matters now. My grades drop down worse than ever. Teachers send notes home to my folks.

Mama silently mouths every word as she reads the notes before sitting at the dinner table. She wads each one in a ball and chucks it on the floor. She flings off her apron and bangs her hands on the oak table. I don't feel too good about what's coming next. Pops looks up from his food.

"What's the damn ruckus about, Grace?" He pulls out a Kleenex from his overalls and blows his nose.

"Gerry, listen to this," says Mama. "Your daughter is almost failing two classes." He nods and shovels a huge forkful of mac and cheese into his mouth.

"I wasn't much of a student, Angela," says Mama.

"It's Angel!"

"Listen, you little smart-ass," she says, "I think I know your name. At least I never failed a class, *Angel*." Her voice thick with sarcasm, her eyes drilling through me. She looks to Pops. His cheeks bulge with food.

"She'll find her way," he says. I can see the orangey yellow of his dinner as he talks. He doesn't look at me, not even for a second. They talk about me like I'm not sitting right there. Invisible. I want to scream, but I keep quiet. Pops can blow the roof off the house when he's mad.

"She could already have her driver's license," says Mama. Let's make her wait an extra year. That would teach her a thing or two."

"Come on, Grace. Do you really think that would help? She's her own person, just like her old man." He pats me on the forearm and wipes his mouth with his sleeve.

"That's all you have to say, you cracker?" says Mama, wiping her hands on her dress. She clears the table, dishes rattling all the way.

"Angela, Angel, whoever the hell you are," says Pops, "get a move-on into that kitchen. Give your mother a break." He winks at me. True to form, my folks never mention my bad grades again.

Ace always listened to me—really listened. I told him of my dream to live at the beach. He encouraged me in so many ways. Then he took off and left me behind. Nothing makes sense to me anymore. It's like there's a storm raging inside of me.

I hitch a ride into Copperville with a couple of guys from Pinewood High. I wander in and out of the stores looking at this and that, nothing special. I have no plan, no money, and no idea why I wanted to come here today. I wander into Patty's Pottery Shop and slip a small ashtray into my pocket. No one will notice it's missing. There are plenty of others like it on the shelf. Don't know what I'm going to do with it, but I had to take it.

CHAPTER II

1967

I START WAITRESSING AT THE GO GET 'EM PART-TIME MY senior year in high school. I've known the owner all my life. You would think someone owning a café would look neat and tidy. Not Faye Vespers'. Instead, her scraggly hair and wrinkled clothes remind me of someone who tied one on, fell asleep on the bed, and forgot to set the alarm. But everyone loves her.

Faye has the biggest heart of anyone in Pinewood. Her heart cracked into pieces when she lost her son, Buddy, at thirteen. Even then, she kept The Double G open, knowing how Pinewood folks depended on her. She always gives a free meal to some sad sack down on his luck.

Faye Vespers' folks opened the Double G in 1935. A blackboard lists the daily specials, like chicken-fried steak or beef stew, still the same menu since the beginning. Folks around here would go loco if it changed. Bright-yellow oilcloth printed with red cherries covers the tables. A hodgepodge of black-and-white photos of old Pinewood families hangs on the walls, dating back to the early days.

I'm the only young one working the tables. The other waitresses are older ladies that live in Pinewood with husbands and kids. They wear wedding rings, so the truckers don't bother them. Being so young and all, I learn fast. Many of Faye Vespers' customers are long-haul truckers. They spend most of their time on the road. That means they're out for easy pickings. Faye told me to be careful. She teaches me stuff I need to know. How to handle these guys. How to use nice, polite words to customers, like "please" and "you're welcome". No one talks like that at my house. The older ladies hand out their advice, too, whether I want it or not.

"Be polite and smile but don't look them right in the eye," says one. "You don't want to give them ideas." She points a finger to the top of her head to make sure I get the message.

"Don't wear nothin' too tight," says the other, cracking her Juicy Fruit gum. "And only talk about what's on the menu. If they want to talk about somethin' else, keep it short and sweet." These ladies know a thing or two, so I should listen.

A few weeks after I start getting shifts at the café, Rhonda moves into our neighborhood. Says her mother named her after some old-time movie star, Rhonda Fleming. She's been married and divorced four times. Hair dyed a phony bright red. She always wears tight clothes and high heels. The town gossips whisper, but loud enough in the café for me or anyone else to hear. No surprise, the first one to speak is Leila the Righteous. It's what everyone calls her behind her back.

"Lord have mercy," she says, "could that dress be any shorter?" She fingers the cross hanging around her neck. Her friend, Marvel, nods in agreement. But then, that's what she always does. Some of us wonder if Marvel can speak at all. Leila keeps going.

"Doesn't anyone tell. Rhonda looks like a ho-oar?"

One night, Pops invites Rhonda over for a drink. What could she be thinking in that short red dress and matching high heels? No one around here wears high heels. Each time she crosses her legs, I can almost see her wazoo. Pops pours her a Bourbon and Coke. Then he lights her Salem cigarette. I have never seen him do that for Mama or anyone else. Rhonda takes a long deep drag and recrosses her legs. There is a run in her black stocking.

"Oh yeah!" she says. "I do love me a smoke with a good drink!" She and Pops laugh too loud like it's the funniest thing anyone could ever say. Mama glares at them and slams a kitchen cupboard door. Pops turn on the TV, he and Rhonda laugh their heads off at any stupid thing, and smoke comes out of Mama's ears. When I can't take it anymore, I escape to my room and put some cotton in my ears. I learned to do that when Mama and Pops have their blow-ups. And I draw horses and dogs, and sometimes flowers and trees. Tonight, I draw a beach with palm trees. I pull out a *Photoplay* magazine. My pup, Ducky, cuddles close to me, like always.

Mama and Pops said I could have a dog when I turned fourteen. That was one time they didn't let me down. Pops took me to the pound in Geiger Springs, where all the dogs begged us to take them home. A lady in her fifties with a volunteer badge walked us up and down the aisles. We looked at every dog, so sad in their cages, so many I liked and wanted to take home. But the little one with brown and white spots stole my heart.

"Pops, I think it's a girl," I say. "Look! She's smiling at me."

"She's a cutie," he says. He turns to the nice lady. "What can you tell us?"

"We think she's a beagle mix. A very sweet girl," she says. "I'll take her out of the cage so you can walk her." She opens the cage, puts a leash on the pup, and hands it to me.

"The vet said her leg was broken," says the volunteer lady, "nobody took care of it, so it never healed properly." She reaches down to pet the dog. "She's been here for over six months. See how funny she walks? She waddles. It's even worse when she runs. That's why no one wants her." The lady turns away as her eyes tear up.

"You can do better than that," says Pops. "Look at this pooch with the floppy ears and shiny black coat."

"But it's my birthday. I like this little pup that waddles. She's the one I want."

"You are a strange one," he says. He shakes his head and shoves his hands into his jean jacket. The lady turns to me.

"Bless you," she says. "I have a soft spot for that dog, too." Pops rolls his eyes.

"I already decided on her name," I say. "I'm going to name her Ducky. Ducky Waddles."

Since we brought her home, Ducky has slept right up against me. Her little dog snores make me happy. She stays by my side when my folks drink too much and fight. Whenever I draw pictures of her, she knows not to move. Whenever I go with Mama to the Co-op in Copperville, I lift a small toy for Ducky and stash it in my jacket pocket.

CHAPTER 12

POPS LOSES A TON OF WEIGHT. I HAVE NO CLUE WHERE HE buys these new shirts he wears with bright colors and big flowers. He splashes Old Spice behind his ears, shaves every single day, and makes sure his hair looks neat. Soon he spends most of his spare time at Rhonda's house. I know Mama is upset but doesn't say much about it. She spends even more time in her bedroom and closes the door, so it's just me and Ducky most of the time.

I learn to cook since Mama can't be bothered.

Faye Vespers knows everything that goes on. "When no customers come in, you can watch what they're making in the kitchen," she says. "You know, how to make simple things like eggs, pancakes, and burgers for starters so you don't starve at home." She makes a tsking sound like she's worried about me. Sometimes she wraps up food for me to take home for dinner. There are some good folks in this world, and Faye Vespers is way up there.

One day Mama and I go into Geiger Springs to shop for my high school grad night dress. When we get home, the closet doors in my folks' bedroom hang wide open like somethin' escaped. Sure enough, it's Pops's clothes. Gone.

He moves in with Rhonda two weeks before I graduate from high school. Then he has the nerve to bring her to my graduation. I can't stand to look at either one of them. Mama almost busts a gut by now, she's so mad. Most folks know what's happening, and everybody stares at Pops, Rhonda,

Mama, and me. This is supposed to be a happy day, but I want to die of embarrassment.

How do I get through it? Drink four bourbon and Cokes at grad night, strip down to my underwear, and jump into the Pinewood Inn swimming pool. Sandy jumps in after me and drags me out. Sue and Dede help dry me off, get me dressed, and drive me home. The next morning I look in the mirror and see Mama staring back at me through my own face. It scares the living bejesus out of me.

Living her whole life as a housewife, I worry about Mama. Even though they didn't get along that great, she and Pops have been together since she was sixteen. At thirty-five that's more than half her life. She's never been alone before.

Boy, does she surprise me. Four months after I graduate high school, she brings a young guy home to meet me. "Angel, this is my new boyfriend, Gus."

He stands there, still as can be, with a funny look. It's Gus, the guy with the gas station, the hideaway for Ace and me. What does Mama see in him? His overalls are dirty, grease under his nails, and even his rim of hair looks grubby. Mama blushes like a schoolgirl.

"Oh, hi," I say. Feels like my eyes are bulging out of my head. "Nice to meet you, I guess."

"Ahem . . . nice to meet you, too, Angel." He looks over my head, across the room, to the wall above Pops's rocking chair. Above it hangs a framed needlepoint. It's Mama's pride and joy. It says, *Hotter than a Hoochie Coochie*. Gus laughs, kind of a strangled laugh. I don't know what to do with myself. Mama grabs Gus by the arm.

"I didn't forget that promise I made you," she says, her voice like sugar, eyelashes fluttering like Betty Boop in those old cartoons on TV. I never saw Mama act this way before in my life. I think my mouth must be hanging open. Am I the only adult in the room? The two of them giggle and whisper all the way upstairs. When I see the loose change he left on the dining room table, I sweep it up and shove it in my pocket.

The following day Mama strolls into the living room, not a care in the world, mellow as can be in her lavender terry cloth robe, another find from Miser's Mercantile, even though it has a few bleach spots in the front.

"Good mornin' Angel!" she says. She almost sings it out.

"Hey, Mama." I don't look up from my bowl of Cheerios.

She sashays over to me. "So, what about Gus? Cute, don't cha think?"

"He's okay," I say, my voice flat.

The dull morning light lands on a single carton of milk gone sour on the counter.

"You know, he could be with a lot of women," says Mama, "but he wants me."

"Really? What other women?" Ducky jumps on my lap.

"Don't give me your lip," says Mama. "I think he's a good-lookin' guy."

"You do?" I can't help but laugh a little bit. "Gus? But he's bald and skinny."

"He's trim, not hangin' over his belt like your father." She brushes a few invisible crumbs off the front of her bathrobe.

"Well, fine," I say. "Whatever you think. So where did you meet him?"

"At the gas station. You know that's *his* gas station." You'd think he was a millionaire with that look on her face. "We got to talkin' one day," she says. "Felt bad how your Pops ran out on me with Rhonda. Asked if I would like to have a drink with him sometime. You know, just like that." She glows, thinking about it. I finish the Cheerios, worrying that Gus will tell her about Ace and me. I'll have to be decent to him.

"Isn't he too young for you?" I say. Mama's nostrils flare, and she cinches in the belt of her robe.

"Listen, you little smart-ass . . . ." Her voice like a witch on a broom. Ducky starts to tremble in my lap. I stroke her head to calm her down. Mama smacks me on the top of my head.

"You mind your own business, Angela!"

"It's Angel!"

"He's my boyfriend, so you better get used to it, *Angel*!" As we hear Gus plodding down the stairs, she changes from poison ivy to blushing rose.

"Good mornin', darlin'," she rings out in a phony musical voice. He ambles into the kitchen, sleepy-eyed, bald head shining.

"Good mornin' ladies."

I pick up Ducky and go to my room.

I never really knew Gus—only met him once before. But he knows Ace and I spent most of our time at his place. It gets me thinking about Ace all over again. He helped me through tough times with my folks, always believed in me, told me I was smart and had artistic talent. Not sure if I'm happy or sad with him on my mind. I think sad wins out.

Whenever Gus comes to the house, Mama's a giggling fool. I don't want to think about her and her skinny young stud doing Lord knows what in that bed at night. After a month of them carrying on like horny teenagers, more than ever before, I know I'm on my own. I pull Faye Vespers aside at work.

"I don't know what to do. I need to get out of my house."

"I understand," she says, resting a warm hand on my arm.

"Can't stand living with Mama these days." I look out the window. A heavy storm still pounds down since early this morning. "Any chance you can give me some extra hours? Then I could rent a room somewhere." A crack of lightning booms out and brightens the café.

"Good idea, Angel," says Faye. A soft squeeze on my arm tells me how much she cares about me. "You *should* get your own place. You know Pinewood is buzzing like a hive of bees over your Mama and her boyfriend."

Only three days later, all excited, she winks and waves me over as I start my shift at the café. Her hands are covered with flour from baking her famous pies. She wipes her hands on her apron like she has somethin' important to say.

"Angel," a big grin on her kind wrinkled face, "things are looking up. You know the old lady who lives across the way from here?"

"Sure, I know her," I say.

"You won't believe this" She takes a big breath and smiles a secret little smile. "Last week, her tenant took off in the middle of the night. At her age, she needs every nickel. She wants someone to move in right away."

"Honestly?" I say, "I wish I could, but I don't have enough money saved up." She twirls me toward her.

"Listen to me, Angel. I'll loan you the first month's rent. We'll work out a plan. It's no good for you to be in your mama's house anymore. Let me help you," she says.

"That sounds like a crazy good offer. Too good to turn down."

"I'm glad I can help you out, Angel. You've had it rough. The place is small," she says, "but it's a good start for you."

"I don't even need to see it first." Maybe my luck is about to change. "Please tell her I'll take it."

CHAPTER 13

POPS AND RHONDA RAN OFF SOMEWHERE AND GOT MARRIED. Must have been a minute and a half after the divorce from Mama. They didn't tell a soul. Now he's Mr. Rhonda Number Five. Sometimes Pops and Rhonda come to the Go Get 'Em, sloshed and sloppy, her boobs popping out of her blouse. All the locals know the whole story. They stare at the two of them and then at me, the pathetic daughter of this loser and his whorey wife.

Why do they have to come here and torture me? I want to walk across the room and knock their heads together.

Living across the street from the Double G makes my life nice and easy for work. But heaven is not one small room with a hot plate. I found an old plaid chair someone left out for trash and dragged it inside. That's about all I can fit in there besides the bed. Once I get off work and go home, if you can call it that, the walls close in. Slipping a few bucks from the cash register into my pocket helps. It's not that often, maybe a couple of times a week. Faye Vespers is so good to me, much better than my own folks. I don't think she'll miss the money. I need it more than she does. Sometimes I pocket other things besides dog toys from the Co-op or the market.

It also pays to go the extra mile with my customers.

"How you folks doing today?" I ask. The guys that like to tease and flirt always leave the worst tips. What do they think? That their great personalities make my day? The best guys are usually married or traveling, on their way to some place more interesting. And that's how I meet Randy on a Thursday night I wish never happened.

"I'm not just driving through one time like a lot of these guys," he says. He puffs out his chest and talks in a too-loud voice. I try to hide a yawn. Then I remember to act interested for a good tip.

"How come every few weeks?" I ask.

"I drive a truck for Sears," he says. He must be six-foot-two, with broad shoulders, and full of himself. I've been down this road before. "You are pretty, aren't you?" he says.

"Guess you're married, right?" I say.

"You could say that."

"I just did." He shrugs.

"When I'm on the road, I'm a free agent. My wife and I have a nice little agreement. We each do our own thing."

"For real?" I say. "You don't care what she does when you're gone?" He shrugs his shoulders again and sighs out loud.

"Thing is," he says, scanning the room, "I'm gone a lot." He drums his fingers on the table like he doesn't want to talk about it. I never heard about a wife and husband who agree to cheat on each other. The craziest story I ever heard was about Charlie Booker and his two wives. Never would have guessed someone like Charlie, with his yellow teeth and combed-over hair, could have two different families at the same time—one of them right here in Pinewood, the other one straight over McClure Pass in Paonia, less than 30 miles away. Over time word reached from Paonia to Pinewood about Charlie's double life. This is a different story but just as crazy to me.

"And your wife doesn't care what you do?" I ask. He stands up and smacks his hands onto the tabletop, rattling the silverware and jiggling his untouched glass of water.

"I'm a young guy," he says, "I have needs." He hangs his thumbs on his leather belt like some Hollywood actor, ready to grab his pistol and pull the trigger.

"Catch you next time," he says, winking at me. He reminds me of Ace a little bit. He's a good-lookin' hunk and doesn't doubt himself for a minute. But he doesn't come close to Ace. In all this time, nobody has come close to Ace. I sure do wish I could see him again. I know, in my heart, that will never happen. Right now, I have to deal with this cocky guy.

"Yep, catch you next time, for sure," he says, on his way out the door. "My name is Randy."

A few weeks later, Randy plants himself at my table. The old man at Table 5 puts some coins in the jukebox for a Glenn Campbell song. It's quiet tonight, with only three customers.

"Hey there, beautiful," says Randy, "good to see you again." He makes himself comfortable at a table meant for four, scans the menu, and smacks it down to let me know he's ready to go.

"What'll it be, cowboy?" I have my pencil and pad ready to jot down his order.

"I'd like the chicken-fried steak with mashed potatoes and peas. That is if they're not canned."

"They are."

"Forget the peas. And I would like you for dessert."

"Aren't you the slick one? The answer is no." I make a U-turn and place his order in the kitchen. When I come back with his food, instead of digging in, he takes a deck of cards from his jacket pocket and shuffles them.

"How about you pick a card?" he says, lasering into my eyes. "If I guess right, you and I get together later."

"No way you'll guess the right one." I pull out the King of Hearts and place it face down on the table. He closes his eyes and frowns hard. He puts his hand on his forehead like it will send a picture of the right card to his brain. There is no chance he can figure out the card I picked. He flashes a big confident smile.

"King of Hearts," he says.

"What? That's crazy good." He couldn't have seen the card. "How did you do that?"

"I'll be here when you finish work and show you." He reshuffles the cards and puts the pack back in his pocket.

"What time do you get off?"

"Hang on. I didn't say yes."

"I guessed your card, didn't I?"

"Yeah, you did."

"So, a deal is a deal. C'mon, we'll have fun. All I need is your name."

"It's Angel. Hmm, I don't know about this," I say. He gives me a 100 kilowatt smile.

"I forgot your name," I say, butterflies in my stomach.

"It's Randy." I make an invisible checkmark in the air.

"Oh, I remember now," I say. "I get off at 8:30. This town rolls up early. You know, we're mountain folks. Early to bed and early to rise."

"I'd be happy to rise early," he says, his mouth curling into a sly grin.

"You know," I say, "Randy is the perfect name for you." He pays the bill and presses a few dollars tip into my open palm.

My stomach twists into nervous tight knots, but I ignore the warning as I pocket the cash.

By 8:20, the Double G has emptied out. I loosen my wild curly hair from its rubber band. It springs out free and loose, just how I like it. I change from my big black waitress shoes and pull on my favorite cowboy boots. Randy strides through the café like he owns the place.

"There she is," he says, like we've known each other forever. "Been thinking about you."

"Don't say that. It's downright weird."

"I bet men are after you all the time." He takes in the café with its black-and-white photos, oilcloth covered tabletops, and u-shaped counters. "Never thought I'd see a gorgeous chick like you in such a hick town."

"Real nice. I may not love it here, but this is my home," I say. I've wanted for years to escape Pinewood. I'm surprised how his words cut into me.

"I think you're meant for bigger things than this town, if you can call it that."

"I think so, too. But please knock it off." A chill goes down my neck. I don't want to go with him. I don't know what to do.

"Until I can make my getaway," I say, "this is where I live." He stands in front of me, head cocked off to the side. He is full of bluster, for sure, but a hunk of a man.

"Okay, fair enough." His voice softens up. "Where would you want to live?"

"My real dream is somewhere with beaches like Hawaii," I say, "or maybe even Los Angeles. They have beaches out there, right?"

"Yes, there are beaches. Ever heard of Santa Monica or Malibu?"

"Maybe," I say. "I'm not sure."

"Well, anyway," he says, "I do the long haul between Colorado and Southern California." He grins at me. "And Los Angeles is my base. How about them apples?"

"You live in Los Angeles?"

"It's really Hollywood. Just a few blocks from Paramount Studios."

"Whoa, you live in Hollywood? Are you an actor?"

"Sometimes." He drums his fingers on the table as his eyes dart from left to right. When Faye Vespers left early, she turned off the heater. I pull my sweater around me to hold off the chill.

"Never met an actor before," I say. "Ever been in a movie?"

"Not yet," he says. He fidgets with his belt. "Listen, Angel, you could catch a ride with me. It wouldn't cost you a thing. It could be a great adventure. How about it?"

"Ha! I don't even know you."

He buttons his city boy jacket, and I grab my brown mittens and fringe suede jacket. He takes my elbow and moves me toward the front door. It's my night to close the lights and lock up. Randy and I step outside, bundled up, but not enough for this cold dark night.

"I have way too much time on the road to think," says Randy. "Hours and hours of driving. You could keep me company and make your getaway." He's like a salesman with his foot in the door.

A wind blows through, and I hug myself.

"Think about it," he says. "You know what, it's cold standing here. Can we go inside somewhere and talk?

We walk across the street to my room. As I unlock the door, he puts his arm around me. But once inside, he pushes up against me and kisses me hard. His teeth grind into mine, and our noses smash together. He pins me up against the wall and grabs onto my crotch.

"I want this," he says. "I've been waiting all night." Ducky growls and bites his pant leg.

"Stop it!" I scream. Faye warned me. So did everyone at work. They all warned me about these truck drivers, these horny long-haulers. Why didn't I listen? He kicks at Ducky.

"Leave her alone!" I scream.

"Come on, Angel, you know you want it. Besides, I want to see more of that strawberry blonde." He tugs at my pants. I fight as hard as I can.

"Get your hands off me!" He pins my arms behind my back and pushes me out the front door. Ducky tries to come too. He kicks her across the room and slams the door shut. With his hand over my mouth, easy as can be, he pulls open the heavy door of his big truck. Monkeys chatter from way in the back. What are monkeys doing here? I want to fight him off. Instead, I go numb. Then he throws me onto the front seat of his truck. My neck snaps as my head hits the gearshift knob. The monkey chatter turns to frantic screams as if they know what's about to happen.

"Ow!" I squeeze the words out. "You'll pay for this, you sick creep!"

"Who're you kidding, you little slut? You know you love it." My head throbs, and blood runs down my neck onto my tan jacket. Not a soul anywhere to help me. *Zip*. Randy undoes his pants. It's the most sickening sound I've ever heard. His hand still clamps on my mouth. Adrenalin shoots through me, powering me up. I swing my arm and punch his right ear.

He grabs his ear, then slaps me hard across my left cheek. So hard I think my teeth will fall out.

"This'll teach you, you stupid little bitch." He climbs on top of me, holding down my shoulders with hands of steel. I scream as loud as I can.

"Shut up, you're ruining everything," he says, his eyes dark and empty as a madman. A blinding light comes through the passenger window.

"What's going on here?" says someone used to giving orders, like a cop. He shines his flashlight on me. "Are you okay, young lady?" I can barely speak.

"N-n-n-o, I'm not okay!" Tears flood my face, and my head pounds like someone is hitting me with a hammer. He yanks Randy out of the truck and pulls out a badge.

"Officer, my girl and I had a little argument. Didn't we, honey?" Randy the Worm comes up with this dumb excuse. He squirms.

"Listen, you piece of crap," says the officer, "it's all over. We've had our eye on you for some time. Trafficking animals across state lines in your bullshit Sears truck. Now we also have you for attempted rape. Right, miss? Attempted rape?"

I nod, not able to speak. My hands, arms, and whole body limp from this nightmare. The policeman fastens handcuffs onto Randy's wrists so they're behind his back.

"I'm taking him in, miss. My partner is on his way. He had to deal with a barroom brawl in Copperville. Are you in much pain?"

"My head . . . my neck. Everything hurts."

"You're bleeding . . . ." He pulls a handkerchief from his pocket.

"I'm taking you to a hospital. First, I need to get this bastard into my car."

"But officer she and I—" Minutes ago, he was a raging monster. Now he's a whining, pathetic worm.

"Shut up!" says the cop. "I don't want to hear another word from you. Understand? Into the car!" He opens the door, shoves Randy into the back seat, and locks the door.

"Your name, miss?" asks the cop.

"Angel. Angel O'Reilly." I hug myself to keep from shivering. Seems I can never do anything right, at least not for long. How could I be so dumb?

"Where do you live, Angel?" he asks, along with other questions. I don't want to answer, but I do, knowing he's here to help me.

"I'll stay with you," he says, "until my buddy gets here. You will need to file a report." I keep hugging myself and stare out the window as a fierce wind howls through the trees.

"Miss? Did you hear me? A report—"

"I don't know," I say, rubbing my hands back and forth across my head. "I can't think."

"Listen to me," says the no-nonsense cop. "This guy is slime."

He stands close enough as if guarding me, but not too close. I think he's a good man, probably in his thirties, with a wife and two or three little kids. He could be home with them, but he's out here tonight. And he saved me. He nods over at Randy without looking at him.

"We've been tracking him for a few years," he continues. "Plain and simple, he attacked you. You need to file a report."

I do my best to listen, but the hammer bangs between my ears.

"I'll file the report. Honest, Officer."

"Okay."

"What about the monkeys?"

"Don't worry. We'll make sure they're safe and sound. Truth is, I'm more concerned about you. My partner will get you to Geiger Springs Hospital, and I'll take this piece of shit over to the jailhouse and book him." Pops always bad-mouthed cops. Said they were criminals who hide behind a badge. I believed him for a long time, but tonight proved him wrong.

If looks could kill, I would be dead right now. Randy's snake eyes drill a hole through the patrol car window. I hope they lock him up until he rots from his own stink. If they let him out in a few years, he could make his way back to Pinewood and come after me. The policeman reads the worry on my face.

"Don't worry, miss," he says. "He's going away for a long time." I take a deep breath and sink into the upholstery. If this officer has kids, they are lucky to have a dad like him. He knows how to keep people safe. I can see his face in the headlights of a massive truck as it passes through town. With deep furrows in his brow, a strong crooked nose, and a thick neck, he could have been a wrestler or football player before he joined the police force.

"I thought he would kill me," I say, my voice all ragged. "Not just rape me but kill me." The officer starts to put his arm around me but changes his mind.

"Angel," he says, "this guy is going to a Federal Pen far from here. The feds could even send him to California. You're going to be okay."

By the time we reach the hospital, it's 1:30 in the morning. You would think from all the blood I would need a ton of stitches over my right eyebrow. It turns out I only need nine, but I do need to wear a whiplash collar and take a drug called Percocet for pain.

I named Sandy my emergency contact when they checked me into the hospital. They must have called her. She's not an early bird, but she arrives at 7:30 sharp in the morning. You can't ask for a better friend than that.

"Angel, just look at you all bruised," she says, "bandages over your eye."

She bursts into tears and places her arm with tender care around my shoulder. I am dog tired and don't have any words for now. Sandy guides me to her car and eases me in. At last, I feel safe, now I'm with her. Warning signals flash in my head: no more long-haulers, trust my instincts, and learn everything I can about life from Faye Vespers. Everybody in town loves her, so she's doing something right.

Sandy eases her old gray Chevy up the sharp mountain curves to Pinewood. As I drift in and out of sleep, I can't wait to return to my little room with its one plaid chair and two burner stove top. As Sandy steps around to help me out of the car, Faye rushes across from the café. When she sees us, deep lines furrow her brow, her deep-set eyes trying to take it all in.

"Sweet Jesus, what happened to Angel?" she asks Sandy as she struggles to help me out of the car. "Here, let me give you a hand." Sandy fills her in on the nightmare of last night. I still don't have the words or energy to talk. My knees buckle as they both hold onto my arms to support me.

"Angel, this is an order," says Faye. "Take it easy for at least a week, maybe two. I'm saying this as a friend, not your boss. No work. You need to rest and heal. And listen, I don't want to preach, but watch it with customers we don't know. Thank the Lord you'll be okay."

"Yeah, I guess it could have been worse," I say. Sandy hands me a glass of water with a pain pill.

Faye Vespers looks around my room. "Boy, this place is small." She clears her throat. "I mean, it's really cozy."

"I know," I say, "I barely have room to change my mind."

Sandy chuckles behind her hand. "Even all banged up and in pain, you make jokes." She eases me into bed and pulls the covers over me. Sandy snuffles but tries to hide it by coughing. "I'll stay with you today. Now, get some rest."

Ducky doesn't leave my side. I know she's helping me heal. Her soft doggy snores lull me to sleep. Sue, Dede, and Sandy—all such great pals—take turns walking her. I pass the long week by drawing whatever I have in my tiny apartment. I sketch the kettle, some dried flowers in an old bottle, the plaid chair, and too many sketches of Ducky to count. Sue comes by herself one stormy afternoon.

"Sue, how about letting me sketch you?" A shy smile crosses her face.

"Well, okay. Can you make me look skinnier?" Her playfulness takes me by surprise.

"Ha. I'll try." She sits down in my one and only chair. She rests her chin in her hand, a perfect Sue pose. I open my box of charcoals and go to work. A sudden crackle of thunder jolts her. She jumps up from the chair and peers through the curtains. An onslaught of rain pounds the roof and splatters the windows. She closes the curtains, slips back into her warm jacket with the fake fur collar, and settles right back into her chin-in-hand pose, like a professional artist's model. I'm proud of her and give her a wink as if to say, let's do this. I work hard on getting the basic shape of her on paper.

"Can I talk?" asks Sue.

"Uh, no," I say, "hold still."

"Okay, only for you. Just one thing—how are you feeling?" She moves her hand away from her chin and sits up straight.

"I'm doing better," I say, with every bit of focus on the drawing. "Now put your hand back where it was and hush up."

I add the finishing touches an hour or so later. Sue peeks over my shoulder.

"You know what? That's pretty darn good. You even got the dimple in my chin."

"Glad you like it, Sue." I smile for what may be the first time in days. "Dang, that makes me feel good!" I tear it off the pad and hand it to her. Sue gives me an air hug.

After a week, I better get back to work at the Double G. Faye, figuring I am still tender with bruises. Thank the Lord, not one nosy question from my co-workers. Even so, they all look at me like I just crawled out of a swamp. Once I smile, they all seem to relax as the worry drains off their faces. Crazy tired on my shift at work, I drag around from nightmares of the attack. I wake up in a cold sweat almost every night. It wouldn't have happened if I only said no to that creep, Randy. If only I never went out that door with him and sent him packing. I'm so mad at myself, I could spit.

CHAPTER 14

ALL HEALED AT LAST, I DRIVE BETSY, MY DILAPIDATED BUICK, into Copperville. Faye's old-time customer gave it to me when he stopped driving. First time I've escaped Pinewood in a month. Driving down Ashby Lane, I spot somethin' I've never seen before. What used to be Lola's Café is now Tommy's Tattoo Parlor.

Without a second thought, I wheel my car right in front of Tommy's. A good parking place always means good luck. As I peek through the plate glass window, a giant photo of Janis Joplin sporting her tattoos fills the wall. I inch through the door, trying to keep as quiet as possible. But the *ring, ring* of the front door turns the heads of the only two people in the room—the tattoo artist and a young guy with an eagle taking shape on his forearm.

"What can I do for you?" asks the man, who must be Tommy. He looks Apache with his dark skin and long black glossy hair. Even with a raw-boned face, he carries fifty extra pounds on him. His apron is smeared with brown, black, and blue ink.

"I guess you're Tommy," I say.

"Well, yeah," he laughs.

"I want a tattoo."

"Yeah, no kidding. Never would have figured." He pushes up his sleeves and adjusts his glasses, the same kind John Denver wears. "If you can wait about half an hour . . . ."

"I can wait." Truth is, I never thought about getting a tattoo before, but I'm going through with it. Tommy keeps working on the guy's eagle. He glances over his shoulder at me every once in a while.

Too bad Lola's Café is gone. Pops took me there for banana cream pie a few times on his day off. Lola's banana cream pie is good—*very good*. But Faye Vespers is the Queen of Banana Cream Pies. After Lola's young husband, a firefighter, died a hero, she moved to Roanoke, Virginia. Then Vinny's Vinyl and Sheet Music moved in. I heard that Vinny never left home without a flask of whiskey. He crashed his pickup into a pine tree in Marble and died on the spot. We don't see much change here, but this location has had some crazy bad luck. Even so, that eagle tattoo is looking good. Tommy glances over at me again.

"Where do you want your tattoo?" he asks.

"On my bicep," I say, "like the soldiers."

"Don't see many women that want a tattoo," says Tommy, "'specially good-lookin' young ones like you. They're always in the military. Are you a WAC or a WAVE?"

"Nope," I say, "just a local girl who's fought a few battles."

He better stop asking too many questions. I may walk out of here if he keeps it up.

"Can you just give me two words? NO ANGEL," I say, hoping he won't be a snoop. "That's all. Just NO ANGEL. And I don't want it too big."

I glance at all the tattoo magazines on the dusty side table. I've never seen one before.

"Whatever you say, princess." He laughs to himself. "I wonder if your look alike, Ann-Margret has a tattoo," he says. "That's a compliment, miss. You do know you look like her, right?"

"Yeah, except when I smile," I say. "I have a gap between my two front teeth, and she doesn't. That's why she's a movie star, and I'm not." I laugh, and he joins in.

"Why you want to go and do that, pretty girl like you?" says his customer. Tommy gives him a playful smack on his head.

"Mind your own business, bud. If she wants a tattoo," says Tommy, "she can get one. What's good for the goose is good for the gander. Right, miss? Or is it the other way around? Anyway, hang loose; I'll be right with you."

I thumb through *Tattoo Revue* magazine with men and women covered in tattoos on their arms, legs, and backs. One lady is covered head to toe in ink except for her face. Where could she work without people staring at her? In a factory? In a cemetery? Digging graves?

Tommy finishes up the eagle. It looks pretty good. His customer gives him a high five and pays.

"I'll be back," he says, on his way out the door. "And Tommy, I want that cobra we talked about wrapping around my other arm."

"Happy to do that for you," says Tommy. "See you next time." He hands me a shot of tequila. "This should help," he says. I down it in a jiffy.

"I never got your name," he says.

"It's Angel," I say, "as in NO ANGEL." I set the magazine back on the table.

"Okay, I hear you. NO ANGEL," says Tommy, his hands guarding his face like he's in a boxing match. "I won't ask what that's all about."

"That's good," I say. "I wouldn't tell you anyways." He nods and doesn't bring it up again. Instead, he hands me a notebook with different styles of print. I choose small block print. NO ANGEL. It should look good.

Tommy works on me for a few hours. It hurts like hell. How could anyone want to do this more than once? I thank him, pay, and start out the door.

"See you again?" asks Tommy, chomping away on a Mars bar.

"I doubt it," I say. "Thanks anyway. I think I'm done."

A few weeks later, my tattoo has healed. I show it off to my Pinewood friends.

"That is very cool," says Sandy, looking at it from every possible angle.

"Why would you go and do a thing like that?" asks Sue, sounding just like her mother.

"I think I might get one, too," says Dede.

Otherwise, I keep it covered, especially when I visit Mama. It's my private badge of honor.

CHAPTER 15

1970

NOT MUCH HAS CHANGED SINCE WE GRADUATED HIGH school. All four Pinewood friends struggle to keep the wolf from the door. I make diddly squat as a waitress. Same for Sandy as a wildlife photographer. She cleans those big fancy houses in Copperville to keep her head above water. Dede runs the only B&B in town.

She took over when her Mama had a heart attack and died at forty-six. Now Dede works around the clock. Her lazy dog of a husband, Richard, can't hold down a steady job. Over six feet tall and maybe 120 pounds soaking wet, he spends half his time tugging up his jeans. He and Dede have been together since eigth grade. I guess he became a bad habit. With zero personality, nobody remembers his name. We all call him Mr. Dede.

None of us went beyond high school except Sue. She makes the drive every day to Colorado Mountain College over there in Geiger Springs. Poor thing still lives with her old fogey mother. I swear that woman drains the life right out of sweet Sue. I still remember her hiding behind her mama's skirt when she was a little girl. Sue has that scratchy LP record voice.

All four of us girls always had big dreams, much bigger than our town could offer. None of us came from much. Pops used to say, "Just a bunch of hard-working folks."

I lie on my bed and stare out the bedroom window. Nothing but mountains with cottonwoods and pine trees stretch for miles and miles. I close my eyes and dream my dreams about Hawaii. How can I ever make it happen?

I start taking a little more from the register at the Café. At the market, I switch price tags on the apples or, sometimes, walk out without paying. If a good-looking guy passing through town leaves me a big tip at the café, I often wonder if he could be my ticket out of Pinewood.

CHAPTER 16

MAMA FELL DOWN THE RICKETY STAIRS AT OUR OLD HOUSE yesterday afternoon. Purple bruises cover her nose, forehead, and right cheek. Plus, she knocked out her two front teeth. The dentist says she has four others that are rotten to the core, that she better go to a guy in Denver to fix her up.

"Please go with me, Angel. I get lost in that city."

"I've only been there once before," I say. "Remember we went with Pops when I was a little kid? I don't know my way around there at all."

"Don't be like that," says Mama. She smiles to soften me up. She looks like a Jack O'Lantern with the gap from her two missing front teeth. "I need your help," she whines. She doesn't think about it, but I worry how she'll pay for all the dental work. Time for me to be her parent, as usual.

"Well, okay then," I say. "Hope we're not like two country bumpkins looking like fools."

We go to The Pinewood Health Clinic for an interview. Thank the Lord they will pay the bulk of the expenses.

"Phew," says Mama, "that is some good news."

But not a word of thanks to anyone.

We catch the train out of Geiger Springs the next day and make it to Dr. Hertz' office in Denver right on time for our appointment. Streamlined couches, everything brand new, and sparkling equipment make me realize what a Podunk town we live in with our old-time dental office and its scratched-up fake wood paneling and ancient chairs.

"Dr. Hertz will see you now," says a lady with perfect teeth. She shows us into an examining room. I help Mama onto the chair as she moans and groans from all her bruises. Dr. Hertz steps into the room in his white uniform. His two soft hands close around mine, making me think he will be kind and careful with Mama. Once he examines her teeth, he clears his throat.

"Your mother will be just fine. We'll replace those incisors she knocked out. And it is essential that I extract all her molars. They can't be saved. But the plate for her missing teeth will look completely natural."

"Ya know," says Mama, "you can talk to me. I'm not deaf, dumb, and blind."

"I'm sorry, Mrs. O'Reilly," he says, explaining all over again.

"I heard you the first time," says Mama. Dr. Hertz looks at me and winks. The woman is a handful.

Dr. Hertz studies me for a minute.

"You know," he says, "we could fix that gap between your front teeth. Has anyone ever told you that you look like Ann-Margret?" He looks proud of himself.

"All the time," I say.

"Well, get yourself some lunch," he says, adjusting his glasses. "Take your time, and we'll see you later."

I kiss Mama's leathery cheek, so she understands I won't be staying. She shoots me a look of despair, but I leave anyway.

Cars jam the Denver streets, more than I see in a whole month back home. After a short walk, I escape into Le Petit Café, with its bright-blue door and blue-and-white striped awnings. It must be pretty good since it's packed with people. The hostess sticks me at a table next to a couple arguing loud enough for everyone to hear.

"Why can't you ever be the one to watch the kids?" says the haggard young woman. Her husband glares at her as if he hates her guts.

"Damn it," he says. "Why? Because I work hard to support y'all, okay?"

"*And I work around the clock*," she snaps, "cooking, cleaning, wiping snotty noses."

"This is what you want to do? Pick a fight?" His nostrils flare. I close my eyes for a minute. An annoyed nasal voice jolts me.

"Have you decided what you want?" The waitress looks bored to death, asking the same question for the millionth time.

"Oh yeah, sorry," I say. "How about a bowl of chili and a Coke?" I open my eyes wide and tilt my head toward the battle at the next table as if to say, *can you believe it?* The waitress shrugs her shoulders and walks away.

A man sitting across the aisle smiles at me in sympathy. I nod and smile back at him.

He understands that these dipshits are ruining my lunch. Once the waitress brings my food, I gobble it down. When I look up, here comes the old guy from across the aisle. Tall and skinny, he wears a jacket with a little green cactus stitched onto each lapel. Fancy rings cover his fingers. His dark hair styled like Elvis Presley. He doesn't look like anyone I've ever seen.

"Are you lunching by yourself?" he asks.

Uh oh, what could he want? I cough into my napkin.

"Er . . . well . . . yes, I am."

"Perhaps you might like some company?"

"Well," I say, staring down at my bowl of chili.

"Oh, I'm terribly sorry," he says, "I didn't mean to intrude."

He has some kind of weird accent. His ostrich cowboy boots look like the ones the rich ranchers in Copperville wear.

Hmm. He must have a few bucks.

"No, that's okay," I say. "You can sit down."

He gives a funny little salute and sets his glass of red wine on my table. Before sitting, he straightens out his jacket. He bares his chalky white teeth in a smile. I wonder if they're real. I hope Mama's new ones don't look like that. I wonder if he goes to Dr. Hertz.

"Well, this is an unexpectedly pleasant day," he says. I take a smaller ladylike spoonful of my chili.

"My name is Zoltan. And yours?"

"Angel."

"Lovely suitable name, my dear."

"I've never heard the name Zoltan before," I say. "What kind of name is that?"

"It's Hungarian. I suppose it sounds strange to you. In my country, it's as common as John or Bill in the US." He adjusts his jacket again and looks hard at me. "You certainly are a beautiful young woman." He must be at least fifty, maybe more. He looks at me like he's trying to figure me out.

"What are you doing here alone?" he asks.

"I left Mama at the dentist's office and stepped out for some lunch. This place looked nice, so I took my chances." He gives me that chimpanzee smile again, but his eyes stay cool.

"You made a good choice," he says and cocks his head to the side. "You're not from Denver," he says, "am I right?"

My face heats up. "Why? Do I sound like a hick?"

"Oh no, my dear, not at all." He dabs at his mouth with a cloth napkin. "I certainly didn't mean to imply—"

"I'm from Pinewood," I say, taking another spoonful of chili. "Probably don't know where that is, being from Hungary and all. Small town up in the mountains."

He leans forward, clasps his hands together on the table. When he breathes, a whistle sound comes through his nose.

"Love everything about Colorado, the people, the mountains, the beauty. I used to watch *Hopalong Cassidy* movies when I was a boy in Budapest. I always dreamt of coming here. You can see I love the western clothes." He points to the lapel of his jacket. "Custom made by my Polish tailor, Bronislaw of Denver. See the cactus on the lapels? Hand sewn."

I nod dumbly and try to listen as he rattles on.

"And the boots?" He lifts a foot so I can see up close. "These were handmade by a very gifted bootmaker. But look how I've been talking about myself. Please excuse my bad manners. I do want to learn about you. Where is your town of Pinewood exactly?"

He takes another big swallow of wine.

"We're about an hour from Aspen," I say.

"I have business colleagues in Aspen," he says, dabbing at his mouth again with his napkin.

I never saw a man do that before. Funny, but he reminds me of the wolf in *Little Red Riding Hood,* a wolf in expensive clothes.

He dips his napkin in his water glass and attacks a red stain on his shirt sleeve.

"Where is Hungary anyway?" I ask. "Isn't that some place in Europe?"

Remembering the wine, he takes a gulp as he tells me that Hungary is in Eastern Europe.

"We have some German people in Pinewood," I say, "a few Swedes, some Irish folks, and lots of people from Texas."

I finish up my lunch and sneak a look at my Bulova watch. It's the one I got from Pops and Rhonda for graduating high school. That was some close call, but I made it.

"Uh oh," I say, "wait a minute, I lost track of time. Need to pick up Mama at the dentist's office."

"I've truly enjoyed our little chat, young lady. Is there any way we can meet again? Perhaps for a cup of tea or glass of wine?" He pats his Elvis-do. "Please don't think it's more than that. I simply like your company."

I check out his pricey clothes again.

"Sure. Here's my phone number in Pinewood if you ever get out that way." He tucks it into his shirt pocket.

"Are you staying in Denver much longer?" he asks.

"Only tonight. Mama and I took a room at the Old Maiden Inn. She had four teeth pulled today, so she needs to rest. We leave at 8 tomorrow morning to catch the early train."

I start to pay for my lunch. He waves me off, strips a Benjamin Franklin from a silver and turquoise money clip, and leaves the waitress a 20 percent tip. I'm glad he's not cheap and understands that waiting tables is hard work.

"Bye-bye, Angel, 'til we meet again," says Zoltan, his nose whistling as he speaks.

CHAPTER 17

WHEN I GET BACK TO THE DENTAL OFFICE, MAMA LOOKS miserable. Crazy nice Dr. Hertz pays for a taxi to take us to the Old Maiden Inn.

Once we arrive, I look around and wonder how she found this dump. Two chairs with a purple pattern face a stained dark blue couch. Two kittens run back and forth through the reception area. I almost trip on the tiny things. Mama closes her eyes and holds on to the reception desk to steady herself.

A pock-marked lady with thinning hair stands behind the reception desk. She drums her fingers, then sneezes into a handkerchief as she watches me look around. She hands me a folded up note. "Humph!" she says, "not even checked in, and you have a message."

I unfold and quickly glance at the note. Mama's still so out of it that she doesn't notice.

> *Would you have a glass of wine with me this evening? Just tell the receptionist yes or no. I will check in with them. If yes, I will come by at 7:30.*
> *Zoltan*

I whisper to the lady. "Tell him yes,"

"Humph!" says the lady again.

I hold onto Mama for the two flights of stairs to our puny room. She can't eat a thing and wants to sleep. I won't feel too bad leaving her alone. She falls into a loud, snoring sleep. I tiptoe out the door around 7:20 to meet Zoltan. I bet the peeling wallpaper in the halls looked good about fifty years ago. I perch on the reception area couch playing with the kittens as I wait.

When Zoltan strides in, dressed to the nines, I'm embarrassed with my jeans, old cowboy boots, and a pale-yellow sweater. Decked out in a turquoise suede jacket and bolo tie, he nods and salutes.

"Good evening, Angel." This must be the way they talk in Hungary.

As we walk out the front door, I can feel the burning gaze of the old woman at the reception desk on my back.

"I hate to repeat myself," says Zoltan, "but you are such a natural beauty. Lovely deep-brown eyes. That strawberry blonde hair. And smart, too. Shall we have a glass of wine right across the street? I suspect you want to stay close to Mother."

"That's real nice of you," I say. "I can't stay too long. Maybe an hour or so."

"I understand."

McGregor's might be the fanciest restaurant I've ever seen, with red, green, and white plaid wallpaper and dark-brown leather booths. A lamp rests on each table along with an ashtray and box of matches in the same plaid, with McGregor's in gold letters. I pop one in my pocket. As soon as we settle into our seats, Zoltan calls out for the waiter.

Dressed in black slacks, bow tie, and a vest that matches the wallpaper, he rushes over and hands us the menus.

"What can I get you, sir?" the waiter asks. He waves his hand around like a fly might be ready to land.

"Tell me," asks Zoltan, "do you have Dom Perignon?"

"Yes sir," he replies, standing at attention, "we most certainly do!" Zoltan doesn't even look at the menu.

"We would like a cheese platter and a bottle of Dom, please."

"Sounds fancy," I say. "I can't wait to taste it!"

He winks at the waiter. "Only French champagne for this young woman." I learn that Zoltan travels for business between London, New York, Denver, and Los Angeles. He never explains his work, but he does seem to have the big bucks. The waiter opens the champagne. The pop of the cork sounds like money to me. *Big money.*

"So glad our paths have crossed, Angel. To you!" We hold our glasses high in a toast and clink them together as he shoots me another toothy smile. I take plenty of time to sip the delicious French champagne.

"This is crazy good!" It slides down my throat, and I ask for seconds. Zoltan has the same joyful look on his face as Reverend Brown when the children's choir sings Christmas carols. He pats his tall Elvis-do. It sits on his head like a small dead animal.

"I don't know much about you," he says, "yet, I am convinced you have a taste for the good life—French champagne, fine dining, and such?"

"To tell you the truth, my life's been like a train ride to Nowheresville. Some folks may think living in a small town is charming. Truth is, I gotta say, it is *boring.*"

At the next table, all the girls wear fancy dresses, and the boys wear suits and ties. Zoltan sees me glance down at my jeans and boots.

"Don't worry, Angel. You look lovelier than anyone at that table." What a nice thing to say. This is like having a nice rich uncle.

"How old are you, Angel?" asks Zoltan. "I'm guessing nineteen, maybe twenty."

"You sure do like to figure people out, don't you," I say. "I just turned twenty a few months ago. Born in 1950. I'm a waitress in a café that's much older than me. The Go Get 'Em Café. Been working there since I was in high school."

He reaches over for the bottle. "Another glass of champagne?" The stones from his rings flash as he pours. I love looking at the bubbles. I stare at them for a long time as they race up to the top of the glass. Zoltan smooths down both lapels of his jacket before he sits up straight in the booth.

"Angel, I need a small package delivered to a client in Aspen. I have important matters in Denver that make it difficult for me to go myself. The client would like to have it by the end of the week. I wonder if you would deliver it for me. I would be happy to pay you two hundred in cash for doing me this favor."

"Are you kidding me? Two hundred? What's inside? *Solid gold?*"

"As you may have guessed, I am involved in high-level business dealings. The package contains confidential documents and such. I don't trust the post office or parcel post. I always deliver it myself. And I believe you are someone I can trust. Would you be willing to take on this responsibility?"

I'm woozy from the champagne. Zoltan looks like he has three eyes now. My head thick with fog, but I hear him loud and clear.

"You bet I can do it. But Mama and I leave for Pinewood tomorrow."

"Perhaps you could drive to Aspen on Thursday."

"Sure, I can do that."

"Excellent. You won't be sorry. I will meet you at the Old Maiden Inn tomorrow morning right before you leave for the train station. Oh, and don't mention this to your mother. This is strictly between the two of us. Okay? A business deal."

"Sure, I understand. I moved out a while back. I never tell my mother a thing about my life."

"That's smart. I believe you have a bright future ahead of you, my dear." He puts one hand under my elbow and helps me up from the booth.

"Thanks, Zoltan," I say. "This is the most exciting thing that's ever happened to me." He rests his hand on my shoulder and locks his eyes on mine to ensure I get the message.

"I'll have detailed instructions and a package for you," he says. "Do not open it. Everything must stay in its original condition. Is that clear?"

"Yes, I get it. Don't open the package."

"That's right. Once you hand it over to Mr. Conway, you'll receive two hundred in cash."

"*Okay.*"

"Good girl," he says, patting me on the back, his new Golden Retriever.

"Mama and I leave tomorrow morning at 8 for the train station." He takes my elbow to guide me again, like I can't get across a street by myself. I start to pull my arm away.

"My dear, I just want to make sure you get back to your hotel safe and sound." It's not cold outside, but he has a few drops of sweat on his forehead. "You did give me your telephone number in . . . what was the name again? Oh yes, Pinewood. Lovely name. This way, we will be able to stay in touch."

Back in our room, Mama's loud snores tell me she's still down for the count. I strip off my clothes and fall into the too-soft bed. Within minutes I pass out until the sun blasts through the window onto my face. Mama climbs out of bed as slow as molasses.

"C'mon, Mama," I say. "Let's move. We have an 8 o'clock train. And the next one isn't until 10:30."

"Okay, don't rush me," she says, her eyes droopy, her voice whiny and weak.

"We can't be late," I say. First time I ever bossed her around.

As I stuff our few clothes into the suitcase, I leave enough room to fit Zoltan's package. Peeling pink rose wallpaper and sad dark wood furniture cry out for help.

"Bye-bye, room. Hope I never see you again." I slam the door shut. Mama hangs onto the banister with a tight grip, shuffling down to the reception area.

While she settles the hotel bill, from a dark corner, Zoltan gives me that funny salute.

"Mama, I need to use the bathroom before we leave. Better here than the train station, right?"

My new boss follows me and hands off the beige package, about the size of a high school notebook, tightly wrapped in cellophane tape. He said it's important documents. I slip it into my suitcase. He winks, gives me one more salute, and heads out. Once on the train, I can't imagine anything but my new job. Two hundred bucks for delivering a package.

At last, a chance to make some money and break out of my little life. I know I can't tell anyone. Not even Sandy. Late Wednesday afternoon, I take Star, our neighbor's bay mare, out for a bareback gallop to work off some steam. A sudden wind kicks in. She goes loco. My heart thumps like crazy. Me, the rodeo rider on a bucking bronco. Only thing missing is the crowd cheering me on. I clamp my legs onto her sides and grip her mane. Once the wind calms down, so does she.

CHAPTER 18

*T*HURSDAY MORNING, THE CRISP AIR SAYS AUTUMN HAS arrived in full force. The aspen leaves have turned from green to gold. I enjoy the hour drive more than ever, knowing this could be a new beginning. To be safe, I arrive an hour early to meet this Mr. Conway. I must've read Zoltan's instructions about fifty times. I sit in Betsy, my Buick, and read the note once more.

> *Dear Angel,*
> *Your contact, Mr. Conway, will meet you in Wagner Park on Mill Street at 11 sharp Thursday morning. He is a gentleman in his forties with light brown hair. He will be wearing jeans, a tan leather jacket, and a green bandana around his neck. Once you see him, give a discreet salute. Once he nods, you will follow him to a safe, sheltered spot. Hand off the package to him. He will hand over $200 cash. That is all there is to it. Good luck, my dear.*
> *Zoltan*

I see a man that fits the description but no bandana. Maybe he forgot to wear it. I give him the Zoltan salute. He looks at me funny and turns away. I look in another direction for Mr. Conway. Only minutes later, another guy comes by in a tan leather jacket and jeans. No bandana, hair more brown than blonde. Maybe it's dirty blonde; I can't be sure. And maybe he forgot his bandana, too. I give him the salute. He walks over to me with an ugly smile.

"Working a little early in the day, aren't you?" He doesn't nod or show that I should follow him. He's a hungry dog and thinks I'm a piece of meat.

"Hey, leave me alone. I made a mistake. Okay? I thought you were someone else."

"Sure, I'll leave you alone, you little tease. If I wasn't such a fuckin' gentleman . . . ." He stomps away like I'm his girl, and we just broke up. My heart pounds until I can't see him anymore. At last, no doubt about it, I see him with everything on the list: blonde hair, green bandana, and tan leather jacket. I give the salute. He nods. I follow him to a spot hidden away from the street, behind some boulders. He speaks fast and low.

"Does anyone know you're here?"

"Not a soul."

"Good. Hand off the package. Do it fast. You don't remember ever meeting. Right?"

"All right," I say. "Now what?"

"Your job is done. I take it from here. And that's that. Get it?"

"Okay, I got it." My heart pounds so hard I think he must hear it. I hold out my hand for the money. He slips two folded hundred dollar bills into my hand.

As I look down at all this money, he disappears. At least he didn't shortchange me. I have never seen so much cash in my life. My heart pounds, blood rushes to my head, and I want to run to my car. Somehow, I manage to stay calm and cool. I stroll through the park like I have all the time in the world. Once inside good old Betsy, I lock the doors and gun the engine to head towards home.

Who cares what they have in that package? I don't really care, and I don't want to know. I made a quick, easy $200. *Crazy good*. If Zoltan asks me, I'll do it again. I turn on the radio. Who comes up but James Brown. He sings "I Feel Good" straight to me.

Halfway home, Betsy starts to sputter and drive all jerky-like. I roll her into Geiger Guys Repair Shop. A big man with a basset hound face steps up to the car. Once I tell him my problem, he looks at the engine and slides under the car.

"Sorry to tell you this, darlin'," he says, shaking his head, "it's the carburetor."

"Oh no. That's bad. I can tell that's crazy bad." I hold on to Betsy's hood to steady myself.

"It ain't good, I'll tell you that," says hound dog man. "We could start work on it right away." I picture the money flying away like little green birds and take a deep breath.

"How much will it be?"

"Around 150 for everything. Maybe a little more."

"You've got to be kidding me. A hundred and fifty bucks?"

"Yeah, I'm afraid so. It's a big job." I can hardly breathe.

"Would you take a hundred cash?"

"Let me think for a minute." He licks his lips and frowns for a good ten seconds. "Yeah! It's a deal. That's between us, okay? The boss is on vacation."

"Okay, deal. How long does it take? I need to get up the mountain for work tonight."

"It should be ready about 3:30 or 4."

I tell him I need to go to the bank to get the money. Who walks around with a couple of hundred dollar bills in their pocket? But, damn, I wanted to celebrate and buy myself somethin' special. Instead, I go to Miser's Mercantile and buy a royal blue coat with a little hole near the hem, probably from a moth. I guess nobody but a little kid would see it.

I make it to the Double G in time for work.

"Look at you all smiley and cheerful," says Elmer, as I bring his burger. "What's up? Got a new boyfriend?"

"None of your beeswax, Elmer. I just feel good, that's all."

Once I get home and stash what is left of my money away, I wonder if I look any richer. I take a gander in the mirror. No difference. I always think rich people look different. They're way more relaxed and not so wrinkled. Even their suntan looks better with more of a swimming pool glow than building-a-house burn. As I reach for a bar of Ivory soap to wash my face for bed, the phone rings. Nobody calls me this late.

"Angel, it's Zoltan. Where in the hell have you been? Been trying to reach you *all day long*." Right about now, he doesn't sound so Hungarian.

"Sorry, Zoltan. I gave the package to Mr. Conway, and then my car broke down outside Geiger Springs. I waited all day while they fixed it. Then I had to hustle to get to the café on time for the dinner shift."

"Yes, I understand," he says, annoyed. "Listen, your contact confirmed that everything went according to plan. Still, I wanted to check with you. What did you think?" His Hungarian accent is almost *entirely* gone. I reach for my pack of Salems, knock it against my hand, pull one out, and light up.

"There were some other guys in leather jackets and jeans, but they didn't have a green bandana." He coughs a few times like he's going to choke to death. I blow a couple of smoke rings up to the ceiling, waiting for him to stop.

"Hang on, let me get a glass of water," he says. Then he puts the phone down, and I hear the water running. He takes one of those big noisy swallows, then a nose whistle. He picks up the phone again.

"Of course," he says, "I already know you waited for Mr. Conway." His voice strained now.

"Yeah, sure. I waited." He whistle-breathes into the phone.

"All's well that ends well, Angel. That's what Mother always said." His accent returns.

"Mr. Conway said you did a professional job. You handled yourself well."

"The easiest two hundred I ever made. You know how many tips it takes for me to make two hundred bucks?"

"You will do it for us some other time, yes?" He always asks me what I want to do. He's good like that.

"Sure, I will. Betsy won't let me down again."

"I'm not sure what you're referring to, my dear."

"I'm talking about Betsy the Buick, my car. Don't worry; she won't break down on me again for a long while. You can call on me any old time."

Two weeks later, the phone rings as I'm coming through the door from the Double G. I pick up the phone while I flip the lights and turn on the heat.

"Hello, Angel. It's Zoltan."

"I'm happy to hear from you. I sure could use some extra money right now. I can *always* use the extra money."

"Here's your chance," he says. He clears his throat for so long it makes me want to gag. "Are you available to get another package from me on Saturday?" I light up a Salem, sit back in my plaid chair, and take a deep drag. Ducky whines for her dinner.

"Yeah. I can do that." I lean over to shush Ducky as quietly as possible.

"And deliver it the next day?" he asks.

"Sure. I can deliver it the next day." He trusts me. This is crazy good. If I work for him long enough, I might be able to break out of Pinewood.

"I'll see you at the petrol station," he says, "across from the Buffalo Bill Hotel in Copperville."

"Petrol station?"

"It's what we say in Hungary. You would say gas station." I hear him mumble to somebody else, but it sounds like his hand is over the phone.

"Do you know the Buffalo Bill Hotel?" asks Zoltan.

"Sure I do. It has been there forever and a day. There was a big shoot-out there about five years ago."

"Yes, yes," he says. "Very interesting detail."

"So right across is the Gulf Station," I say. "Is that the one you mean?"

"Yes, that is correct," he says, "the Gulf Station. I'll meet you there at 10 a.m. on Saturday. Capiche?"

"What?"

"Never mind, my dear."

He clears his throat again. I wish he would stop with all these weird noises.

"You are taking notes, are you not?" he asks.

"Uh . . . no, but I will," I say.

"Yes, please do. Here's your next note: You will meet up with Mr. Conway in Aspen on Sunday morning at 9, at a different location this time. Better if it's a different place each time. Do you understand?"

"Sure, I get it, Zoltan. I can meet you Saturday at 10, and meeting Mr. Conway on Sunday at 9 is good, too."

"*Excellent*. I will give you further instructions when I see you."

"Okay then. I'm ready to do some business for you."

"How lucky we met. A shame I'm too old for you, my beauty."

When I show up on Saturday morning at 10 sharp, Zoltan leans against a black Cadillac picking his teeth with a gold toothpick. And always the Zoltan salute. This time he wears all black: jacket, pants, boots, and Stetson hat. He looks like a piece of beef jerky. A Denver Dry Goods shopping bag, along with the package, rests on the ground near his right foot. He hands it to me with written instructions. His rings sparkle their own Morse code that says big money. Mr. Conway will wear the same jeans, jacket, and green bandana that he did before.

The next day everything goes as easy as pie. Mr. Conway and I recognize each other in no time. This time I know what to do. He slips me a couple of hundreds, again folded up tight. It's all there. I must be the luckiest girl around. I walk at an easy pace back to Betsy the Buick and make my way back to Pinewood.

Over the next few months, I deliver packages three more times, always at a different location. Mr. Conway and

I don't say a word to each other. I have the routine down pat, like a real pro. When a whole month slugs by without a word from Zoltan, I wonder why. Everything has gone so well. He knows he can trust me to do the job. I can't figure out why he wouldn't be happy with my work. And I sure do miss the extra money. I'm saving it all in an old Heinz pickle jar on the shelf above the refrigerator. That way, I can always find it.

CHAPTER 19

On a Monday night, I'm at home straightening up the place. Monday nights are good for that. With more money working for Zoltan, I moved into a one-bedroom apartment. Tonight, on *Ed Sullivan*, a special bulletin grinds the show to a halt as I dump cigarette butts into a wastebasket.

"After years of investigation, international drug kingpin Vincent (Skinny Vinny) Garofalo was taken into custody in New York City. A part-time resident of Denver, Garofalo is also known by an alias of Zoltan Szabo."

Wait a sec . . . that's Zoltan they're talking about on television. *Holy Moly*.

The ashtray slips from my hands and crashes to the floor.

"The alleged mastermind," says the newscaster, "of a drug ring stretching from London to New York, Denver to California, Garofalo grew up in an Italian working-class neighborhood in New Jersey."

Drug ring? I'm delivering drugs? And Zoltan is *Italian*?

The newscaster continues. "Authorities say he has trafficked drugs his entire adult life yet evaded prosecution all these years. Also arrested in Aspen today, is his accused accomplice, Jack Conway, also known as Handsome Jack Jones."

And there I see it, no doubt about it, Zoltan's face on TV. *My Zoltan*.

That isn't even his real name. My brain flip-flops, trying to make sense of it all. Then Jack Conway's face is flashed on the screen. *That's him.* The same man I would meet in a park, or a gas station, or wherever, and I would hand off a package to him. I hold on to my stomach with both hands as I gasp for air and sink into my new couch.

*I've been delivering drug*s. I knew it was too good to be true. Two hundred dollars for delivering a package. I could be in *big trouble*. My heart speeds around and around like a miniature racetrack. Maybe the cops will come *after me*.

The newscaster goes on. "Authorities say it is hard to estimate at this time, but they believe a conservative figure would be at least fifty million dollars in profit for the Garofalo drug ring over the years."

What? Zoltan and Conway made millions of dollars selling drugs worldwide, and I thought a lousy two hundred was a lot of dough. What a laugh. Those two cockroaches really screwed me over. They could've paid me way more. I want to tell Sandy, but I best keep my trap shut. I fire up a new Salem, grab a bottle of Old Crow from the cupboard, take a few slugs, and slump back into my (paid for with drugs) couch.

"Authorities," continues the newscaster, "will have their work cut out for them to investigate, what they believe, is a huge network of drug runners across the country."

Zoltan acted like I was special, but he had lots of people doing his dirty work. *HOLY CRAP.*

Next morning my head screams out from the bourbon. "Of course, it was too good to be true," says the grown-up voice in my head that I don't listen to. Now I could be going to jail. I ran drugs for these two guys. I knew it couldn't be good. But Zoltan told me I was delivering important papers. All this time, I wanted to believe it. This is seriously bad news.

Wherever I go, everybody talks about the drug bust non-stop. As if it makes their lives more exciting, people in the neighborhood jump up and down because a lot of the dirty work happened nearby. And to think I can't tell a soul. I will miss that easy money. I should have known there was something crooked.

Maybe I should go to church and repent. *Dammit.*

But I didn't know, I thought it was important papers. Why'd they have to go and get caught now? Just as I was saving up some money. He only paid me two hundred bucks a shot. That creep really ripped me off. But worse than that, the Feds will be looking for me.

CHAPTER 20

A Clark Kent look-alike sits at table number 3. Out of step with the other customers, Clark's for sure not a country guy. Dressed in a blue pinstripe suit, long-sleeve white shirt, dark-blue tie, and black-rimmed glasses, he motions me over.

"This place looks like it's been here for ages," he says. No kidding. He says the same exact thing folks coming through town always say. It gets on my last nerve. Faye Vespers should put a little sign in the window that says, *Founded in 1935*. That would save me some grief.

"Yeah," I say, "place opened in 1935 and still going strong."

"What do you think of the chicken-fried steak?" he asks. "Would you recommend it?" He must be in his early thirties. His face as pink and smooth as a baby's bottom.

"Well," I say, "the chicken-fried steak has been on the menu since day one, so I would say it's a winner."

"Alright, I'll have that and a Coors. It's a Colorado beer, right?"

"Yep. Local to Colorado," I say. "Coming right up."

When I bring him the food, he gives me a sad little smile. It's a slow night, so I stand near his table. He takes off his black-rimmed glasses, removes his city boy jacket, and rolls his shirt sleeves. His arms and hands are as pale as a pike, nothing like most guys around here. Most locals work outdoors, building houses, fixing cars, and plowing snow—mainly muscle jobs. On the weekend, they fish and hunt. I notice Clark Kent's short nails, so neat and clean. He pokes at the food, sets down his fork and knife, and breathes deeply.

"My wife left me a year and a half ago. Said she didn't love me anymore. That she wants her own life." Oh no, here we go. They don't pay me the big bucks for that. Maybe he's a Fed, trying to throw me off-guard, and wants to ask me about Zoltan. My breath almost stops, and the blood pools up in my head.

"She left you, huh? Sorry to hear that," I say.

"Well, thanks." He takes a handkerchief out of his pocket, wipes his brow, and shakes his head. He picks up his glasses and puts them on again like he's trying to hide.

"That's right," he says. "I came home to an empty house and a note on the kitchen counter. Honest to God, I never saw it coming."

He's telling this to me, a stranger. I guess he just needs someone to listen.

"I had to get out of Columbus," he says. "Now I manage Soldiers Bank in Geiger Springs."

Hmm. This is getting interesting.

"That's a good job," I say.

He looks up at me and shrugs. "It's okay." Everything about him is neat and tidy. His haircut, his clean-shaven face, his crisp white shirt.

"Do you like Geiger Springs?" I ask.

"It's fine for work, but I don't want to live there." He looks better with that little smile on his face. "I rent a place up here in Pinewood," he says. "One of the most beautiful drives I've ever seen. That's what sold me. Plus, I love the peace and quiet."

"That's 'cause you haven't been looking at these same mountains your entire life," I say. I lean over his table and lower my voice. "Want to hear somethin' amazing? I've never seen the ocean. Not even close." He laughs.

"Guess what?" he says. "I'm from Ohio. Neither have I." He cocks his head and looks at me like he sees me for the first time. "My name is Arthur." He blushes when he tells me. None of the men around here blush, that's for sure.

"Nice to meet you, Arthur. I'm Angel." His shoulders ease up, and he removes his glasses. Without them, he's not bad looking.

The more he talks, the more I think he's for real. That he isn't with the FBI. Still, I'm on edge that Zoltan and Mr. Conway will talk. He shows up for dinner every night at Table 3. He always gives me a huge tip. And he never asks me about those two.

After a few weeks, Arthur asks me out on a real date. We go to dinner at Luigi's in Copperville. Only twenty minutes down the mountain, but I've never been there before. Everyone is dressed up so nice, waiters in spiffy black slacks, white shirts, and little bowties. It reminds me of that McGregor's place in Denver, where Zoltan got me drunk on champagne. I can't believe the crazy high prices and order a hamburger, the cheapest thing on the menu. I have to say it is the best burger I've ever tasted.

Arthur drives me straight home and says goodnight at the front door. Not a kiss. Not even a hug. I don't get it. Most guys ask me over to their place for a drink and some nooky, and that's about it. Maybe it's different with older guys from the city. He takes both my hands in his. "I'm glad we did this," he says. "Let's do it again." He is *so* polite.

"Dinner was crazy good," I say. He squeezes my hands and waits for me to go inside my front door. I throw my clothes on the chair. What does Arthur see in me? He's much older than me. At least ten years. And he manages a bank. I wash my face, brush my teeth, and change into my flannel PJs, printed with different dog breeds. I always sleep the best in these pajamas. I pull the covers up to my chin and try to picture Arthur and me with our clothes shucked off. I wonder if he sleeps in flannel PJs, maybe the ones with the trap door at the back.

The following week Arthur and I go for a walk near McClure Pass. He talks nonstop the whole time. I don't mind. He's smarter than anyone I've ever met. He explains all kinds of things, like the reason for the Vietnam War and what goes on in the world. I never met a man like him before, at least not someone who wanted to spend time with me. I'm used to folks talking about Pinewood and the local gossip. That's about it.

He asks me to go to a movie in Copperville on Saturday night to see an old movie from the 60s called, *The Nutty Professor*. I laugh so hard the Pepsi comes out of my nose. It doesn't seem to bother him. He looks at me like he's glad I'm having fun. On the way home, Johnny Cash sings "Folsom Prison" on the radio. It cuts off mid-way by a man's loud excited voice.

"Another suspect was taken into custody in the drug scandal that rocked the country a few months ago. Johnny "Pastrami" Cohen was arrested at his luxurious apartment on Fifth Avenue. Cohen is the alleged main conduit for the international operation based out of New York."

Arthur dials down the sound.

"One of these characters operated just an hour away in Aspen. His name was Conway. Have you heard about it?"

The color drains out of my face.

"Well, sure I have," I say. "Loco, huh? So close to Pinewood and all." My mouth turns dry as dust. Arthur keeps his hands on the wheel and doesn't say a word. I feel like a time bomb is ticking.

"They were dealing Heroin," he says, "the worst drug around." I want to end the conversation, but I can't help myself.

"Whoa, that's bad," I say. "They must have made a ton of money." I wonder if he can tell I'm as nervous as a church lady in a saloon.

"They got away with many millions of dollars," says Arthur. He laughs a mean low chuckle. "Good thing these criminals will be locked up for a long, long time." He turns up the music again.

"You want to see my place?" he asks. "Maybe listen to some music and talk?"

"Sure. We can do that for a while." Pine trees block his two-story cabin from the street. He holds the front door open for me. *What a gentleman.* Could be the first guy ever to hold a door open for me.

"Welcome to my palace," says Arthur. The cozy living room has a leather couch with a folded blanket on the back. No shirts lying around, old newspapers piled up, and dirty dishes in the kitchen sink. It smells clean, like fresh pine. So old-fashioned and proper it makes me nervous. I wonder where the cops will find me if Zoltan talks. Maybe they would arrest me at the café in front of all my customers.

"I could go for a glass of wine," I say. "Do you have some?"

He goes into the kitchen. There's a creak of a cabinet drawer opening and closing.

"I have an open bottle of red," he says, sticking his head through the door. "Red sound alright?" I stay on the couch, uncertain if I should join him.

"Anything wet is fine with me," I say. Arthur sets down two big goblets with *Bottoms Up* in red letters. He gets a fire going in the fireplace. We sip our wine as the fire crackles and pops. At long last, the tension drops from my neck. He holds my hand for a long while without either of us saying a word.

He scoots closer to me and kisses my neck, then my lips. Most of the guys I've been with are fast and rough macho men. This guy is smooth. We kiss on the couch for a while. Without a word, he retakes my hand and walks me into the bedroom. He slowly unbuttons my blouse, unhooks my bra, and looks at me.

"Beautiful," he says.

Once I'm undressed, he lays me on the bed and runs his hands over my body so gently that I gasp. After all the one-nighters, I can hardly believe it. He kisses me on my lips, neck, and shoulder, working his way down until he covers every square inch of me. He takes his time and waits for me. This is way better than I ever dreamed. I never expected someone as buttoned up as Arthur would make such beautiful love to me. Afterward, he looks into my eyes and strokes my cheek. He looks handsome with his hair flopped down on his forehead.

"You know why I wanted to wait before we made love?" he says.

"Tell me," I say.

He props himself up on his elbow and looks up at the ceiling for a minute like he can't put his words together so fast.

"There is something extraordinary about you, Angel," he says. "Yes, you are beautiful, that's obvious . . . and intelligent. But I sense there is even more . . . I must say, I am intrigued."

He's not street smart like I'm used to, but he does manage a bank, the go-to-college kind of smart. In a million years, I never figured someone like Arthur would be interested in me. When I slide out of bed to get dressed, he pulls me back under the covers and rolls on top of me. He smooths back my tangled hair.

"What's your rush?" He is full of surprises. And we start all over again. I don't like to stay overnight with a guy. In the morning they want to talk and have coffee together. But Arthur convinces me to stay. He holds my hand all night long while we sleep. He must really like me.

CHAPTER 21

1971

THE PINEWOOD GIRLS MEET AT DEDE'S B & B FOR OUR annual T-shirt party. She has couches and chairs all over the place with sweet little handmade pillows. Even the toilet paper rolls in the guest bathrooms are wrapped in lace.

There's the green room with fern wallpaper, the red room like a French bordello, a white one with little doves on branches above the bed, and a blue room. That one has a pale-blue ceiling with puffy white clouds. Quaint little sayings in needlepoint hang on the living room walls. Some say: *Home is Where the Heart Is* and *Money Can't Buy Happiness.*

"Out-of-towners love this crap," says Dede.

"Can't believe it's been a year since we had our last T-shirt party," says Sue in her croaky voice.

"I know," says Sandy, her lipstick as red and glam as always. "We started in 1965 when we were fifteen, and here we are six years later. Unreal. A whole new era of fun T-shirts."

"Here's my latest one," I say. I open my jacket and flash my T-shirt. *Rich or Poor it's Good to Have Money.*

"Right on," says Sandy, raising her fist up in the air.

"That's our girl," says Dede. "Hope it happens for you!"

"What does yours say, Dede?" I ask.

She pulls open the beige cardigan she stole from her husband, Richard. Underneath, a red T-shirt with bold black letters reads: *I Want to Get Stoned with the Stones*. We all laugh even more.

"Isn't that the best?" she asks, pulling her sweater back over her toned stomach. She pours each of us a bourbon and Coke.

"Okay, Sue," says Dede, "your turn."

"It's not as exciting as yours, Dede." A blush creeps down her short neck.

"Don't worry about it, Sue," says Dede. We know you're not the craziest girl in town. C'mon, let's see what you've got."

Sue removes her fake leather jacket and places it on the side table. Her oversized T-shirt is emblazoned with a flower that reads: *War Is Not Healthy for Children and Other Living Things*.

For a moment, all of us hold our breath. Sandy breaks the silence. Her eyes snap with emotion.

"Sue, you always put us to shame. That's a beautiful message you have there." She takes a deep long sigh and opens her favorite blue coat to show us her T-shirt message: *Live the Life You Want, No Matter What It Takes*.

"Crazy good, Sandy. I love that," I say. "Yep, no matter what it takes."

Sandy nods and winks at me.

"Speaking of no matter what it takes, what about that movie *Bonnie and Clyde?* Did you all see it?" asks Dede.

"Loved it," says Sandy. "That Warren Beatty is yum." She closes her eyes and kisses the air. "He could talk *me* into robbing a bank." Everyone laughs.

I drift into a bourbon and Coke haze to daydream of Ace and our wild times together. It's been five years. I've never stopped thinking about him.

"Hey Angel, you with us?" asks Sandy.

"Oh yeah, I'm with you." But I'm not with them at all.

My head spins with confusion. Arthur treats me better than anyone I've ever met. Why do I still think about Ace, my favorite outlaw? I was only a kid. He dumped me, yet I still think of him as the love of my life. On her way to becoming a schoolteacher, Sue gives a meaningful stare that forces me to snap to attention.

"He's not Warren Beatty," I say, "but I met a nice guy. He manages Soldiers' Bank in Geiger Springs."

I told Sandy about him already, but not the others. Dede, *with the unemployed husband*, lets out a whistle.

"Bank manager, huh?" she says. "Way to go."

"That's great, Angel. I wish I could meet someone," says Sue, still stuck at home with Mom. She wrings her hands. "I can't remember the last time I had a date."

Sandy's bright brown eyes cloud over. "My last fling was a married guy I met on a photo shoot. It was fun while it lasted. But that and a nickel gets you nothing." She looks at her empty glass. "Can you pour me another drink, Dede?"

Sue notices Sandy's mood and changes the subject.

"Let's go see another movie with lots of action," says Sue. "There's one I heard about with a con artist. He fools a lot of people and gets away with a ton of cash." Sandy's face brightens.

"How about you, Angel? Want to see the movie about Charles Ponzi? He's the biggest con artist of all time," says Sue. I laugh for the first time all night.

"Count me in," I say. *"I want to see what he can get away with."*

"Tell us more about the new guy in your life," says Sandy.

I've told her a little bit, but not too much. Her face is filled with curiosity as if I might have the answers. Wish I did.

"He's the kind of guy your mama says you should marry," I say. "You know what I mean?"

Now all the girls are hanging on every word I say.

Sandy smirks at me. "I hope he's good in the sack."

"For heaven's sake, Sandy," says Sue, "is that all you can think about?"

"It's not easy to meet a nice guy," I say as a big sigh escapes my mouth.

My friends nod like those little dogs in the back of a car window. Wish I could be content with someone decent like Arthur. He could be my ticket to a better life. That is if the cops don't connect me to Zoltan and Conway, the con men.

I wonder what Arthur would think of Pops and Rhonda, who are still the town joke after all these years. Mama best get it together, too. She drinks too much, talks too loud, and still lives in the same old house on Beaver Drive. She busted her teeth, falling down those rickety stairs. Now she's in worse shape than ever.

Early Monday morning, the phone rings as I'm washing my hair in the shower. I don't answer. A few minutes later, it starts ringing again, like someone needs to get ahold of me. I grab a towel and pick up on the fourth ring.

"Angel, it's Sandy." Her words rush out faster than usual.

"What is it? What's wrong?" I ask, water dripping all over the kitchen floor.

"Sue's mother died. Just over an hour ago."

"Oh no. What happened?" I mop the water, juggling the phone against my ear.

"She and Sue were having breakfast. Sue went into the kitchen for her toast. You know how she likes her wheat toast so well done it's almost burnt?"

"Yeah, yeah. What about her mother?"

"By the time the toast was finished, Sue found her face down in her bowl of Lucky Charms, deader than a doornail."

"Oh no," I say. "That is too sad. Poor Sue. What a nightmare."

"I know," says Sandy. "She had such a grip on Sue, not letting her date or do much of anything."

"That's true. She was under that woman's control. Sue is finally free," I say. "At last, she can have a life." I hope she makes the most of it.

I thought I would have a better life once I went to work for Zoltan. That didn't last too long. At least the cops haven't come after me. At least not yet. Some luck has been on my side. Maybe they don't care about small-timers like me. They go after the Big Fish. Even so, I sure do miss the excitement of passing off a package to Mr. Conway and that easy money. I thought that was my escape from Pinewood. No matter what, my Pinewood girls and I need to stick together.

"Sandy, let's go over to Sue's house so we can be with her. We're all she has now."

CHAPTER 22

*I*T ISN'T ALL THAT LONG BEFORE *I* SPEND MOST NIGHTS AND weekends with Arthur. One Saturday morning, he wants to head out of Pinewood to explore a few of the small towns. This time I'm the expert. We hit the road after a quick breakfast of orange juice, coffee, and English muffins.

Every single time I leave Pinewood, my heart lifts. It's a reminder of the whole big world out there. We sail past the market, liquor store, and thrift shops in Copperville. Arthur wheels onto the I-70. We pass small towns with names like New Castle and Silt. The Colorado River roars right alongside the road. Off to the right stands the big co-op, where they sell horse feed, bridles, and dog food. My kind of place.

"Coming up in eight miles is a town called Rifle," I say.

"Rifle? That's quite a name for a town," says Arthur, his city boy background coming into the foreground. He laughs. "Rifle!" he says again. "It couldn't get more Western than that."

"True enough," I say.

"Why don't we stop there," he says, "and walk around?" I don't mention that the whole town could fit in your back pocket.

"That would be fun," I say. He turns off the highway onto narrow dusty streets. From the looks of it, Rifle must be older than Pinewood.

"Look at that café across the street," says Arthur. "It's called Sharpshooters Café. Maybe that's the name of the owner, Mr. Sharpshooter."

"Right," I say. "And his first name is Eagle-Eye. Eagle-Eye Sharpshooter."

Arthur nudges me with his hand and laughs.

"I've got to see the inside of that place," he says. "Let's have lunch there."

We head on down to Sharpshooters Café. Three waitresses, decked out in cowboy hats, jeans, and boots, rush around. Each wears a low-slung leather belt and holster and packs a .22 pistol.

"My God! I thought I'd seen everything," says Arthur.

"Don't forget you're in wild, wooly Colorado," I say. Our waitress appears in a flash, pencil in hand, ready to go.

"Howdy, folks! What can I get you?" Her hat looks a little too small for her head.

"Two burgers with fries and two Cokes," says Arthur. Even though he knows what I want for lunch, it bugs me that he doesn't ask me first or let me order for myself. I don't say anything but flash him a warning look, which he ignores.

Our waitress scribbles down the order on her pad while chomping on chewing gum. The yellow and silver of the Wrigley's package peeks out from her breast pocket. Once she writes down our order, her hand rests on the handle of her gun. I wonder if she's ever blown a hole straight through her foot. Arthur glances nervously at her and then at me. She walks away, still chomping like crazy.

He leans across the table and whispers. "I guess you can't complain about the food or the service around here. They might shoot you for sending back cold soup." I can tell he's only half kidding. I like showing him my part of the world.

On our morning hike on McClure Pass the next day, Arthur plays Moses and walks with a long stick he found on the trail. The sky is as deep blue as the flax wildflowers I love to pick along the trail. Arthur stops and takes my hand, his face happier, relaxed, and more handsome than usual.

"You know," he says, looking up and all around us, "it doesn't get better than this." He leans onto the stick. "People travel far and wide to see this kind of beauty, to enjoy a hike like this."

I suppose he's right, but I would love to see beautiful beaches with palm trees. We hold hands as we start up a steep section of the trail. Who do we see but Sandy and the girls coming toward us. No surprise since we have all hiked this trail for years.

"Hey there," I say. All three of them have big grins plastered across their faces as they walk toward us. Sandy wipes her brow with a bandana.

"You must be Arthur." She reaches out to shake his hand.

"And you must be Sandy," says Arthur. "Angel has told me a lot about you."

"Yep, it's me. I hope she hasn't told you too much." She laughs her unique Sandy laugh, loud and boisterous, with her head thrown back. Arthur gives me a look that says, I see why you like her. Sandy puts her arms around our gal pals.

She takes charge as the ringleader. "This is Dede, and that's Sue. We call ourselves The Pinewood Girls."

"Good to meet you all," says Arthur. "Angel said you've been friends all your lives."

"That's right," says Sue. "I'm sure Angel must have told you her real name is Angela. She started calling herself Angel when she was about sixteen." I glare at Sue, but she doesn't notice. He stares at me with a question mark in his eyes.

"You never told me that," he says, frowning.

"To tell you the truth, I kind of forgot Angela was my real name," I say, hoping this is the end of it.

"Why did you change it?" he asks.

"It's just easier to say."

Dede breaks the awkward moment like only Dede can do. "You two lovebirds will have to come over and have a drink with us at the B&B."

"A very nice invitation," says Arthur. He wraps his arm around me. "Okay, sweetheart?"

"Sure, that would be fun," I say, hoping I sound like I mean it. What would we talk about? Richard's job interviews that never pan out? "Thanks, Dede," I add. "Well, I think we should push on." Arthur takes my hand, and we continue up the mountain.

The next morning Sandy shows up at my door at 8:45. The house is quiet, with Arthur somewhere on the 133 headed towards Soldiers Bank.

"Hey," says Sandy, "thought we could catch up for half an hour."

"Sure," I say. "Come on in. I just made some coffee." She helps herself to a mug, then sits with her arms planted on the table, like she's ready for business.

"So that's Arthur," she says. She whispers like he may be in the next room listening. "He's better looking than you said."

"You think so?" I say, "I do like it when he wears jeans. He doesn't look so much like Clark Kent."

"Clark Kent!" Sandy laughs. "Does he ever become Superman?" We laugh, like always. "We only had a minute to talk yesterday on the trail," she says, "but he seems like a decent guy. I didn't realize he was so much older than you."

"He's thirty-three. So, yeah, twelve years older than me. Married once before for seven years, but no kids. So that's good."

"He's kind of stiff compared to other guys you've been with. Right?"

"Maybe 'cause he's older," I say. "Or maybe they're all like that from Ohio. I don't know."

"He seems like a gentleman," says Sandy. "That's hard to find around these parts."

"He teaches me about other places in the world, like India. He said cows roam the streets because they're considered sacred. Things like that. Yesterday I showed him what *I* know, so I took him to Sharpshooters Cafe. He almost peed in his pants when he saw the waitresses with guns."

Sandy cracks up again. She tosses her hair off to the side, Sandy style.

"He must be pretty good in the sack," she says, "or you wouldn't stay with him. Maybe Superman?" I laugh but don't answer her question.

"Sometimes, he bosses me around. I ignore it. He does treat me pretty good most times."

With Ace, I had my big love. With Zoltan, I had money. Now I have Arthur.

CHAPTER 23

1971

ARTHUR TAKES ME TO THE PINEWOOD INN FOR DINNER on a Saturday night. The place is packed, as usual. Jimmy, the bartender, is going full speed ahead. The daily specials are written in chalk on little blackboards. Today it's top sirloin with baked potato, yummy cold-weather food.

The Pinewood Inn restaurant overlooks the swimming pool out back. Flashes of that brutal high school grad night when I jumped into that same pool, drunk, in all my clothes, take over my thoughts. I do worry that Arthur will find out about some of my crazy past with Ace and handing off packages for Zoltan. He would drop me like a hot brick.

Folks stand shoulder-to-shoulder at the bar. Tonight seems rowdier than usual. Five macho bikers in black leather sit at the round table near the window, smoking, laughing, and slamming down their drinks. I've seen bikers galore stop in Pinewood over the years. Arthur looks their way, raises an eyebrow at first, but decides to pay them no mind. The bartender pops over to say hi to us. He just met Arthur a few months ago, but he's known me for years.

"Hi Jimmy, good to see you," says Arthur, with a small tight smile. "We'll each have a glass of your house red."

"Comin' right up, Artie!" Jimmy slaps Arthur on the shoulder. Arthur winces.

In less than five minutes, Jimmy places two glasses of wine in front of us. "Speedy Gonzales," says Arthur.

He turns to me and raises his glass. Several big groups celebrate birthdays, an anniversary, or the simple fact that it's the weekend. Arthur leans towards me.

"Cheers, darling." We clink our glasses together in a toast. "To more good times." He leans over and gives me a light kiss. Over his shoulder, I can't help but notice one of the Harley guys staring at me. I could never forget those piercing blue eyes and sun-streaked hair.

Holy Hell, it's Ace. After all this time. He gives a thumbs up and sashays out the door. Blood wooshes to my head. I want to chase after him. If only I could see him one more time. He's back here in Pinewood, so close to me right now. I don't know how I manage it, but I stay nice and still, quiet as a church mouse, lean back in my chair and take a deep breath. I can't mess this up with Arthur.

"What's wrong?" says Arthur. "You have the strangest look on your face." His own face darkens with concern. "Who are those people?" he asks.

"Uh, no clue!" I say. "These biker guys always stop in Pinewood." I swallow and squeak out the words. "They all look alike after a while."

"I have to agree," he laughs, "kind of like outlaws. I wouldn't want one of them coming in the bank." He pretends to wipe the sweat off his brow. I laugh with him, but more out of relief than anything else.

"Well, anyway," he says, "let's finish our drinks and order some dinner. We can throw on our jackets and go for a walk in the nice cool autumn air."

"I would like that top sirloin," I say. "It's kind of expensive, though."

"You can order whatever you want, sweetheart."

I kiss Arthur on the cheek. "A walk after dinner sounds great." I wonder if Ace flew out of Pinewood or if he's going to stick around. It's been five years, and I still dream about him. I know he left me hanging and ran out on me. I do believe he loved me. But here I am with Arthur, and Ace just walked out the door. Again.

When the food arrives, my mouth waters from the aroma of the grilled steak. I smother it with A-1 sauce, plunk a wad of butter into the baked potato and dig in right away. I even close my eyes. *It tastes so good.*

"Angel, remember to put the napkin in your lap," says Arthur. "And slow down! You're acting like this is your last meal."

"Sorry, I'm really hungry." Not everybody wants to cut their meat in small perfect little bites the way he does. He glares at me.

"And you might want to cut that steak into smaller pieces," he says.

"Okay, I will." I hide my mouth with my napkin. He reminds me of my 11th grade math teacher, Mr. Strange, the perfectionist. I hated his class, and he knew it. That was the year when Ace ran out on me. I could hardly drag myself out of bed to go to school. And I almost failed a few other classes besides math. I wonder if Ace stayed outside with the other bikers. Never thought he'd pass through Pinewood again.

"Another glass of wine?" asks our waitress.

"I'll have a vodka?" I say. "Straight up with a twist." Arthur looks at me funny, but I don't care. Once she brings my drink, I toss it down.

A young couple in their twenties walks into the restaurant, arms wrapped around each other. They gaze at each other like the world could stand still and it would be okay. Arthur notices me looking at them. He touches my arm.

"You're so quiet, sweetheart. Do you like your dinner?"

I did at first.

"Well, sure, it tastes good."

"Alright, then. When we finish, what do you say we grab a little dessert in town. Let me see that beautiful smile of yours." I give him a camera-ready smile, then set down my fork and knife on the right side of my plate, like he showed me. He said it signals that I'm finished with my meal.

"Ready?" he asks. I nod.

Arthur helps me with my coat. I pull out my white knit hat, a Christmas present from Faye Vespers, and scrunch it over my head.

"See you, Jimmy," says Arthur. Jimmy waves and returns to his high-speed bartending. He could win the bartending Olympics.

Arthur puts his arm around me as we leave the Inn. I still hope to see Ace. Just to see him again would make me happy. When I spot a few bikers in the parking lot, my heart skips a beat. I squint my eyes against the dark. Maybe Ace is out there waiting for me. As Arthur and I move away, I look over my shoulder but don't see Ace.

"What are you looking at?" asks Arthur.

"Nothing, really, it's such a beautiful night," I say, and give up my search so I don't set him to wondering. He hugs me close as we stroll through town. After a while, I take a deep breath, wipe my mind clean and sink into Arthur's shoulder. A bright crescent moon hangs high in the black sky.

Most shops close at 5:30, but Sally's Sweet Shoppe is still open. Arthur buys a couple of chocolate-covered honeycomb bars. As we walk along, nibbling on our candy, he stops at the picture window at Jofer's Family Jewels. The lights in the window are bright enough for us to see inside. Arthur points to a ring with a sparkling-blue stone surrounded by small diamonds. I'm shivering from the chilly night, and he hugs me closer.

"I know you like blue," he says, eyes all aglow. "That ring would look beautiful on you."

"I'm not much for jewelry. I'm more of a jeans and boots kind of gal. It's a pretty ring, though, I'll say that."

"You sure you wouldn't wear a ring like that?" I never heard him sound so unsure, except the first night at the Double G when he said his wife walked out on him. Why is he talking about this fancy ring to me?

"You're so funny," I say. "Why you ask?"

"Because I want to marry you," says Arthur. "That is like the one I bought for you. I've been waiting for the right moment." He smiles and drops down to one knee right there on the sidewalk. A soft sprinkle of rain doesn't stop him. He dips his hand into his jacket pocket, pulls out a small velvet box, opens it, and holds it up to me.

"Will you marry me?" he asks, all choked up. Three young boys walk past at that exact moment and stop to wait for my answer. They snicker and elbow each other in the ribs.

"Are you kidding me?" I say. "Holy shit . . . I mean, yes. I do, Arthur. I want to marry you, too." He slips the blue topaz ring on my finger. When we kiss for a long time in front of the store, our little audience applauds.

They yell out, *"Get a room."*

We laugh along with them.

"We will," says Arthur. I never saw him lit up like a Christmas tree before. "This is the beginning of a new life for us, Angel."

The drizzle steps up to a heavy downpour and breaks the spell. We run back to the car, his arm around me, to escape the rain. My mind now floods with confusion. He treats me right. He's smart. He has a good job. He may boss me around a little but has never let me down. Not once.

But Ace . . .

The next day at work, I tell Faye Vespers that Arthur asked me to marry him. I flash the fancy topaz ring, big as can be on my finger, so she knows it's true.

"How about that for some good news?" chirps Faye. She steps out from behind the cash register and waves her arms up like she's saying Hallelujah in church. Then she yells out to the customers.

"Angel's getting married!" Everyone cheers, whether they know me or not.

"I've known you since you were a tiny little thing," she whispers, "and now you're getting married. I'm so excited for you!" She wipes her hands on her dress. "Do you know when?"

"We're talking about sometime in the spring," I say, unable to believe I'm talking about my own wedding. "Maybe the last week in May."

"Have the ceremony here at the Double G," Faye Vespers says, looking like she's ready to burst into tears.

She pulls a hanky from the sleeve of her dress and pats her watery eyes.

For as long as I can remember, she always kept a hanky there.

"Yes, it has to be here," she says. "After all, this is where you met your prince." The customers are raising coffee cups, their glass of coke or water or whatever to me in a toast.

"*Congratulations*," shouts everyone in the café. I never had so much attention before.

"That sounds perfect, Faye. I would love to be married here."

When I tell Arthur, he says he wants a formal wedding at the Inn, but I put my foot down. For once, I get my way with him. I never cared about the white dress, church wedding, or lots of people throwing rice. No fuss and keep it simple. That's me. It makes sense to have it at Faye Vespers' café. The Double G has always been a big part of my life.

CHAPTER 24

1972

ON OUR WEDDING DAY WE LUCK OUT WITH PERFECT weather. But all is not perfect. My thoughts turn to Ace. I always thought somehow, some way, we would end up together. When I saw him at the Pinewood Inn with the bikers, I thought he might come back for me. Crazy, I guess, but I thought we would escape Pinewood together on his motorcycle. But I was wrong.

My friends, all smiling ear-to-ear, look so happy for me. Arthur never looked more handsome than he does today. His eyes have the sparkle of love. I'm a lucky girl. I better push these thoughts of Ace out of my mind. It's a stupid dream that could never come true. Ace would never settle down, says the voice in my head. You're right, I say back to it. I smile at the people who matter the most to me. My folks, Faye Vespers, and my Pinewood girls.

I asked everyone to wear cowboy boots and jeans. Mama, in new dark-blue jeans, her hands twitching for a cigarette, stands as far away as possible from Pops. Rhonda plants right next to him, trying to steal the show in a low-cut red blouse and blue jeans with appliqued red flowers. Looks like she splurged on brand-new red boots, too. The whole group forms a semi-circle around Arthur and me, with Sandy, Dede, and Sue standing together.

My jeans are studded with dark pink and white rhinestones, and so are my white boots. Mama styled my hair in long waves with a few pink flowers woven here and there. My sweet pup, Ducky, is the Maid of Honor. She matches my outfit with a huge pink bow tied around her neck. I hold a small bouquet of white roses. Somehow Arthur looks more dressed up than everyone else. I guess it's the sharp crease down the front of his jeans. Reverend Brown keeps it short and sweet like I asked. I'm shocked that Mama cries the whole time. I can't figure out what that's about.

The Reverend announces, "You can kiss the bride."

Arthur and I share our first kiss with Ducky sandwiched between us. Once Pops hears the words that we're man and wife, he plants a drunken kiss on my cheek.

Rhonda stays in the background, her boobs popping from her flashy blouse.

"We have champagne, everyone," announces Faye. The whole gang toasts Arthur and me as we sample the bite-size brownies and oatmeal cookies, still warm from Faye's oven. I told her not to bother with a cake. Nobody likes wedding cake.

Some goofball put a cardboard sign that says *Just Married* in the back window of Arthur's Buick Skylark and tied tin cans to the bumper. They clink, clank onto the street as we drive off for our honeymoon in Denver, planned by Arthur, so he could *surprise me*. About a mile down the road, he pulls the car over and throws the cans and the sign in the back seat once we're out of sight.

"We don't need to advertise to the world," he says. I think it's fun for other people to wave and cheer. He wants to keep it between us. I never saw him so happy. What a difference from the sad guy I first met at the Double G. He never did tell me why his wife left him. I guess I'll find out now that we're married. Funny, I didn't consider it before, but I wonder why Arthur didn't invite anyone to our wedding. I guess I'll find that out, too.

On the drive to Denver, we don't say much. He puts his hand over mine. A clap of thunder and a crack of lightning comes out of nowhere. The sky darkens, and it pours down. One of those May storms you never see coming. I hope it will end soon. It scares me that it's a sign from God. I don't exactly believe in God, but you never know. I fidget with the knobs on the radio, trying to drown out my worries. Is this the beginning of a new life or a new trap? Mama and Pops didn't have much of a marriage. None of the Pinewood girls have had the greatest parents. I don't know a soul that has what I'd call a happy life. *Here's to hoping.*

We approach a fancy old brick hotel with a dark-green awning stretching along the front. Parking attendants in red jackets with black collars stand waiting and then rush to our car the moment we stop. Could that be their whole job, just standing there like that?

"Welcome to the Palace Hotel," says one of them as he opens my door. I reach into the back seat for my suitcase.

"No honey," says Arthur. He frowns at me, like I'm a simple country bumpkin, catches himself, and smiles. "Don't even think about it," he continues. "They'll take the luggage for us. That's their job."

I walk away like a princess. Arthur squeezes my hand as we walk into the lobby. Arches everywhere with lighting inside of them. The orange velvet upholstered couches and high polished wood tables look like they would be in a palace. I need to keep my mouth from hanging open.

"This is amazing," I say.

Arthur smirks.

"I can't believe you've only been to Denver two times before in your whole life," he says, "just three hours from Pinewood."

"Yep, only twice before," I say. "So now I'll be here three times."

Arthur chose an Italian Renaissance-styled hotel built in 1892 because he says it has a history. I don't want him to think I'm dumb, so I don't ask what Renaissance means. He went through a lot of trouble to find the right place. He's good that way. Since we're only staying two nights, we don't have much to unpack. Our room has pale-green walls and white drapes. A round wood table smells fresh with lemon oil. A dozen peach-colored roses in a real crystal vase grabs my attention. *I need that crystal vase.*

Arthur opens a bottle of champagne waiting for us in a silver ice bucket. He pops the cork, and we hold our glasses up, looking at one another like in the movies.

"To you!" He wipes his hand across his mouth like he's erasing the words. "Correction, to *us*."

"Yes, to us," I say. He sips his champagne for a minute.

"I have a thought, sweetheart," he says. "I'm going to take you to dinner at one of my favorite places in Denver. It's called McGregor's Bar and Grill." I almost spit my champagne across the room. Somehow, I manage to keep my cool.

"Oh, okay, that sounds nice," I say. "A customer at the Double G mentioned it one time. I hear it's a nice place."

"Yes, it is, darling. I only want the best for you." Holy shit. He said the same thing Zoltan said that first night when he took me to McGregor's—about me deserving the very best.

Is there a connection? But they threw Zoltan in jail. And now I'm Arthur's wife. I swig down the champagne. I wonder if the Feds will ever find me? When Arthur steps out for a minute, I pour one more glass of champagne to drown my fears.

I wear my rhinestone jeans and boots to McGregor's. Most ladies are dolled up in dresses or skirts. Arthur doesn't comment, which surprises me. My neck stiffens up as I wonder if Zoltan will show up. I know, without a doubt, he couldn't be here, but my mind keeps fighting me, shouting out that Zoltan might walk through the door any minute.

The waiter stands at the table, like a soldier ready for his orders. I sink into the brown upholstery when I realize he is one and the same man that waited on Zoltan and me. Same flattop, same long pointed nose, same thin lips. I don't look up at him. Instead, I bury my face in the menu.

"Ahem," says Arthur. "Let's start with a nice cocktail." He smiles over at me. "How about a Screwdriver, sweetheart?" he asks.

"Sure," I say, keeping my voice quiet, trying to disappear.

"Alright then," says Arthur.

"Hors d'oeuvres to start?" asks the waiter. He focuses intently on Arthur for a few seconds. He glances back my way. He continues to study me, unsettling me even more.

"Didn't I wait on you once before?" he asks. "Maybe a year ago?" I sink a bit lower. "I remember that beautiful hair color of yours. You just don't see it that often." I better think fast.

"Oh no," I say, "it had to be someone else. I've never been to this restaurant before. We're celebrating tonight." I flash my teeth in my most winning smile. "It's the first night of our honeymoon."

"Hmm," he says with a slight frown. "I'm pretty good at remembering faces, but I guess I was wrong this time. So, how about some Rumaki?"

"Sure," says Arthur, "we'll take an order of your Rumaki."

The waiter leaves us alone, with me wondering what in God's name Rumaki could possibly be. Arthur turns to me, a question mark planted in his eyes.

"That was very odd," he says. "Why would he think he saw you before?"

I shrug my shoulders.

"You've only been to Denver twice before, right?" says Arthur. "Once as a child and once when you brought your mother for dental work. Isn't that what you said?"

"That's exactly right. Those were the only two times I've been to Denver." This isn't my idea of a honeymoon conversation. Hope this'll be the end of it.

"You have a great memory, Arthur."

"Thank you, my Angel," he says. "One thing I'll say for myself is I do have a good memory." He excuses himself and goes to the men's room. I wrap the McGregor's ashtray in a cloth napkin and slip it into my purse. He returns as I'm snapping my purse shut.

"That was fast," I say. "By the way, what is Rumaki?"

"Chicken liver with a water chestnut wrapped in bacon. It's delicious."

CHAPTER 25

"**H**ONEY, I'VE CLEARED OUT THIS CLOSET FOR YOU." Arthur points to the open doors with ten wire hangers dangling there for my clothes. "I moved all my things to the closet in the spare bedroom," he says. "The top three drawers of the dresser are yours."

A hundred tiny birds flutter in my stomach. Welcome to a new life, living with Arthur in his perfect tidy house.

"You know, Arthur," I say, looking around the spotless house. "You're neater than I am."

I've never seen dust on the furniture, or his clothes tossed onto a chair. You'd think he never sat on the couch, ate food, or slept in bed. He never spent much time at my apartment.

"Spend the weekends with me," he'd always say, "where we have plenty of room to stretch out and be comfortable."

"I'll do my best to keep your house tidy," I say.

"It's fine," says Arthur. "Don't worry about it. I love you the way you are." But even before we hit six months of marriage, I'm not convinced he loves me the way I am.

I'm not the greatest cook on the planet, but that's okay. He takes me to the Inn. If I don't make the bed, he doesn't fuss. And he doesn't mind if I go to the Ale House with the girls on Friday night.

"No problem, sweetheart," he says. "I'm fine staying home and finishing up my book." Six months later. *Six months*. He stands and shakes his head the way you do at some birdbrain who doesn't understand a word you say. He points at my clothes—a pair of jeans, a few sweaters, one jacket, and a nightgown, piled up on the bedroom chair. He picks up my cotton nightgown between his thumb and forefinger, drops it on the floor, and stares at it like it will give him a disease.

"My God," he says, "how can you stand the mess? Can't even see the back of the chair."

"When we got married, you said you didn't mind." Boy, was I wrong to believe him.

"Maybe I did, but *not like this*." He points at the pile, mouth puckering up in disgust.

"Sorry, I'm such a slob," I say, wondering what happened to that white sweater of mine.

"No, honey, don't say that. Just try a little harder, okay? Besides, I want to get you a few nightgowns. You could use some new ones."

"Arthur, I don't care. It's just to sleep in. Besides, I'd rather sleep naked."

"Do it for me," he says, "okay? And maybe we'll get you some other lingerie, too." He has a dreamy look on his face that I don't understand. What is the big deal?

"Stuff like that doesn't matter to me," I clarify. "You know that. I guess it's safe to say it's important to you?"

He smiles, which answers my question, but that grin wipes off in a few seconds.

"Do you realize I've only seen you in corduroys and jeans," he says. "You even chose to wear jeans at our wedding. Who does that? I have never seen you in a dress. Not even once. And I know you have beautiful legs. Especially when they're wrapped around me." He has a wicked expression on his face that I ignore.

I lift my pile of clothes from the back of the chair. What do you know? There's that American flag sweater, and the white one, too. Okay, what else is here? Arthur continues with his shopping plans, whether I like the idea or not.

"This Saturday, we'll drive to Grand Junction," he says. "Geiger Springs probably doesn't have much in the way of lingerie. Let's make a whole day of it." A whole day of shopping? I've never in my life spent more than twenty minutes buying clothes. He must be joking.

"A whole day to buy underwear and nightgowns?"

"We'll have a good time," says Arthur.

He wants to do what he wants to do. It doesn't matter what I think or say. After folding the pile of clothes, trying to be as neat as possible, I glance at the wilted lilies on the nightstand. They were so beautiful. Now they're done for.

"It sounds like going shopping is what you want," I say, "so I guess we're going shopping."

"Great," he says. His face goes pink with happiness, and his voice turns excited. "Let's get an early start."

"Whatever you say. But we're taking Ducky. I can't leave her all day long trapped in the house."

When Saturday rolls around, I put Ducky in the backseat. Soon enough, she climbs onto my lap, buries her face in the crook of my arm, and falls asleep. I stroke her soft head as I look through the window at the deep dark blue of the Colorado River.

Once past Geiger Springs, we head into wide open spaces. We pass Haven Horse Ranch. I point out the window. "Look at that beautiful colt! He must only be a few weeks old."

Arthur doesn't even look over to see. Instead, he drives straight to Sexy Siren Lingerie without checking a map, almost like he's been there before. He leaps out of the car and takes my hand. I wonder why his palm is so sweaty.

With all the salespeople busy with other customers, we mosey to the back of the store. One rose-colored nightie with tiny black ribbons catches his eye. I've never seen somethin' so fancy to sleep in. He keeps running his hands over the silk and closes his eyes.

"You have to try this one," he says.

"Okay, I'll try it now."

"No, wait. Let's get a few more so you can try them all at once." He reaches for a short nude-colored gown with thin little straps, touching it in a way that gives me the willies.

"Yes," he says, "and how about this pale blue one?"

I shrug my shoulders.

"You have to try it," he goes on. "With your brown eyes and strawberry blonde hair, it's perfect." He continues to stroke the silk gowns. A little shiver goes down my spine as I stand back and watch. He buys a blue, nude, and a black one. All silk. As a kid, I slept in flannel pajamas. In the summer, I wore an oversized T-shirt and panties. I mean, you're sleeping. What else do you need? Arthur takes forever and a day to choose ten silk panties and three fancy bras I must try. I tap my toe out of frustration and boredom with these shopping shenanigans. The salesgirl behind the register smiles at Arthur as if she recognizes him somehow.

He doesn't return her smile.

"Anything else I can help you with, Mr. Turner?" she asks.

"That should do it, thank you," says Arthur. He glances around the store as she rings up the sale, taking it all in. "Just curious," he says, "what is the largest size you carry in this store?"

"Extra-large in the nightgowns and panties," she cups her hands before her chest. "44 Double D in the bras."

"Hmmm, interesting," says Arthur. "You must have some large women customers."

Our saleslady winks.

"Oh yes, some of them are quite large," she says. "We want to accommodate anyone who comes to shop in our store."

"How nice," says Arthur and picks up the packages. I tug on his sleeve like a little kid would do.

"Let's go, Arthur. *Puh-leeze.*" He grips my wrist to shut me up.

"Hope to see you soon, folks," says the saleslady. He releases his grip.

"We've come all this way," says Arthur. "Maybe we can find a dress that shows off your lovely trim figure."

"Do we have to?" I ask.

"Come on, Angel," he says. "Is this really so painful?"

"Jeez, Arthur, I feel like a dolly that you want to dress up."

His nostrils flair. "Can you stop being a tomboy for just one day?" I go silent. We carry on shopping since that is what Arthur wants to do. I tag along, never so bored. I didn't even spend this much time planning our wedding. I squirm as he watches me in the mirror trying on my fourth dress at Donna's Dress Shop.

"Don't look so unhappy," he says. I give him a big fake smile.

"Turn around one more time," he says. I make a slow circle. Arthur beams.

"Look how well it fits," he says. "The light green is very flattering." I remember Dede's mama telling me I would look good in a green dress. I feel like a fool. Arthur glows like a proud papa.

"That's perfect," he says. "I want to buy it for you."

"Okay, fine," I say. Please, someone put me out of my misery.

"Do you like it as much as I do?" he asks.

"Yeah, love it. Let's get it." Nothing more I want to do than jump in the car and see the horses running free in the fields.

The following Saturday, I wear the dress to dinner, just like he asks me to. When I return from the ladies' room, he sits up straight in his chair and adjusts his jacket with a shit-eating grin.

"What's up with that grin?" I ask.

"I like it when all the men in the room look at you."

"You do? How come?"

"Because you belong to me!" he says.

"Don't say that. You don't own me. I'm your wife. I'm not a thing."

"You're so touchy," he says. He throws his napkin on the table. My stomach tightens up as I push away my hot fudge sundae. Once home, I make a beeline through the living room and straight up the stairs, shouting as I go.

"I have a stomachache from that dinner. I'm going to take some Pepto-Bismol."

No nooky tonight. That should teach him.

CHAPTER 26

WEEKS LATER, HE DEMANDS THAT I ONLY WORK THE LUNCH shift at the Double G. Then he lays down the law by getting me where it hurts the most. I can't go to the Ale House with the girls anymore.

"We're still newlyweds," he says. "I want you home with me on Friday nights." He likes to unwind from the week by reading or playing solitaire. Saturday nights, he takes me out to dinner. The same dumb-ass, boring routine every week.

One night, as I come through the front door from work, Arthur walks toward me, rattling the change around in his pockets.

"Have a seat," he says. "We need to talk." He pulls up a chair. He clears his throat like I'm a customer at the bank with a stack of bounced checks.

"Jeez, Arthur. What's going on?"

"Where should I start?" He loosens up his tie and pulls at the neck of his shirt. It's not the shirt he needs to loosen up. He stares at me with hard unblinking eyes.

"You're scaring me," I say. "What's wrong?" He motions for me to sit down.

"Okay, I'll jump right in."

"Good!"

He twiddles his thumbs, then lasers his eyes on me. "You've been a waitress your entire working life, right?"

"C'mon, you know that."

He stops the twiddling. "How long exactly?"

"I started at sixteen, and now I'm almost twenty-three," I say. "What're you getting at?" He's tapping a pen on the table.

"Well, sweetheart," he says, "you're capable of so much more. Besides, you should stop this kind of work." I wish he'd stop tapping the damn pen.

"Why?"

"Well . . . someone from Soldiers Bank might recognize you from the café. You know what I mean? Not good for business." I glance out the window at the pale moon.

"What?" I say, struggling to take in his words. "I was good enough for you before." He's taking my whole life away from me.

"Oh boy," he frowns, the rat-tat-tat of the pen driving me crazy, but I don't say a word, too worried about what he'll say next. "I was afraid of this," he continues. "You're so capable. That's the point. Go back to school. Or don't work at all." What did he say? Did I hear right?

"I don't have to work?" I can't believe what I'm hearing. I don't love working as a waitress. But still, I'm used to making my own money. Will I have to ask him for every cent? I'd miss my customers, no doubt about it. I sink back into the cushy armchair, take a deep breath, and roll the news around, unsure if this is a blessing or a curse.

I tell Faye Vespers first thing when I arrive at work. Her face droops in disappointment, but she doesn't say it. My head swirls in confusion. Arthur's ashamed that I work as a waitress. It's the only job I've ever had. Well, Zoltan and all that, but still, the Double G has been in my life from the beginning. I wonder what that man sees in me.

CHAPTER 27

*I*T'S MY LAST DAY AT THE DOUBLE G, ALMOST LIKE PACKING my bag to leave home forever. My feet drag across the linoleum floor. My energy is as low as I can remember in a long time.

"So, what you gonna do with yourself now?" asks the longtime chef. He's been working at the Double G forever and a day, maybe since before I was born. Over the years, he's changed from a fun-loving guy in his thirties to a grouchy old codger. He wipes his hands on his not-so-white apron as he searches my eyes for an answer.

"I'm not sure what I'll do. Take a little break, I guess, and think about it."

"Maybe it's time to pop out a kid or two?" His eyes go dark. "Easy street, right? Now that you're married to a banker." He whips off his chef's cap and takes a deep bow as if I'm royalty. My face heats up.

"Hey, stop it! The Double G is my second home. I'm still the same. I won't be busting out of my britches." He pretends to see a bird, or something more interesting than me, out the window. I look up at him.

"I'll be seeing you around."

"Yep. See you around." He wipes his hands on his apron, ready to return to the same old kitchen. I pack my scuffed waitress shoes into an old paper bag to leave my job forever. Faye Vespers throws her arms around me, tears streaming down her face.

"I only live six blocks away," I say. "You'll still see me all the time." A loud honk as she blows her nose with Kleenex. She dabs at her eyes.

"I love you like you're my own," she says. When did those deep lines show up? I see her every single day but never noticed how much she has aged until now.

"I feel the same way about you. I really do. Thanks for everything. You've helped me out too many times to count. It's just that I need to move on. Besides," I whisper in her ear, "Arthur doesn't want me to work anymore." Her mouth shapes into a silent O. She hands me a pink bakery box with a warm pie inside. A bear hug with Faye, and I'm free. But free to do what? I have no clue.

The first few weeks, I sleep as late as possible until my pup whines and wakes me up. I make myself a bowl of Cheerios or scrambled eggs, then Ducky and I go for a walk. Afterward, I lay around the house like a slug and watch *As the World Turns* on TV. In the afternoons, I take Ducky on extra-long walks. Friends from the old neighborhood let me ride Star, still my favorite horse, a few times a week. I always loved riding horses.

Today is a perfect September afternoon, with a picture-perfect blue sky and fresh cool air. I throw a blanket over Star and ride her bareback. As we ride alongside a golden aspen grove, my brain lights up, and a buzz moves through my whole body. *I could be a rodeo rider.* That would be the perfect job for me. I'm so excited that I swing the horse around and gallop her back to the barn. The wind rushes through my hair. I'm happier than I've been for weeks now. I know what I'm supposed to do with my life. I take the blanket off Star, brush her down, and kiss her on her velvety nose.

"Thank you," I say, wrapping my arms around her massive neck. "Look how you helped me." She whinnies and shakes her head as if she understands every word.

Once home, I leaf through the yellow pages in the phone book. They have rodeos in Copperville every Saturday night. Maybe there's a school nearby. Sure enough, I come across Ride-A-Bronc School, halfway to El Jebel, less than an hour from Pinewood.

I set up an appointment for later in the week, on a Friday morning. I don't tell Arthur so I can surprise him. He'll be so proud of me. Wednesday and Thursday drag by.

The next two days and nights, I'm jumping out of my skin with excitement. On Thursday night, I can't sleep. As Arthur snores away, I bundle up in my robe and fluffy slippers. Nighttime is a special kind of quiet. I pad through the chilly dark house and sit back in the easy chair. The world looks soft and mysterious in the moonlight. Nature has her private life when the world is sleeping. My eyes shut, and I drift off into dreamland.

At last, Friday comes. When Arthur leaves for work, I head out to El Jebel and give myself plenty of time to find Ride-A-Bronc School. My spirits always lift when I'm on the road. Once I take the El Jebel exit, I make a quick left turn, a right turn for a mile, and one more right. In front of me are two large corrals.

Off to the left is a decrepit building with a sign that says, "HOWDY! Come On In."

I stop for a minute and watch a couple of young cowboys roping calves. They lasso them around the neck, wrestle 'em to the ground and tie up their legs. I don't think that's for me. Looks like the calves can get hurt. Stayin' on top of a wild horse sounds right up my alley. The old man who runs the place has thick cocoa-colored skin, deep lines run like riverbeds down his face, and two black braids trail from his cowboy hat. We talk for an hour.

"How well do you understand horses?" he asks. How many times have I been thrown? Do I have much fear? What kind of injuries have I had? He doesn't crack a smile. He speaks slowly with few words, like centuries of wisdom fill his head. I answer his questions the best I can, as true and honest as possible.

"I don't have any fear," I say. "Riding feels natural to me, like I was born on the back of a horse."

"You start on a bucking machine," he says, giving me a thumbs up, "not a live animal. You've passed the first hurdle. Next step is signing up for the classes," his voice a deep rumble.

"Okay!" I say. He explains the two-week course to me and hands me a brochure. Now I can do what I love: spend my days with horses. And one day, I can make money doing it.

Arthur will be so proud of me. Roaring up the mountain to Pinewood, I picture myself riding wild broncos, holding on with one hand and waving a cowboy hat in the other. I open the front door and pop a couple of turkey TV dinners in the oven. He deserves a nice hot dinner, maybe some wine, too.

I pour some Gallo for us and wait. He closes the front door before the cold air gets in.

"That smells good," he says.

"You can thank Swansons," I say. "I made some canned peas, too."

"Well, at least it's a hot dinner," says Arthur. He washes his hands first, like always. He sits at the table for a few minutes without saying a word.

I raise my glass to him.

"Guess what?" I say, "Big news."

"Good to hear. Please tell me." He stops eating, holds on to his knife and fork, and waits.

"I figured out what I want to do," I say, wondering if he'll like my idea. "I've been thinking hard about it."

"Good girl." A rare smile crosses his face. "I can't wait to hear," he says, leaning towards me. "Tell me all about it." He forks some peas into his mouth.

"I want to go to school." Even with those good table manners, his mouth hangs open with excitement as the peas almost fall onto the table.

"That is *great news*," says Arthur. "How many classes?"

"Just one."

"That's fine," he says. "It's a start. So, you'll be going to Rocky Mountain College?" I twist my napkin in my hands.

"Uh, no, not Rocky Mountain," I say. "I'll be going to Rodeo School."

"I've never heard of . . . wait a minute, did you say rodeo school, as in cowboys and bucking broncos?" He sputters the words and bangs his hands on the dining room table.

"Yeah, that's right," I say. "I've always loved everything about horses. You've never seen me ride, but I'm good. I love the smell of stables, fresh hay—even horse shit."

"Are you kidding me? What the hell is wrong with you? I think you're dead serious."

"I am serious," I say. "And I'm excited." He turns a bright angry red.

"I'm sorry to break it to you, but there is no way in hell that you, my dear Mrs. Turner, are going to rodeo school. You really believe riding broncos is better than being a waitress?" His nostrils flare. Ducky cowers under the dining room table. Arthur now grips his knife and fork in a stranglehold and points them straight up, ready for battle.

"I really want to do this."

I thought he would be proud of me. But no, he shakes with rage.

"You can forget about it." He shakes his head back and forth. "I mean it," he says, "no fucking way."

"Why? Why do I have to forget about it?"

"I don't like all those men sniffing around you. Understand?" His mouth trembles. "And you need to improve yourself, to learn, to grow, and not spend your days around a bunch of horny cowboys. *Jesus Christ.*" He slams the silverware down and yanks his chair away from the dinner table. I've never heard him curse, never seen him so fired up. I'm afraid he may come over and smack me across the face.

He speeds out the front door and slams it, keeping the invisible noose tight around my neck. I've cried maybe two times in my life. Once over Ace, my biker boyfriend. And that crazy bad night when that maniac Randy almost raped me. Even my crazy parents never made me cry. Tonight, I can't stop the tears. I finally think of something I can be good at, and he hates everything about it. I can't do anything right in his eyes. The tight rubber band on my hair gives me a massive headache. I pull it out and lie face down on the couch. Ducky sidles up next to me; I put my arm around her and pull her close.

When Arthur walks back in a few hours later, he won't even look at me. Exhausted from the topsy-turvy day, I stay on the couch and fall asleep. Next morning, he shakes my shoulder.

"Wake up. It's already past 8. I'm leaving for work." He reeks of his favorite English Leather cologne.

"I'm awake," I say, yawning. Arthur's mouth pulls down at the corners, so I know he's still got his knickers in a wad.

"Are you still mad?" I ask.

"No, I'm pretty well past it," he lies. "But I never want to hear about rodeo school again." He leans over to kiss me on the cheek. I dodge it.

That night, the air as thick as cotton, he pulls out a stack of LPs, all of them by Pat Boone, his favorite singer. He opens a bottle of scotch, Gallo for me, and we never get around to eating a speck of dinner. Arthur throws down four drinks in a row, and I polish off the entire bottle of wine by myself. Both of us end up drunk as skunks in no time.

I fall asleep slumped on the floor. Snoring his head off, tangled in his clothes, Arthur passes out cold on the couch. About 3 in the morning, we stumble into bed without a word.

With rodeo school a no-go, I still need to figure out what to do with myself. I watch a ton of cooking shows on TV. What a waste of time. My casseroles burn up. You could play Frisbee with my piecrust. I overcook the burgers when I leave them cooking and wander over to catch up on *Days of Our Lives*. I want a life like those folks with fancy houses and everyone looking good. Even their problems seem like good problems. Arthur has a new full-time job: to correct my grammar, boss me around, demand to know where I've been and who I've been with.

CHAPTER 28

*H*ere's the topper. I come home early from Sandy's house one Saturday afternoon. I open the bedroom door a sliver and can't believe my eyes. He stands there at the full-length mirror he insisted we buy. My husband—*Mr. Perfect*—prances around in red silk underwear and bright silver high heels. I always wore silk underwear for him. Never guessed he'd wear it himself.

"Everyone should have big mirrors like this," he told me once. "That way, you can see yourself from head to toe. You know, have the complete picture." I never understood why that was a big deal. I went along with it. Never in a million years would have guessed . . . .

I don't think he sees me. He heads straight to the bathroom without looking my way. Hope he didn't hear me. I almost puke up my lunch and blast down the stairs, so he won't catch me spying on his secret frigging life. Holy hell. What next? Does this mean he's queer? I never saw him look at men. He loves having sex with me. Now I understand why he acted so weird in that lingerie store, stroking the silk negligees.

Sitting at the dining room table, I light a cigarette as my mind goes loop-de-loop. A muffled *clomp-clomp-clomp* as he makes his way down the stairs in normal man clothes, a sheepish look on his face that turns into a big phony smile.

"Back from Sandy's early?" His voice unnatural and high-pitched, like he's nervous.

"Yeah, well, Sandy left early for a photo shoot," I say, thinking my voice sounds okay. I could spit nails right now. How could I be married to this freak?

"Oh, well, good for Sandy," says Arthur. I want to smash him in the face with my fist. Maybe knock out a few teeth to ruin that phony ass smile.

"I thought I heard you coming upstairs when you first got home," he says. His voice is still a fake kind of cheerful.

"I changed my mind," I say, "and got myself a beer instead." His face relaxes.

"It sure hits the spot right now," I say. I tip back the can and take a few swallows.

"Oh, okay, sure, good," he says. He gulps down the words and goes outside to do who knows what. I sit and draw wildflowers to try and calm down. I open a package of spaghetti for dinner, pop it in boiling water and heat up some ragu. I need to keep my mind off this circus I joined.

We eat dinner in silence, chewing our food slow and thorough like our lives depend upon it. When Arthur flips on the TV, we glue ourselves to *The Carole Burnett Show*. So odd that we sit side by side, laughing our asses off without looking at each other, like strangers in a movie theater. The air hangs thick between us for the rest of the night 'til we both fall asleep.

The house is empty when I wake up. Thank the Lord, Arthur already left for work. What a nasty dark morning. A hard Colorado rain pounds down on the roof. I head straight to the fridge for a Miller High Life. Not what I usually do at 8 in the morning, but nothing feels normal right now. Jesus save me, my banker husband in high heels. I thought this marriage couldn't get worse. And now . . . look at yourself,

Angel, I think. How did you end up in another mess? I cover up with a blanket on the couch and stare out the window. Spencer should be here soon to fix the leaky kitchen faucet. Ducky jumps up to cuddle, placing her head in my lap. She can always tell when something bothers me. I put my arms around her and bury my face in her neck.

Spencer bangs on the door, doesn't wait for an answer, and pushes straight on through.

"Hi there. It's pissin' rain," he says. "Sorry to bust in on you. Figured you wouldn't mind." The lunatic didn't wear a hat or jacket today.

"C'mon in and dry off, Spence. I'll get you a towel." I snatch one from the hall closet and hand it to him. He still looks the same as in high school, only better.

"Hey girl," he says, "is that alcohol on your breath? You been drinkin' this morning?"

"Well, yeah. Can't help it. I'm not too happy right now," I say.

"Why? What's going on, Angel?"

"I made a giant mistake." I hide my face in Ducky's neck again.

"What do you mean," his voice gentle and kind, "what kind of mistake?"

"Marrying Arthur . . . ."

'He's not beatin' on you, is he?" He reaches out and touches my arm.

"No. But we don't have much in common," I say, "except maybe our underwear." I laugh too loud.

"What the hell you talkin' about? Are you drunk?"

"Could be. But I feel like crap right now." I back into the cushion embroidered with *Pinewood Colorado, A Little*

Piece of Heaven. My arms hang like dead weight off of my body. My voice cracks.

"I don't know what to do," I say. Spencer's well-worn tool belt sits low on his narrow hips. He pulls at his goatee, just like his pops always does.

"You always had a smile and a joke at the Double G," he says. "Cheered me up so many times when I had a bad day."

"Yeah, we always had fun kidding around." I always liked his crinkly smiling eyes.

"Anything I can do to cheer you up right now?" he asks. "You really seem low. Drinkin' this early in the morning. That's not good." He runs his hand through his long hair. I shrug, glad he ignored my underwear comment.

"What can I tell you?" I say, "I'm just down."

"How about a hug," he says. He reaches out his arms. "That might help." I could use a good man snuggle right now. Once he holds me, my arms spring back to life and wind around his neck. I press up against him for comfort. His raw male energy kicks into gear. I bet Spencer never wore ladies' silk panties. He leans back with both hands on my shoulders, as if he's about to say somethin'. But he doesn't say a word. He leans in and kisses me, soft and loving, like he cares. He drops his tool belt to the floor. Within no time, we're teenagers who can't get enough of each other. We stumble into the bedroom, his jeans down around his ankles, me tearing off my bathrobe and rose-colored nightgown.

"Do you have a condom?" I ask. "We better be careful."

"Sure." He pulls me onto the bed, confident and knowing. We melt into each other. His muscular body, a crude skull tattooed on his chest. We ride the waves together like we've been doing it for years. Well, there was that one time we did the deed in his car after Jimmy Jones' nineteenth birthday party. He touches my face and kisses my forehead when it's over. It doesn't last long enough for me, but he holds me close afterward, and I rest my head on his chest.

"Man, I was a little too excited," he says. "Tell the truth, I've always wanted to make it with you one more time. You are one sexy woman." I smooth the hair back from his forehead. He looks so relaxed right now.

"I do feel bad," I say. "Never thought this would happen. Your wife is a nice person."

"Let's not talk about her right now, okay?" he says. I kiss him on the shoulder.

"Okay, you're right," I say. "We better get up, Spence. And don't forget the leaky faucet."

"Good thing you said that," he grins. "I almost forgot." Dede calls me while he's in the kitchen, wrestling with the repairs.

"Can you help me out?" she says. "I forgot about a dinner tonight for the Bed and Breakfast Guild. Not one pretty dress to my name. Can I borrow that green one with the short sleeves?"

"Sure. Just be careful not to spill on it. And get it back to me as soon as you can. Arthur would go bat shit if he knew you borrowed it. He just loves that dress."

"Can I send Carmen to pick it up?" says Dede. "She'll finish cleaning the rooms pretty soon. I'm knee-deep in paperwork right now."

"I'm kind of busy right now," I say. "Tell her to come around 1:30." Once in the shower, I let the scalding hot water beat down on me. Reminds me of those religious folks I saw once on TV carrying crosses and hitting themselves with branches. Spencer yells from the hallway.

"Everything is working fine right now. Faucet's in good shape. Sorry to leave so soon. I'm late for the next job. Gotta say you are somethin' else, girl. You won't say a word to your friends, right?"

"Don't worry, Spence. Not a word. Take care." Once I throw on my favorite faded jeans and cozy flannel shirt, I toss the covers back on the bed and pat them down. At 1:30 on the dot, a timid knock on the front door.

"Come on in, Carmen," I shout. "How you doin'?"

"Very good, Missy Angel," she says, "I come for the dress for Miss Dede."

"Follow me into the bedroom. I'll get it for you." My little Ducky follows right behind us. I step into the back of the closet and pull out the dress, covered in plastic for safekeeping.

"Missy, Missy, look! The dawg!" she shrieks. I can't see what she wants me to see.

"What is it?" I step out of the closet with Arthur's favorite dress draped over my arm.

"*Mira . . . look*," says Carmen. "*En la boca* . . . her mouth. The dawg has a cone-dome." I chase Ducky around the room, the used condom clamped between her teeth. Carmen cowers in the corner, not moving a muscle. Ducky dashes around like it's the most fun she's ever had in her entire life. I have never spanked my dog, but it might happen right now.

Tongue-tied, I know I'll have to speak up.

"Bad girl, Ducky," I say, my voice as creamy as butter, "come here." She slinks over to me, tail tucked between her little legs. I yank the thing away from her and hope I don't get splattered. At least it was Carmen, not Arthur, who found it.

"Missy," says Carmen, "how'd that happen?" A blush heats up my face, so I back into the closet to avoid her.

"Beats me, Carmen." I stand between some clothes. "Well, thanks for coming by. I hope the dress works out for Dede." Holy moly, I could wring Spencer's friggin' neck. Who leaves a condom on the floor? I flush it down the toilet. Once she leaves, I pour a beer and one more after that. The rain beats down and stays in full force for the entire afternoon. I toss a few logs in the fireplace and build a fire the way Pops taught me when I was eight. Perched on the couch, I concentrate on the flames devouring the logs and crack open the last Miller High Life in the fridge.

CHAPTER 29

1973

WHEN I CALL SANDY TO ASK IF SHE WANTS TO HIKE, she agrees and doesn't ask me why. That's what I love about her. She senses somethin' is up. I get my hair under control, pull it back into a ponytail, and grab my blue baseball cap embroidered with *Aspen is for Lovers* left behind at the Double G. Sandy stands outside her front door, ready to go. We head up the mountain in Betsy the Buick, still going strong after all this time. Arthur makes fun of my old jalopy but doesn't buy me a new one either.

"What's going on?" asks Sandy. She knows me so well. She can read my face like nobody else. "You look worse than bad," she says. I can't hold back. My words tumble out in a raging river.

"Every chance he gets, Arthur patrols every dang move I make. I can't take it anymore."

She gives a comforting squeeze. "I was afraid that's what you were gonna tell me. Gotta say," she adds, "I had a bad feeling about the two of you from the start." I wipe tears with my left hand and drive with my right. With our arms around each other's waist at the top of McClure, breathing in the crisp air, Arthur is right about one thing: people come from all around the world for this view.

"Remember what the tourists said every summer?" asks Sandy.

"How could I forget?" I say. "Look at this view. The mountains and sky so close you can touch them." We shriek with laughter.

"Talk to me," says Sandy. "What's going on?" My mood sinks deeper than a fifty-pound weight in a pond.

"I hate being married," I say. "I thought I felt trapped in this town before." I laugh. "Man, that was nothing compared to being stuck with Arthur." She studies me, flipping her long thick hair off to the side.

"C'mon," she says, "you know you can always be honest with me. We're sisters." She looks me in the eyes and holds onto my shoulders. "Do you love him?"

I glance down at my hiking boots. "I used to like him." My voice comes out in a whisper. "He's smart and stuff like that. And he used to be nice to me. Now he's a different guy . . . in so many ways." We don't speak for a while.

"Tell you what I want to do," I say. "Get the hell out of here. I know I've said it for years. Now I am ready to figure out how to do it . . . ."

"Me too," she says. "We've got to come up with a plan." We walk down the fire road. I pluck a red paintbrush wildflower from the ground and tuck it behind my ear. Sandy does it, too.

"I thought marrying Arthur would make my life better," I say. Sandy takes hold of my hand.

"Yeah, I get it. Seriously though, you have nothing in common."

"I know . . . and you have no idea." My throat closes.

"Oh no, like what do you mean?" she says.

"I saw him the other night," I stutter, "in ladies' panties and silver high heels." She drops my hand.

"What?" she shrieks. "C'mon now, you're joking, right?" The words keep tumbling out of my mouth. Having no control, I describe every detail of the scene, the mirror, the heels.

"But I never let on," I continue. "I'm not sure, but I don't think he saw me." I kick some loose stones down the road, explaining how he pranced around, the weird way he touched the lingerie when he took me to Sexy Siren. Sandy slaps her hand against her forehead to make space for this crazy news.

"You *are* serious," she says. "I can't believe what you're telling me. I am so sorry, Angel." Then Sandy claps her hand over her mouth to keep from laughing. "Seriously? When you said he was a different kind of guy, I had no idea what that meant," she says, laughing even more. A cold wind stirs up the aspens, rustling their leaves and chilling me to the bone. I rewind my wool scarf to make it more secure. A big magpie lands on a half-rotted log across the trail, cocks its head and speaks to us: "Ka-ka-ka-ka."

"My poor friend," says Sandy. "Now what?"

"Just call me Calamity Jane," I say. "My life is one crazy hot mess."

"Sorry to laugh," she says. "I'm right there with you, Angel. I feel so bad for you. I don't even know what to say right now. I'm always stuck with my own worries about money every day of my goddam life."

"I know you're always worried. And I know it's gone on for a long time. Since Arthur made me quit my job, I don't have any money of my own. But you know that." She links her arm in mine, and we keep walking.

"What should I do?" I say, hoping she has the answer. She throws her arms up like an Italian mama.

"I wish I knew," she sighs. "I wish I knew."

"If we could only bust out of here."

"Wouldn't that be great?" says Sandy. "How to get the bucks is the problem." She flips her hair to the right, showing her clear rosy complexion. She always looks good for someone with no money and, in fact, better than the rest of our Pinewood friends. I take a deep breath.

"Yeah, the bucks," I say. "No kidding. That's always been the problem."

"There must be some way. Other people do it." She flips her hair to the left.

"Who do we know that ever escaped?" I say. "No one!"

Sandy shrugs her shoulders.

"I wish I had the answer," she says, "but it is time to go into high gear."

"Yep, there's no time like the present. Truth is, the only one I know close to money is Arthur. You know, working in a bank and all." Sandy's face screws up tight like she's wracking her brain for ideas.

"It's not his money," she says. "So, how does that do us any good?"

"I don't know," I say. We face each other as if we're in a church or somewhere private, not outside in the middle of the mountains. But nature is my religion, and when I do my best thinking. Still, nothing comes clear.

"You could divorce him," says Sandy. "That way, you could get some money." She stops to point at four little chipmunks darting across the road.

"Divorce him?" I say. "I guess so."

"You should get some dough out of it."

"But it's only been a few years . . . ," I say.

"Never been through it, so I don't know a thing about it," says Sandy. "If only my photography career would take off. People say they love my work but don't buy it." She pulls at her sleeves.

"Listen, Sandy, I don't have a penny to my name. Arthur will blow his top if I start waitressing again." My mind spins like churning butter.

"Keep thinking, Angel. I will, too. Let's get out of Pinewood. We need a plan."

"You're right. We do need a plan." I stumble on a stone. Sandy grabs my arm and steadies me.

"C'mon now," she says, "you should eat something. You'll feel better." She hands me some trail mix. We prop ourselves against a rock and chomp away, each in our own world grasping for ideas on how to escape, only to come up with nothing.

"Phew, I feel better now," I say. "Didn't realize how hungry I was." I sip water from the canteen Pops bought me a lifetime ago. "Let's go, Sandy. I'm ready to move."

"I'll race you to the top of the ridge," she says. "C'mon. Like old times."

"Okay. Let's do it."

We take off at full speed until the sky turns dark and thunder roars out a warning. The downpour soaks us to the skin as we dash to the safety of Betsy the Buick.

Another sleepless stretch of night with Arthur leaves me with puffy black circles under my eyes. Air thick as cotton as he readies for work. As soon as he leaves the house, I rush into the extra bedroom. In the closet hang more clothes than

I've ever had in my life: pants, jackets, grouped in colors. All the blue shirts face in the same direction, including the white and striped ones, which are in their own section with a perfect amount of space between each item.

I shove the hangers aside, reach into the back of the closet and poke around to find a black cover placed over a stack of boxes. Inside is the truth of Arthur's secret life *right before my eyes*. I stand on my tiptoes. On the top shelf, the silver shoes, red ones, black sandals stand in a perfect row. I gulp to get some air. Holy moly! This little hobby has been going on for a while. Maybe years! How did I end up in this freak show? This explains why his first wife ran out on him. What about those business meetings at night? He must be somewhere prancing around with other weirdos who like to dress up. Could he belong to some weird club? I can picture it all now.

"Charlie, how do I look in my purple nightie?"

"You look gorgeous, Arthur!" I could puke. The only way to handle this? Tune him out the way I always did with a pain-in-the-ass customer at the Double G. I dial the phone.

"Sandy," I say. "We have to talk." I almost strangle on my words.

"Angel? What is wrong?"

"I just discovered Arthur has a wardrobe fit for Marilyn Monroe. I am sick to my stomach. We need to come up with a get-away plan soon."

"Hang in there, Angel. Don't do something nuts. We'll figure it out."

Another long night of torture staring into the TV without a word between us. I follow Arthur up the stairs. We undress in silence, slide under the covers, and face away from each other.

I run on a white sand beach in a bikini. A breeze lifts the hair off my neck, taking me to a calm place I've never been before. A golden-skinned beach boy hands me a coconut with a straw coming out the top.

"What is it?" I ask.

"A magic drink," he says in his island accent. "You will feel a special happiness. Please take. Enjoy."

"That sure looks good," I say. I stir the milky liquid with my straw, take a small sip, then savor every bit. I drag a beach chair to the ocean's edge and gaze at the rolling waves. I've wanted to do this my whole life. Now I'm here. I breathe deep and take in the perfect moment. Next thing I know, something clamps down hard on both my legs. An octopus raises its rubbery head out of the water. He laughs as his long tentacles add more pressure to my legs.

"Help me," I yell. "Someone, help me. Please, please help."

"Angel, what is it?" Arthur shakes me. "You're having a nightmare." My chest beats so hard Arthur must hear it.

"I dreamt an octopus was squeezing my legs!"

"Ducky, get off. Right now," says Arthur. He pushes her off my legs and sweeps her onto the floor.

"Oh, that's better," I say.

"You're okay," says Arthur, "it was only a dream." I sit up in bed. It wasn't real, I think. I'm okay, it was a nightmare.

"But it was so scary," I say. "It felt so real."

"I know," he says. "It's over now." He turns away from me. His back like a brick wall, shutting me out. When we were first together, he would have held me and made me feel safe. He faces the window and falls into a deep sleep in a few minutes. I lie awake, wondering when the real nightmare of this marriage will end.

CHAPTER 30

I SPENT THE ENTIRE DAY TRYING TO COME UP WITH AN escape plan. As I sit across from my banker husband, I can't help but think he works at a bank with money, money, and more money. Arthur digs into his Hamburger Helper while I stare at mine. I can't stand his neat friggin' haircut. Or the way he cuts his meat so perfect and nice. I push my noodles around. I make a little hill of it, then smash it down again. Arthur's face scrunches up. He slams down his knife.

"Can you stop playing with your food? You're barely eating a thing. What's going on?"

"I'm bored being at home all the time. Just can't figure it out. Maybe I could be a teller at your bank."

He takes a long time to wipe his mouth with his paper napkin. He stares me down like I'm his prey.

"I don't know if you're equipped for a teller job."

"Why not? I'm not smart enough? Is that what you mean?"

"It's not that. It's essential that a teller is good at math and details."

"What else do they do?"

"They need good customer service skills."

"That's me alright! My customers always loved me at the Double G."

"I'm sure," he says, cutting me to the quick. "This is different, though. Much more complicated. Tellers handle large sums of cash. They balance the cash drawer." He sucks in some air.

"I took the money from customers and always brought back the right change."

"Sorry. It's not the right job for you. The details are extremely important. You've always said you're not a detail person. Besides, it's not a good idea for a teller to be married to the boss."

"Hey, I didn't think you were the boss."

"I am the bank manager, so . . . ?"

"Wow, Arthur, I never thought of it that way."

"Hah! What do you know—it's nice to see you show some interest . . . ." Right now, he has a grin plastered across his face. I wonder if he has some garters stashed in his desk at work.

"I'd still like to come on down and see the place." I wait a long time for an answer.

"Hmm. Well, you know, I'm swamped all day long."

"Hey, you ashamed of me or somethin'?" He looks around the room for a while before answering.

"No, of course not. Well, um . . . we can set it up. Maybe Wednesday. And when you come to see me, please wear that green dress I bought you."

"I get it. Look like a bank manager's wife, not a hick. And cover my tattoo, right?"

"Well, yes. I can't understand why you would put NO ANGEL in ink on your shoulder. What were you thinking?"

"I like it."

"Well, keep it under wraps, okay?" Pretty funny he would say that. He has a whole secret life *under wraps*.

"Fine," I say, "I will make sure no one at the bank sees it."

When Wednesday morning rolls around, I look at myself in the bathroom mirror. I brush my hair a hundred strokes to get out all the tangles and make it shiny. Remembering I have a tube of *Cherries in the Snow* lipstick from our wedding, I dig it out from the drawer. I pooch my lips out as I put it on. Not bad. I cover the freckles on my nose with an old tube of Erase. The dress may be a little tight, but it should be okay. If I meet folks at the bank, I better watch my grammar. It drives Arthur bonkers.

Driving down the mountain, my gas tank reads so low I need to fill 'er up, or I'll never make it to the bank. Arthur will throw a fit if I'm late. When I pull into the gas station, Gus, the owner, is the same young stud who dumped Mama. He never remembers me. Always chomping on gum. Gus chews gum and sells gas. I smile to myself and open the window. He pushes his hat back and scratches his head.

"Fill 'er up?"

"Yeah. The cheapest one, please," I say. "I'm in a hurry, too, so you can forget cleaning the windshield, okay?"

"Okay, won't take long," says Gus. "You're Grace's girl, right?" He does remember. He yells over his shoulder to someone out of earshot. Even in the rearview mirror, I recognize the sexy swagger. No doubt about it, there stands Ace. Always flipped my brain like a pancake. I can barely catch my breath. Even so, I open the car door, step out and look him in the eye. At first, he smiles like you do at a stranger, kind of vague-like. His face lights up as he plants himself in front of me.

"Angel!"

I nod, unable to squeeze out any words at all. My eyes tear up as his muscular arms wrap around me. When he leans in to kiss me, I back off a bit, not by much, and sink into him. With his hands on my shoulders, he stands back and looks me up and down, his lips now smeared with *Cherries in the Snow*. I pull myself together, remembering the hurt when he left town, leaving *me* without warning.

"How come you ran out on me?" I ask.

"I didn't handle that too well. I am sorry." He does look sorry. Never thought I would hear an apology, but it rolled out of his mouth like he meant it. "But I did let you know," he says, "I never stick around for too long. Besides that, you were so young. I was getting in deep."

"Ha! Deep! You can say that again!" We share a laugh as Gus finishes filling up my car. He washes the windshield even though I told him to skip it.

"Ace, you better wipe off that lipstick," I say. "It's not your color." We laugh, just like we always did. Then silence, as if we can't believe the moment. He runs his hand through his hair again and smiles his lazy smile. When I glance at my watch, I panic.

"Listen, I've got to get moving," I say. I hope my voice doesn't shake and give me away. "I need to be in Geiger Springs in thirty minutes."

"Okay. Well, hey, look at you all fancied up. What's in Geiger Springs that can't wait?" Damn, he looks good. The man takes my breath away.

"I'm meeting my husband at the bank." I look down and push some loose gravel around with my foot.

"I should have figured you'd have a husband by now," says Ace. "Meeting him at the bank, huh? Sounds important."

"Well, yeah. He's going to show me around."

"Show you around?" he says, not putting the puzzle together.

"Um, because he's the Manager of Soldier's Bank." He whistles through his teeth.

"Good going, Angel." He looks off into the distance for a minute. When he turns back, his direct gaze sends shock waves through me, like when we first met. Ace digs in his pocket, pulls out a piece of wrinkled paper, and scribbles down his phone number. He closes my palm around it. Gus stands watching us.

"Hey Gus," says Ace, "can you get lost for a minute?"

"Ace, she still has to pay," he says. I hand him the exact change. As he pockets the money and walks away, Ace waits until his pal can't hear us.

"Listen, I'm going to be in town for a while. Call me at that number, okay?"

"We'll see about that," I say. He gives me a sidelong glance, knowing there's not a chance in hell I would do anything but call.

"I never stopped thinking about you, baby. Honest to God," he says.

"That's good to know." My body heats up as he watches me tuck his number into my wallet.

"Ace, I've gotta go." He waves goodbye as my foot hits the pedal.

I give him the old Zoltan salute and swing the car onto the I-70. My sweaty hands slip on the steering wheel. In my craziest moments, I never guessed I would see Ace after that time at the bar. And then he shows up out of nowhere. I weave the car from lane to lane to make good time. Oh no, I spot a Highway Patrol car waiting behind a bush to catch a speeder. He turns on the siren and goes after someone else, going much faster than me. Phew! Only ten minutes late, I roar into the bank parking lot. A few people stand and watch me like they're thinking, *Who's the maniac?*

One old cow wags her finger at me. I jump out of the car, ignoring her as I speed walk into the bank. Once inside, I try to calm my nerves by straightening my dress. Too bad I forgot to polish my shoes. Haven't worn them since who knows when. I smooth down my curls. Sitting at a desk, a fat lady with a port wine stain on her right cheek gives me the eye as I pull myself together.

"Yes, can I help you?" She sits behind a desk in her too tight navy-blue suit, gaping between the buttons. They may go flying any minute now.

"I'm here to see Arthur," I say, careful to have the right attitude.

"Oh yes, Mr. Turner?" she says, looking me up and down. "Is he expecting you?"

I mimic her highfalutin tone of voice.

"Yes, he is expecting me. I'm his wife." Her eyes narrow as she studies me some more.

"Really?" she says, hoisting herself out of her chair.

"Yes, ma'am. Really." I want to trip her.

She mumbles to herself, but loud enough for me to hear. "Hmmm, you never know."

She leans over her desk and dials the phone with a frown on her face.

"Mr. Turner, Mrs. Turner is here to see you. Yes, sir, I will show her in."

She motions to me. "I can see you to his office Mrs. Turner." I don't like the way she says my name. Don't like it at all. As I follow, her fat ass looks like two gophers fighting in a paper bag. That and a rip in her stocking cheer me up. Although I'm not too late, a stick is firmly up Arthur's ass.

Arthur nods his thanks, and she waddles away. As soon as she's down the hall, he taps his finger on his watch.

"You know, my time is valuable. Please be more considerate!" I glue a smile on my face.

"Well, nice to see you too."

"You have lipstick on your teeth," he says.

"Oh. Let me fix that." I rub with my fingers to clear it away. He shakes his head like I'm nothing more than a dumb hillbilly. Lots of plaques and awards hang on the walls. His chest puffs out as he watches me take it all in.

"This bank is bigger than it looks on the outside," I say. "And it's real pretty, too."

"Not a bad place to work," he says," adjusting his cufflinks.

"So, you ready to show me around?" He introduces me to the Assistant Manager, all six tellers, and other important-looking men in suits sitting at their desks. He opens the heavy door to the room with safe deposit boxes. They almost touch the ceiling. Arthur looks at them tenderly as if they're his own flesh and blood.

"What do people keep in those boxes?" I ask.

"Documents, gold bullion, expensive jewelry—all kinds of valuables."

"I never knew that. How much money could be in this bank right now?"

"Could be as much as $100,000."

What I wouldn't do to get ahold of that kind of money.

"$100,000?" I say, "that is loco."

Arthur laughs and puts his arm around me.

"C'mon, I'll take you to the Pigeon Inn for a quick lunch." For a minute, he looks like the nice guy I met at the Double G Café.

That night, I dream I'm first in line at Solders' Bank holding a big red bucket. *The lady teller, an old, wrinkled-up Debbie Reynolds, throws in so much money it starts falling over the edges of the bucket onto the floor. Customers rush around and pick up all the bills. Instead of running off with the money, they stuff it in my shirt pockets, jacket, any place they can.*

"Take the money. Go on, take it," *they say in one voice.* "Take all of it! You deserve it."

CHAPTER 31

Two weeks later, and I'm trying to figure out a move out of this mess. I find Arthur's note near the coffee pot on the kitchen counter:

> *The meeting in Denver will go an extra day. I'll stay at the Holiday Inn tonight. Try to do something productive. ~A.*

I put my feet up, stretch out my arms, and take my sweet time to sip a mug of Folgers out on the deck. Whew! Seeing Ace again scrambled my brain around. The guy makes me feel alive like nothing else in the world. Ducky jumps onto my lap to snuggle. A slight breeze and the soft morning sun lull me back to sleep. The blaring phone wakes me up.

"Hello, Angel?"

"Yeah, who's this?"

"This is Dede's husband, Richard."

"Hey, Mr. Dede, I mean Richard. I conked out right here on the deck. What time is it?"

"It's 11."

"Okay, give me a chance to wake up. How you doin'?"

"Not so good," he says in a soft voice. I struggle to hear the words.

"I'm sorry to hear it," I say. "What's going on?" The phone goes silent. "Uh oh. Is everything okay with Dede?"

"Hard to talk." His voice cracks. "Can you please stop by. Please?"

"I'll be there as soon as I can," I say. I race through the door in less than five minutes. It must be something crazy bad. Why did he call and not Dede? He opens the door before I knock. His eyes are squeezed down to slits in his red puffy face. I barely know the guy. I don't know what to say to him. And I'm worried about my friend.

"Come in, please," he says. He sweeps his arm out like I'm a new customer. He has his left hand wrapped around an open can of Coors. He takes a long slug. When he tries to smile, it doesn't work.

"What's going on? Where's Dede?" I glance around the dead quiet living room. Old newspapers are stacked on the floor along with unopened mail and a slew of crunched beer cans. Dede would never allow such a shambles.

"Where is Dede?" I ask again. Once more, Richard looks about to burst into tears.

"She's gone," he says. I did notice her car wasn't in the driveway when I pulled up.

"What do you mean, gone? To the market or—"

"No, not the market." His voice hot. "She is gone, gone, *gone*. No mas. Finito! Okay? Understand?" He buttons up to hide his pale soft belly. "You didn't know?"

"No, I didn't know! If she's really gone, I can't believe she didn't say anything," I say. "What happened?"

"I don't know where to start," he says, his voice ragged.

"That's okay. Just start anywhere." I pat him on his shoulder like we're the best of pals. He stares down the beer can for help. A quick scratch to the top of his head sends dandruff floating to his shoulders.

"Like I said, Dede's gone. Really gone. She and Carmen ran off together." He sinks into a weathered purple chair. I slide back into its mate.

"Wait a minute, are you talking about Carmen, who cleans your B & B?"

"Yep, that Carmen." Fat drunken tears roll down his cheeks.

"You mean, like ran away with?" He nods and wrings his hands together. The cat jumps on his lap.

"It's true," he says. "They ran off to Chihuahua, Mexico."

"Are you joshing me?" I say, not believing my ears. "Are you saying Carmen and Dede ran off together . . . like a real couple?"

"That's right." He polishes off the beer and belches twice. I sink deeper into the chair and try to take in the news.

"This can't be real," I say. He stands up and motions for me to follow him into the bedroom. We stand at the foot of the bed, as if it will help me understand this crazy story a little better.

"Who would've guessed this was going on right under my nose?" His voice cracks. "My wife and our housekeeper! I still can't believe it either." He stands up and wrings his hands.

"Sweet Jesus," I say. "Tell me what happened."

"A bunch of guys meet at Pablo's Pool Hall on Tuesday nights. Only a few showed up, so we finished early. I usually get home around 9. That night, I got home before 8."

"Okay. Then what happened?"

"I hear loud moaning from the back of the house. I think maybe the cat is in heat again. I follow the sound. Well, no, ma'am, it wasn't the cat. It was Dede and Carmen in bed. Couldn't believe my eyes. I couldn't see their faces at all. They were screaming, 'Oh Dede, Oh Carmen,' so I knew it was them." He shakes his head.

"That must have been one crazy shock," I say.

"Yeah, it was. Only girl-on-girl I ever saw before was in *Debby Does Buffy*."

"And now your own wife."

"Yeah, it was tough to see."

"What happened next? When they knew you were standing there?"

"They both sat up, buck-naked. I never realized Carmen had such big tits. Swear to God, big ones! Anyway, they put their arms around each other and laughed at me." His voice catches. "Dede said, 'Now I know about hot sex.'"

What can I do but hand the poor guy a fresh Kleenex from the nightstand. He blows his nose so hard it sounds like a flock of geese.

"So sorry," I say. His voice drops low as he fixes his sight on the bed.

"Yep," he murmurs. "They ran off to a lesbian free-love commune in Chihuahua, Mexico." My mouth drops open. Who would have guessed this about Dede? And now she left Pinewood for a lesbian free-love commune. I'm still trying to wrap my head around it.

"I can't believe it. Is this true?" I say. "For real?"

"Yep, it's all true," he says. "Now, what am I supposed to do?" He cracks open another beer. He goes on. "Dede grabbed a few things from the closet. That was it. They took off in our old Chevy. She yelled out the window. 'You can have the B & B. I'm done with Pinewood forever.'"

"Have you heard from her?" I ask.

He bangs his hand against the bedroom wall. "Nada. Not a single word."

Everything in the bedroom is some shade of brown or beige, the walls, the furniture, the printed bedspread. Even Richard looks like shades of beige.

"Did you ever have a clue about Carmen, uh, walking the other side of the road?"

"Road? Oh, I get it," he says. "Well, yes and no. She kept that pack of Marlboros in her shirt pocket. Held it kind of tough when she smoked like a man. Come to think of it, she did have a mustache. Not too dark, but it was there."

"What about Dede? Did you ever think—"

"I never had a clue," he says, wringing his hands again.

"Hey, I'm sorry about all this, Mr. Dede." His head snaps around.

"Don't call me Mr. Dede anymore, okay? My name is Richard."

CHAPTER 32

*A*s soon as I back out of the driveway, I dig for Ace's phone number in my jeans pocket. The thought of him almost burns a hole in my pants. I swing the car in front of Bob's Olde Time Barbershop. They have one of the few public phones in town.

Two people are ahead of me in line. Some guy on the phone talks way too loud to his girlfriend. His long bushy beard could be home to a dozen small creatures. He wants to borrow money from her. She's not giving in. He slams down the phone. Next is a lady in a housedress who forgot to get potatoes for dinner. This could be the biggest crisis of her life from the sound of her voice. At last, it's my turn. The dime drops down with a clink. One ring, two, three, four. Where is he? And then . . .

"Yeah, Ace here." I want to hang up, but I can't get out a word.

"Hello? Hello?" he says. "Who is it?" I take a deep swallow and croak out a few words.

"Hey there, Ace."

"Is this who I think it is?" I hear a smile in his voice.

"I don't know," I tease, "who do you think it is?"

"That could only be Angel. How's it going, baby?"

"Completely loco. I can tell you later."

"When is later?" Ace says. "I want to see you soon."

"It's wild with you coming into town right about now," I say. "You know, after all this time." I keep my voice soft as I notice folks lining up behind me.

"Oh yeah? How is that banker husband of yours?"

"He's out of town for a few days," I say. I must be crazy to call him, to start something up again.

"Out of town, huh? What do you know?" he says. "I am happy to hear it." That baritone voice of his sets my blood to tingling, just like the old days. "You want to meet me at that little café in Rifle?" he says. "Not where the waitresses pack guns. I mean the other one." The man is irresistible. When I think how I'm stuck in the mud with Arthur, the uptight banker with his silk underwear collection. I deserve some happiness.

"The other café in Rifle is Mom's Café," I say. "Is that the one you mean?"

"That's right, Mom's," he says. "How about it?" His deep voice rumbles through the phone and takes me back to the first day we met. Ace on his Harley and 16-year-old me with a mile-high rocky road ice cream cone.

"I'll meet you there," I say. "I'm driving an old jalopy, but I'll get there."

"Hang on a minute," he says. "You can leave your car at Gus's. Ride with me on my Harley, like old times. What do you say?" Could this be happening? He's talking to me like no time has passed.

"Is this for real, Ace? I can't believe we're talking."

"Get your sweet self down the mountain," he says. "I can't wait to see you."

"Okay," I say, hoping my voice sounds calm and strong. "See you at the gas station in an hour."

"I'll be waiting," he says in his growly voice.

I race down the mountain, even passing slow-moving looky-loo tourists on the curves. My heart pumps so hard I think I can hear it booming. As I screech into Gus's, Ace leans on his motorcycle, the other hand on his hip, smiling ear to ear. I jump out of the car and run towards him. He pulls me up against him, we wind our arms tight around each other, and we carry on like there's no one around for miles.

"I knew we'd see each other again," he says, cocky as ever.

"Wow," I say. "You know, you did break my heart."

"Can I make up for it now?" The guy makes me quiver in my boots.

"How you going to make up for it?" I tease.

"Hmm, let's see," his eyes flash his own brand of Morse Code. "Let's forget about Mom's Café," he says. "I want you right now."

"Where should we go?" I squeeze the words through my dry lips.

"There's a motel in Rifle right across the street from Mom's. How about that?" he asks.

"It takes an hour to get to Rifle. I could change my mind by then," I say, not even convincing myself.

"I'll take my chances on that," he says. He glances back at me with a sly grin, revs up the bike, and off we go. The soft summer wind on my bare arms sends a thrill through my body. I press up against his back, my lips brushing his left ear.

"It's been a long time," I say, over the sound of the engine. He nods.

"Eight years."

He nods again and steps on the gas. As he checks us into the motel, Mom's Café is a long-forgotten thought.

"Good to see you, Ace!" says the Indian guy behind the desk, his head wrapped in a white turban.

"Hey, Amir, how goes it?"

"They know you here?" I say. He shrugs.

"By name?" He shrugs again. "I've stayed a few times over the years." My stomach squeezes up. Am I crazy to be here with him? I hang back.

"Come on, baby. It's been too long." He slips his arm around my waist and leads me down the dingy hall. We check out the black-and-white photos of cowboys and wild horses. He pulls me close and kisses me.

"I want to wrangle *you*," his voice loaded with sex. Once in the room, we shuck off our clothes, and Ace is inside me within no time. We try to make up for all the lost years, bucking and bolting, wild hot, and sweaty. We carry on for hours. I scream out his name over and over. He buries his face in my neck. Finally, too exhausted to go on, we lie tangled together and catch our breath.

"God, it's good to be with you again," he says. "I have dreamt about you for years. We really do have it together, don't we?"

"I've dreamt about you, too, Ace. More times than you would ever guess." He looks down at my arm.

"Hey, when did you go and get that tattoo? NO ANGEL, huh? Does this have anything to do with me?"

"Maybe." He brushes my hair back as I snuggle up to his shoulder.

"Your folks must have gone wacko."

"Believe it or not, they've never seen it."

"I guess that's one way to remember me." He kisses me on the forehead. "What do you say, we get a little sleep and breakfast at Mom's in the morning?"

"Sure, we can do that." He is out cold in a few minutes. Unlike Arthur's pale, soft skin, I can't take my eyes off his tan, muscled body. I don't want to go to sleep. All I want to do is stay in his arms and stare at him for the rest of the night, imagining the stories in his scars, places he's been.

Next morning, sleepy but happy, we sit in the red Naugahyde booth at Mom's Café. Ace leans across the table.

"I think I'll have the Rancher's Special. How 'bout you, darlin'?"

"I'll have Pigs in Blankets." The waitress takes our order, and we set aside our worn menus. The room is jammed with locals having breakfast before heading out to work.

"Just like old times, huh?" says Ace. "Come to think of it, we never went much of anywhere except Gus's house and the barn, did we?" The café's counter fills with solo men in their overalls, the type that works with their hands. All except for one in the corner with dark hair, dressed in a gray suit and yellow tie. I almost jump out of my seat when I first notice him, thinking it might be Arthur. I tune out the people and the noise and concentrate on Ace.

"At least we were in a bed last night and not on a stack of hay," I say. He chuckles into his cup of coffee.

"How you been, Angel? I'm guessing your marriage isn't that great."

"You've got that right."

"What about when I saw you at the Pinewood Inn with my biker pals. That dude, your husband?"

"Yeah. But we weren't married yet."

"That strawberry blonde hair of yours—I knew it was you right away. I could feel you all the way across the room."

"You know what? That was the same night Arthur asked me to marry him. Boy, did that take me by surprise."

"His name is Arthur?" He chuckles again.

"Yep, his name is Arthur. It's been downhill since then," I say. "Well, not right away, maybe six months after we got married." Our waitress comes by with the coffee pot. Ace waves her away.

"Only six months! What went wrong?"

"He bosses me around and treats me like a dumb hick."

Ace shifts around in his seat. "There's nothing dumb about you." He reaches across the table for my hand. I've met people from all walks of life," he says. "You are one of the smartest, most talented people I know. I could see it right away—the brains, the talent. I hope you know that about yourself."

"Well, I don't know . . . ." I tear up and pull my hand away from him. "I've got to get away from Arthur," I say. "Marrying him was a crazy mistake."

"I'm sorry, darlin'." He shifts again in his seat.

"It hasn't been all peaches and cream for me either." Ace takes a bite of his scrambled eggs. He pushes the plate aside as if his food has turned bitter.

"Why? What happened?" I ask. Our waitress shows up and asks if we need anything else.

"No thanks," he says, "we're fine." He watches until she's out of earshot and moves closer until we're hip to hip. I can't imagine what he needs to tell me. Funny, but he never used to share much about himself years ago. All I longed for at sixteen was to be close to him, hear his stories, and bring me into his world. One day poof, he was gone. Now he's back and wants to tell me something private and personal. I lean into him.

"I went to prison for five years." He focuses on a Felix the Cat clock on the wall and never shifts his gaze. "Yep, five years in Montana State Prison."

I can't take it in. I want to hear his story but can't believe what he's telling me, so I study the picture-perfect family of three at the next table. A young blonde girl in a cowboy outfit sits next to her look-alike mother. The clean-shaven dad dressed in his Sunday best, even though it's not Sunday. They look at their daughter like she's the best thing since sliced bread. That must be nice. Ace gives my hand a sad squeeze and brings me back.

"You went to prison?" I say, my heart sinking fast. "Why? What did you do?" He folds his napkin into a neat square and takes a deep breath.

"You know Gus, my pal with the gas station. Well, his brother Gary and I are tight. We rode our bikes, broke up a few bars in our day, and had some fierce times together."

"I bet you did," I say, not wanting to know about those fierce times. He goes on.

"Ever hear of the Wild Woman Saloon in Chinook? It was famous back in the day as a biker hangout. Not a place you'd like. It always smells of whiskey. Some punk was itching for a fight, calling me chicken shit, giving me the hard eye. I drank too much. Before too long, he got me all riled up. So, I slammed him with my fist. I hit him so hard I broke his jaw. Even worse, the guy had a heart attack and died right there on the floor."

"No! Was he old?"

"Not older than thirty-five. But there he was, belly-up and no pulse. They said he was a local, a troublemaker. I never should have hit him. If I was smart, I would have walked away from a fight. But they got me for manslaughter, and I ended up in the slammer." He looks over his shoulder at the waitress.

"How about some more coffee?" She rushes over with a steaming hot pot. I have no more appetite. My pancakes have gone cold; the syrup congealed. Ace takes a few sips of fresh hot brew.

"Funny thing about people," he says, "my cellmate was decent. Polite, soft-spoken." He holds the mug in both hands like he needs to warm up his mood.

"What was he in for?" I ask. I'm glued to my seat, my hip connecting with his leg under the table.

"Robbed a bank in Billings. Kind of an ugly cuss but a gentleman bank robber."

"What does that mean?" Am I crazy to be sitting here? But there's nowhere else I would rather be. "What is a gentleman bank robber?"

"Not a thug or hard ass. Good manners, soft-spoken. He was well-educated, too."

"So how come he robbed a bank? Couldn't he get a good job?"

Ace rolls up his sleeves as if the coffee warmed him up a few more degrees. "Drugs. He was a good guy that made some bad decisions. The two of us would talk for hours."

"About what? How to rob a bank?"

"No, I'm serious now. We talked about books like *On the Road* by Jack Kerouac."

"Never heard of it. I guess we really don't know that much about each other. I still feel like I'm a kid."

"You always seemed wise, not to mention your street smarts." He drinks down his coffee and points up a finger like he has more to say. He sets down his mug.

"I always thought you were something special." I'm surprised at his words. Him saying it out loud and all. "I mean it, Angel," he says.

"Well, that's good to hear," I say. I don't know what's special about me. I never understood what he saw in me. He always believed in me. I wish I believed in myself more.

"Oh," I say, "I don't know . . . ."

I push my hair out of my eyes. "How smart could I be if I married someone like Arthur?"

"He's a lucky guy," he says. "He should treat you better. You deserve it." Ace plunks down some cash on the table.

"C'mon, let's get out of here. Sure wish we could go back to the room."

"I better get going. Arthur will be home from his trip later today." I turn to Ace as we walk out of Mom's. I'm not sure what this is all about. Will we ever see each other again? I'm not banking on it, that's for sure. My life is a mess . . . . He pulls me up against him and kisses the tip of my nose.

"Oh man, you still have those cute freckles. You know, in my way," he says, holding me close, "I've always loved you."

"I've always loved you, too," I say, slapping my hand over my mouth. Here we are, back together again. We made love, we had breakfast together. Why shouldn't I say it?

Ace doesn't look at me.

"Angel, I need to tell you something." He twists the silver skull ring on his pinky finger. Uh oh. His serious tone makes my gut take a deep dive.

"You want the short or long version?" he asks. Now what? I tap my foot on the asphalt.

"Short version, please." I must remember to breathe.

We start to walk, his arm slung low across my hip, his thumb hanging through the belt loop. Sick with worry, I want to push him away, but I don't. His touch keeps me glued to him, although, without a doubt, I'm in for some bad news.

"I've been living this life-on-the-move for a long time," he says. "Prison knocked the crap out of me. All the bad shit you hear about prison is true. Once I landed there, I knew I should keep my nose clean and stay out of trouble."

"That was good," I say, "right?" The serious look on his face makes me wonder. Eight years since we've seen each other. So much has happened. So much has changed.

"I kept to myself," says Ace, "had a lot of time to think. Too much time. And that's where I was. Locked up when both my folks died." He shakes his head as if he can shake the sad memories away.

"I am so sorry," I say. I take his hand from my hip and hold it between my hands.

"My parents were never happy with me." He swallows hard and pulls his hand away. "They were good people, but I couldn't toe the line and live the life they expected." It's all pouring out of him now. Things I always wanted to know about him.

"What do you mean? What life did they expect?" I ask.

"Law school," he says, "like my old man. Top university. All that."

"That's crazy," I say. "Your pops was a lawyer?"

"Yep, a good one. And Mom was no stay-at-home wife. She ran his practice."

"Jeez Louise, Ace. I had no idea you're from those kinds of folks."

"Not many people know," he says. "So, darlin', this is my chance to get on with it. Start with a clean slate. You know what I mean?"

"I guess so," I say, with no clue of what he's talking about. He stares straight through me.

"I met a woman." His voice is so low I strain to hear what he's saying.

"Oh!" I say. "A woman?" My blood runs cold. I look at him, but he won't look at me.

"... while I was locked up. She worked with the Montana Prisoner Advocate Program," he says, "and took on my case." His words come out slow and careful, different than before. He still won't look at me. "She did a great job. Sprung me out way earlier than I ever dreamed possible."

"Ooo-kay," I say. The word takes forever to leave my mouth.

"A total class act," he says. "I still can't believe she wants to be my wife." My temperature shoots up to 105.

"What did you say? Did you say, wife?" Can he see the steam coming out of my ears? He backs away, a weird grin on his face.

"This is hard for me to tell you." He yanks at his collar. "We're getting married in two months." Once the message sinks in, I pound him with my fists.

"You dirty dog! How could you?" He holds his hands in front of him to block the blows, like two fighters in a boxing ring.

"When I saw you," he says, "I couldn't resist. We always had that special thing."

"Oh yeah? Well, someone should cut off *your thing*." I gasp for air, still hitting him, trying to hurt him. "I hate you! I hate your guts!" He stops holding me off and lets me hit him like I'm nothing more than a tiny bug, and he's a friggin' man of steel.

"I'm sorry, baby," he says.

"You are so full of it, *baby*." I walk to the road and stick out my thumb for a ride.

"Angel, no, don't do that. Please . . . ."

A sudden wind kicks up a dust storm, twirling and whirling around us. Ace rushes over, holds his jacket in front of me to hold off the dust, and wraps his arm around me. I slip away from him.

"Don't touch me," I say. "Leave me alone, you lying bastard!" I walk toward the road, hands shielding my eyes just enough to see the road.

"C'mon Angel, don't hitchhike," he says. "I can take you back to Gus's place."

"Get on that bike with you?" I say, "Not in a million years."

"Angel, I am a shit." He runs his hand through his hair. "I am so sorry."

"No, you're not, you selfish fucker." I swivel further away from him. "I hate you. You liar. You did it to me again." He turns away. The crunch of gravel under his feet breaks my heart. It's the saddest sound I've ever heard. He turns back and throws me a kiss.

"Take care of yourself," he shouts. "I'll always love you."

The roar of his motorcycle ends it the way it started on that summer night eight years ago.

CHAPTER 33

HOW COULD ACE PULL SOMETHING AS ROTTEN AS THIS? I better pull myself together. A grizzled old rancher towing a horse trailer stops for me.

"Hop in, girly."

"No, that's alright." I shake my head to rid my hair of dust and whisk my clothes.

"You okay?" he asks.

"I'm fine," I say.

"Sure would have liked the company," he says.

"Sorry, Grandpa. Thanks anyway." Next, a white Ford Falcon with five rowdy frat boys pulls over.

"Hey beautiful!" says one, hanging out the rear window. "Hop in!"

"Check out the body on this chick," says another.

He wears a baseball cap that says, *Nobody Does it Better.*

"Keep going, guys," I say. "Toss the bottles, get some coffee, and sober up."

"See ya," say the lunatics, peeling rubber as they go. I jab my thumb in the air. Cars race past me at 65 mph or more. At last, a station wagon slows down and pulls up close to me. Just what I'm looking for: A sweet-faced young mother, like Shirley Jones in *The Partridge Family*, with four noisy young kids in the back. She leans out the car window.

"Where to, hon?" she says.

"I have to get home to Pinewood," I say. "Do you know where that is?"

"Quiet back there, kids!" she says. She grins at me. "Sure do. I'm going in that direction, dropping my nephew off at his mom's in Copperville. I could take you that far."

"That would be fine. Well, anyway, that's where my car is. You know Gus's Gas Station on 133?"

"Yep, I know it. Jump in, hon. Sorry, it's kind of a mess."

"I don't mind."

I open the passenger door. Coke bottles clank together on the floor. *Psychology Today* magazines cover the front seat.

"Oh, can you just hold on to those magazines?" she asks. "I could be better organized." She glances in the back. "I need to put them in a binder." I don't know if she means the magazines or the kids.

"Mama, who is the lady?" says a little boy wearing a plaid jacket.

"A friend of mine." The mom leans over and whispers. "What's your name, hon?"

"Angel."

"This is Angel, guys." The kids have already lost interest.

"I'm Maggie." She has beautiful clear skin with peaceful blue eyes, her general expression calm, like she doesn't know the meaning of stress. Soft curly brown hair frames her heart-shaped face. The kids play a game about who can spot license plates outside Colorado. I remember playing with my Pinewood girlfriends at that age.

"Out of State!" yells one of the boys.

"That's not fair. You always see them first!" whines a little mop-headed girl.

"Kids! Settle down back there," says Maggie. "You don't want me to get nervous and have an accident." She leans toward me again. "So, Angel, why are you hitchhiking? Kind of risky, isn't it? A pretty girl like you."

"It's a long story." I face the window. "I can't talk about it right now."

She hits the gas. "I'm sorry, hon," she says. "I didn't mean to pry."

I ease back into the seat. The hum of the car on the highway eases my mind.

Maggie flips the radio dial back and forth 'til she reaches station KMTS. "Here we go!" she says.

"My favorite country station," I say, looking out at the lush emerald-green of the ranchland and the red glow of the mountains.

"Then I'll turn it up!" she says. "I just love the drama of country music." She breaks into song and I join. Her voice reminds me of the time I went to church with Sue Bland and her folks. They thought I needed "the exposure". That it would be "good for me". And that was the end of that.

I'm an alto when I can stay on tune. Maggie and I sing a few more country songs along with the radio. She turns down the volume.

"Have you lived in Pinewood a long time?" she asks.

"All my friggin' life." I want to cheer up for this nice lady but can't yet.

"My hubby and I have the Little Country Market in Copperville. Do you know it?"

"Oh yeah. Everyone talks about your muffins. They're always gone by 8:30 in the morning."

"I get up at the crack of dawn to bake those muffins," she laughs. Her easy way helps to settle my mind, at least a little.

Only five miles from the Copperville turnoff, traffic slows to a snail's pace. A VW bus faces in the wrong direction on the highway. Traffic putts along as people crane their necks to see. Patrol cars and fire engines surround the accident.

I wonder if anyone survived?

"Oh no. Look at that," says Maggie, "a Ford Falcon flipped over."

"Oh no! It's the college kids! They offered me a ride right before you did. They were drinking in the car and acting nutso. No way would I get in the car with those maniacs. Told them to get themselves a strong cup of coffee."

"It could have been you in that car, hon," says Maggie. "How terrible! So many reckless drivers out there."

First Ace, then the college boys, and now me, on my way home to a man who dresses up in women's lingerie. My tears drop onto her *Psychology Today* magazines stacked on my lap. Maggie rests her comforting hand on mine.

"I know you've had a tough day." Maggie plucks Kleenex from the cramped console and hands me a few. "If you need someone to talk to, you can call me. I'll give you my number when we get to Copperville."

"That's real nice of you." I blow my nose and wipe off my wet face.

"Mama, why is the lady crying?" says a little voice from the back of the car.

"She's okay now, kids. It made her sad to see that horrible car accident."

"Oh, okay. Out of State," yells the mophead. "I saw it first!"

Screaming ambulances race the boys to Geiger Springs Hospital. I hope they make it. We'll read about it in the paper tomorrow. So sad, so young. Traffic eases up. We lurch ahead, driving in silence again, each thinking our private thoughts. I surprise myself and blurt it out.

"I just saw my old boyfriend. He's such a shit." Here come the tears again.

"Uh oh! That's not good," says Maggie.

"Yeah, we rode to Rifle on his motorcycle. Spent the night together. First time I've seen him in years. I'm not sure why I'm telling you this," I say, "I don't even know you." I stare out the window thinking, wondering if I should keep talking. My thoughts shift over to the accident. How we never know what will happen from minute to minute. I wonder if any of them made it out alive.

"I'm flattered you're sharing with me," says Maggie, her voice like melted butter, "that you feel comfortable." I shift gears back to Ace.

"I thought," I continue, "well, I guess I *hoped* we were back together again. We spent a crazy good night together. Then you won't believe this one. He tells me this morning he's getting married in two months. After this amazing night. I'm so mad I could spit nails."

"No wonder you're upset," says the nice lady who listens well and reminds me of Sandy. I bet she learned a lot from her *Psychology Today* magazines.

"Yeah, I'm upset! Ace was the love of my life." She glances in the rearview mirror before changing lanes.

"Oh, my goodness," she says, "any chance you're talking about Ace Bernstein? Good looking guy? He rides a Harley?"

"Uncle Ace," screams the mophead. "He plays monster with us."

"That's enough, kids," says Maggie. "Quiet back there!"

"What?" I say. "Are you kidding me? You know Ace?" Why in God's name did I tell her all about us? My thoughts spin out of control. She looks like a regular nice mom with little kids, a station wagon, and the works. But people can be tricky. You can bet I've learned that lesson. "Ahem!" I need to get a handle on my nerves. "I guess you *know him well* if your kids call him Uncle Ace."

"Oh gosh, I know how upset you are right now. Please don't get the wrong idea, Angel. Can I explain?"

"Go ahead," I say, arms planted across my chest.

"Ace is friends with my husband," she says. "They met at the Harley dealership in Geiger Springs a few years ago."

Maggie pulls a soft pack of Winston cigarettes from the console, taps one out of the pack, and lights up. She exhales a long thick stream of smoke.

"My guy liked Ace so much he invited him to our house for dinner. And boy, oh boy, did he appreciate a home-cooked meal." She waves her cigarette in the air as she talks. "We've been friends with him ever since."

I study her face as she tells me the story. I start to relax.

"The kids are crazy about Ace," she continues, "so is my husband." A radiant smile lights up her face as she explains. "They love to take walks and smoke cigars. Ace's stories and his life on the road fascinate my husband. He is the ultimate reliable family man—thank God." She laughs, takes another drag on her cigarette, and turns to me. "Speaking of smoking, I really need to quit. Such a nasty habit."

I breathe a sigh of relief. Maybe time to lighten up the conversation. I think she's okay.

"So, Maggie," I say, "do you think we're good enough to start a singing group?" Her voice might be worse than mine.

She bursts out laughing. I join in so loud and for so long that I may bust a gut.

"Mama, what's so funny?" asks little mophead.

"Just grown-up stuff, honey," says Maggie. "You'll understand when you're older." She gives me a wink.

"You always say that," pouts the little girl, "when you don't want us to know something."

"Kids," says Maggie, as we pull up to Gus's Gas Station, "they're wiser than we think."

"Thanks, Maggie," I tell her. I step out of the car and carefully set the magazines back on the seat. "You are a ray of sunshine in my rotten day."

"And you are a delight," she says. "Please take good care of yourself."

"I'll come see you at the bakery. Maybe we can sing to the customers."

We start laughing again as Gus walks toward me with a welcoming smile and greasy hands. I ignore him. The kids wave goodbye from the back of the car. Their sweet innocence lifts my spirits, at least for a short while.

Racing up the mountain, I hope Arthur doesn't come home before I do. Although I make it in record time, his Buick Skylark stands in the driveway. More bad luck. When will it end?

Arthur booms through the front door with Ducky wagging her tail behind him. Did she think I had left her forever, stuck with Arthur?

"Well, well," says Arthur. "Look who decided to come home," his arms crossed tight across his chest. "And where have you been, little wife?"

The sneer on his face makes me shake. He points at Ducky as if he wants to shoot her.

"This dog of yours never does her business in the house . . . until today." His eyes are colder and meaner than I've ever seen before. "She was starving. I guess you've been gone for quite a while, and I do mean quite a while."

"You know what?" I say, "I had a few rotten days. I don't have to explain a friggin' thing." His mouth drops open. I speak up for the first time. Arthur goes mute as if I kicked him in the shins. Ducky lopes over to me, tail still wagging like crazy. I pick her up, hold her close, and trudge up the stairs with Arthur a few feet behind me. I burrow under the covers with Ducky and hide under the pillow. Arthur stands over me and pulls it off.

"Where were you?" he demands. "Out with rough riders and cattle poachers?"

I sit up in bed and push off the dog. "That's pretty funny," I say. "You're accusing me of a secret life? How about that negligee collection of yours?"

His open angry mouth snaps shut like a lizard catching a fly. He shrinks into himself.

"Just leave me alone," I say. "I am bone tired."

I dive under the pillow again and pass out. Once I wake up, the house is like a morgue with no sign of Arthur anywhere. I pop a frozen chicken pot pie in the oven and finish off some Gallo wine. Tuckered out from two of the craziest days of my life, I stumble back to bed and fall into a dreamless sleep until the next morning.

A pounding headache wakes me up. Blinking from the bright morning light, I toss cold water on my face, brush my teeth, and wrap up in my chenille robe. I scrounge in the fridge for something to eat, but there's not much. Instead, I crack open a nice cool beer. Outside, life goes on as usual. A lone deer strolls across the grass, beautiful and free. I rub the smeared-up kitchen window to get a better look, but she's already slipped out of sight. Gone. This town is nothing more than a noose around my neck, strangling me day by day. Swinging open the fridge door, I pull out the last can of brew.

At first, Arthur treated me better than any man. Took me places, showed me new ways to think, and loved to buy me things. He always wanted me to look pretty, bought me clothes, and spent money without complaining. He treated me special, almost like his doll. He even loved when other men looked at me. That was downright weird. When I first met Arthur, he may have looked like Clark Kent, but he sure as hell never turned into Superman.

I pick up a yellow pencil and a notepad from Soldier's Bank from the kitchen counter, almost tearing through the paper with wild circles and angry zigzags. Flipping to the next sheet, I cover it with triangles in a row, like dragon's teeth. With each page, I unwind more. Halfway through the notepad, I draw big rectangles with triangles on top. It looks familiar. A shiver goes down my spine. A building that drew itself: Soldier's Bank.

I slump back in the chair, take a few deep breaths, and call Sandy.

CHAPTER 34

SANDY PICKS UP HER PHONE ON THE FIRST RING.

"Where have you been?" Her voice is worried and strained. "I tried to reach you all day yesterday," she says, "up until 11 last night."

"I'm sorry. I really am." I stare at the crude drawing of Soldier's Bank again. "I do need to talk to you. I'll tell you why later. Can we meet at your house around 3 this afternoon?"

"Sure. But what's going on? Why wait that long? It sounds important."

"I'm riding Star in a little while. Nothing better to make problems slide off my shoulders than riding that horse. Or any horse. Gotta work off some steam. I'll explain everything when I see you. Promise."

"Okay," says Sandy. She sighs into the phone like she's had enough of my crazy life.

"I can't talk about it now," I say. "I hope you understand." Sandy sighs one more time. I can't blame her. She's put up with me for so many years.

"Okay, Angel cake. Come as soon as you can. Okay?"

At Lindbergh's barn, I take a few minutes to pet Star's muzzle. She tosses her head back and whinnies, happy to see me. Maybe she's as happy as I am to see her. I tell her how fed up I am with my life as I place the bridle over her head, complain about Arthur as I throw the blanket over her back, and share the latest about Ace and me as I saddle her up. I'm at my best when I'm with her, better than I am with people. She understands. I know she does.

We trot briefly, moving into a full gallop once we reach a vast pasture half a mile past Pinewood. We've done this together too many times to count. The pasture drops into a meadow covered in thousands of tiny wild white daisies from weeks ago. Every one of them is dead and gone.

I've been treading water in this marriage for a long time. I'm going under. Ace came back to me, but he's gone. And I blew the lid off Arthur's secret. Early on, I never would have guessed he was two bricks short of a load. Sandy's words come back to me. She said it true how Soldier's Bank would go bat shit crazy if they found out about Arthur's little hobby. Time to take control of my life.

A huge black bear, at least 250 pounds, crosses the trail. They may look cute, but I remind myself that they're fierce animals.

A few minutes to 3, I show up at Sandy's, more relaxed than the morning but still jumping out of my skin.

"What's going on?" Deep furrows trouble Sandy's brow. "I've been worried about you," she says. "Do I sound like somebody's mother right now?"

"You do, but that's okay," I say. She gives me a light smack on the arm.

"You got it," she says.

We sit at the dining room table, the one Sandy has lived with her entire life, handed down by her English grandparents to her parents and now to her. We sat at this table when we played Old Maid as little kids. We sat at this table and talked about horses and high school crushes when we were teens. We even wrote a blood sisters' constitution at this table. We cut our index fingers with razor blades, holding hers up against mine so our blood would mix, and vowed to always be best friends. When her parents went out, we sat at this same table and overdid the Gallo wine. We shared our secrets and spilled our guts.

If furniture could talk, what stories it could tell.

"Hang on, Angel," she says. "Save your latest adventure for one more minute. I'll get you a little snack." She opens the cupboard and takes out a package of Chip Ahoys, knowing they're my favorite cookies of all time. She plops the package on the table and hands me a Coke bottle. I take a huge bite of a cookie as if nothing but that cookie will settle my nerves. She knows what to do. Even when I do something loco, she stands by my side. I hope I'm as good a friend to her.

"Okay, tell me, Angel. What the hell is going on?" Sandy props her arms on the table and leans her chin into her hands, ready to be the best listener on Planet Earth.

I fill her in on the whole story of me and Ace. She puts her hand out like a referee at a baseball game.

"Hold on! What did you say? I can't believe you never told me until now." She blinks her eyes in surprise and maybe hurt, too. I bring her up to the minute – how Ace and I spent the night together in Rifle, how he dropped the news that he is getting married, how I hitchhiked home, how Arthur was lying in wait for me. She listens quietly, like the great friend she is, until I say everything I need to say.

"Whoa, whoa, whoa," she slaps her hand to her forehead. "What a nightmare! You're right about one thing," she says. "I never would have guessed all that!"

"Sandy, the main thing is, I've got to get away from Arthur," I say. "He's nothing like the guy I thought I was marrying. He's turned into a monster."

The phone rings, but she ignores it. Someone knocks at the door, but she ignores that, too. She looks at me like she wants to help but doesn't know what to do. She reaches out for my hand. I don't . . . can't let her take my hand. I pull it close, make a fist, wrap my other hand around it, and hold tight.

"Remember that time Arthur wouldn't agree to me taking rodeo riding lessons?" I say. "He doesn't like one thing about me. The real me! Why did I marry him?" Sandy reaches out and unravels my two hands. This time I let her mother me.

She cups both my hands in hers and waits for me to breathe. When she hugs me, her steady heartbeat calms me down a bit. We sit that way without talking for a long while. The afternoon sun lands on her face through the window. She looks worn and beaten down. The spunky girl I know has left the room.

"Sandy, we have to get out of here," I say.

"Great idea. But we've said this for years. So, let's get serious. But how can we do it? Neither one of us has two nickels to rub together." She sweeps her hair off her face. It always looks so glamorous to me. I can hardly run a brush through my hair.

"You know I scrape to pay my rent every month," she says. "And Arthur won't let you work. Does he give you any money at all?"

"No, not much. Money for groceries, that's about it. I buy everything on sale. I keep whatever is left over. He buys me clothes because, you know me, I don't buy them. I could care less."

"No money is a pretty bad start for a getaway," says Sandy. She almost laughs, but it comes out like a puny cough. She opens a curtain to let in some more light, spots a dime on the rag rug, and pops it in her pocket.

"Listen," she says, "the only one we know with any kind of money is your charming husband, *Arthur le terrible*."

"Here's the thing," I say. "He does make more than most of the folks we know. The real money is in the bank where he works. That's what we need. *Big money!*" Sandy shifts in her chair, the forest-green one, where she likes to read.

"In the bank?" she says. "What are you saying?"

"Well, that's the truth. That's where the money is. If we could get our hands on some, we could live the lives we want."

Sandy cups her hand over her mouth. "C'mon now, are you saying we should rob your husband's bank?" She throws her head back and hangs onto the arms of the chair as if she needs to steady herself. I smile, don't say a word, just smile.

"You must be nuts," she says. "Have you lost your mind?"

"Maybe so. Maybe I've found it," I say. "Well, roll it around in your head. I think it's the only way. Cleaning houses ain't gonna do it for you, Sandy."

Her eyes fill up. "We're trapped, aren't we? Trapped in this rotten town 'til we die in our beds." A deep sob, like I have never heard from Sandy, shocks me. And then a storm of tears. I go over to hug her. She's limp in my arms, allowing me to hug her back now that she needs one. It only lasts for a minute or so. She pushes me away.

"Let's talk tomorrow," she says. "All of a sudden, I'm exhausted."

I close the front door as quiet as I can. The same door where we carved our initials as kids and got a thrashing from our folks. The door groans as I close it, tired of it all, the same as Sandy and me.

CHAPTER 35

I LOOK OUT THE KITCHEN WINDOW, HOPING FOR THE SUN to poke through a thick layer of clouds. I don't know how much longer I can go on with so little sleep. Every night I keep my distance from Arthur, a brick wall between us. Like every other day, I roll the story of my small life over and over in my mind. As soon as the clock hits 8 a.m., I phone Sandy.

"Can you come over? Let's talk. I'll make you some grits and eggs."

"That sounds good. I'll be there by 9." My mood brightens with her familiar knock, knock, knock on the front door.

"Good timing, San," I say. The toaster pops out some golden toasted Wonder Bread. I flip the eggs and grits onto a plate. I slather butter on the toast.

"I hope you're not buttering me up, too," laughs Sandy.

She tucks her food away. I stand watching her eat as I sip my coffee, no sugar or cream, always black and strong.

She finishes off the last of her breakfast and pushes aside the plate like she's ready for anything. Still, she looks worn out, eyes droopy, like she's been through the mill. It's true; she has been through the mill for years. Her parents were decent folks. They didn't have much money and always rented the house like Sandy does today. I don't know why, but Sandy still sleeps in her girlhood bedroom. And she can't explain it. I don't think she knows the answer.

I sit with her, my hands wrapped around the mug as if it will warm up my spirit.

"So, what's going on, Angel," she says. "More crazy stories? More about Soldier's Bank? You want to go to prison like Ace, your dream man?"

"I can't take it anymore," I say, "living with Arthur."

"I know, you've said that many times. And I understand. You hoped for stability, a better life with him. I'm sorry for you. But I'm not too happy with my life either. It's not even close to what I thought it would be." She stares into her coffee. "What happened to my husband? Where is he? I thought I'd be married with a couple of kids and a nice life. Remember how we played Old Maid when we were kids? Now I am an old maid."

"Sandy, listen to me. You're not an old maid. Okay? It's smart to get married a little bit later. Look how I messed up. I didn't marry you-know-who for the right reasons. It all went off the rails in no time. You're lucky you didn't get stuck with the wrong guy. I know it will all work out for you. You'll see." I smack both hands on the table. "So, let's get down to business, okay?"

She sighs, deep and sad like it might be her last breath.

"I've been wracking my brain," I say, scanning the living room. I live in Arthur's house, by his rules, under the thumb of my jailer. Sandy sits on the edge of her chair, waiting to hear what I'll say next. "Listen," I say, "our only way out is going for Soldiers Bank."

"That is completely bonkers." Sandy slaps her hands on the table. "I think you are losing your marbles."

"And you said that before. But listen," I say, "please, just listen for a minute. We could start all over again. We could! Far away on some beautiful beach."

"You know what," says Sandy, "I'm in a rotten mood today. The biggest photo shoot I've had in ages canceled on me at 6 last night. *Six o-clock.* I had all my gear together, ready to tackle this job with everything I've got. I could finally make a good chunk of money. Just as I was ready to eat my burger, they called to say they were canceling. They didn't give a reason or even apologize! These are the folks I told you about, the super-rich family with tame foxes that live in their house."

"I'd rather live with a fox than with Arthur."

Sandy shoots me an annoyed look.

"Pay attention. I'm trying to tell you something. I need to get my hands on some dough." She taps her fingers on the table.

"I know a place where we can get lots of money." I point at my Soldier's Bank coffee mug. "Look, right here in front of you. Soldier's Bank, where my controlling husband works."

"Take it easy," says Sandy. She stops tapping her fingers. "You need to calm down."

"I don't know any other way out," I say. "It's worth a shot to me. Just knowing I can dump this jailer husband of mine and split out of here forever. If I never see another pine tree again . . . ." I tap the coffee mug with my fingernail to make my point. "Are you in, or are you stuck in friggin' Pinewood the rest of your life?"

She wrings her hands together. "I finally got paid after two months from the last photo shoot. So, listen to this one. Their check was no good, insufficient funds." Her voice cracks. "My rent check bounced for the third time in the last three months." She buries her face in her hands. "My landlord was yelling his head off. Told me he's had it with me."

"Sandy, you know I would give you the money if I had it. If I could help you in any way, I would do it. I'm so sorry." Ducky settles onto my lap. I stroke her velvety head as I listen to my friend.

"I am so sick and tired of struggling," she says. "Living hand to mouth all these years. You caught me on a bad day."

"You have had it rough," I say, "no one would argue with that. Just think Sandy, you would never have to worry about money again."

She sweeps her hair aside. "Listen, I need to go. I'm cleaning for the Williams family today."

"Why don't you think about it?" I ask. "Just think about it."

"Thanks for breakfast Angel. I'm at my wits' end. And I think you've gone off your rocker. I don't know what else to say."

"You don't have to say a thing," I tell her. "Just think about it." She opens the front door and turns back to look at me.

"We always knew we didn't have much going for us in this town," she says, "but we never thought it would get this bad." She leaves me sitting at the table with my coffee mug, my thoughts knocking up against the sides of my brain, trying to make sense of it all.

If I take a job, Arthur will find out. Sniffing around me, the nose of a bloodhound, he could be the best private detective in Colorado. He'd find out right away if I returned to the Double G. It would take years to scrape enough money together for a getaway. I need big money, escape money, and I need it soon. I know I need Sandy's help. I don't think I can do it myself. Maybe I should try a minor heist or two and see how it works out. Then maybe I could win her over. Maybe that would bring her around. She's no dummy. I'm no dummy. She got better grades than me, but she always told me I was smart, told me I had brains. I know Sandy is sick and tired of being poor. Life is so friggin' unfair. She's the best person I know. Truth is, nothing is going to change for her. We're both stuck here in godforsaken Pinewood for the rest of our stupid lives. If I divorced Arthur, he would do his best to destroy me.

I think I have what it takes to pull off a major heist. I've done great with all the small ones over the years. Geiger Springs would be a good place to start. Maybe I'll heist some clothes or lift a piece of jewelry. Sandy always said I stay calm in tough situations. I know I can handle it like a pro. I'll give Sandy some time. Maybe she'll come around.

CHAPTER 36

I CAN'T BREATHE FROM THE SUFFOCATING AIR IN ARTHUR'S house. We don't say much to each other these days. He leaves for work without a goodbye. We eat dinner without talking. When he goes out at night, he doesn't bother to explain anything, like where he's going or what he's doing. Last week a small piece of red silk was hanging out of the small leather bag he always takes with him at night. And I could care less where he goes or what he's doing. He said he always locks up the bank. If I could somehow get ahold of those keys.

I've lost eight pounds in the past three weeks. No appetite from living this crazy life. I look like a skinny gizzard. If Sandy doesn't come around, I'll have to move ahead with a plan for me, myself, and I. Anything would be better than this living hell.

A practice run is in order. Two days later, I drive the 30 miles to Geiger Springs. Although Polly Anne's Dress Shoppe has been here for years, and I've walked past it many times, I've never been inside. Dede said she bought her wedding dress at Polly Anne's when she married Mr. Dede, Richard, whoever he is, poor guy. I wonder how he's doing since Dede ran off with Carmen. That had the whole town buzzing. You can bet it gave Leila the Righteous a new reason for living. Sandy asked Sue and me to come to her house one night after word got out. Sue picked up some playing cards and nervously shuffled them as we sat around her oak dining room table.

"We all knew Richard had no personality and didn't bring home the bacon. But what a shock about Dede and Carmen," said Sue. "Did you know anything about this?" Sue asked. Her head swiveled back and forth between Sandy and me. "Did Dede ever let you in on her secret?"

"Not me," said Sandy. "I had no idea . . . I just hope she's happy now."

"I didn't know until Richard told me the whole story," I said. "I guess Dede was too scared to tell us. I sure do miss her."

"I can't believe we may never see her again," said Sue. We talked for hours, laughing about all the good times we've had together. We also wondered if we let our friend down in some way.

As I park the car, I snap myself out of my thoughts and back to the job ahead. Focus on Polly Anne's Dress Shoppe. You can't mess this up. I step out of the car onto the sidewalk, pause, and take a deep breath. Once I open the shop door, the *ding ding* of little bells sets my nerves on edge. Everyone's eyes are on me. But they all turn back to what they're doing. It's a cozy, welcoming shop covered in wallpaper with tiny yellow flowers. The scent of lavender fills the room.

"Welcome," says a saleslady standing behind a big old-fashioned cash register on an oak desk, just like Faye Vespers has at the Double G. She continues to ring up her customer. I notice her pile of silver necklaces and stylish cocoa-colored dress. The other saleslady, maybe in her mid-thirties, with long black hair, stands up nice and straight. If Mama had been here, trust me, she would point it out: "Now that's good posture, Angela."

That woman started harping on me at age twelve and never stopped.

"Look at those round shoulders," she said, too many times to remember. "You'll have a hunchback one of these days."

The good-posture saleslady points to the dressing rooms. "We're busier than usual for a Tuesday afternoon," she says from across the shop. "Would you be alright to change in the bathroom? We'll get to you as soon as we can." I smile and nod. She goes on, "Please let us know if you have any questions."

"I'm fine with using the bathroom," I say, and gather a stack of four sweaters in my arms: two identical purple slip-ons, a chunky white cable knit, and a pale orange cardigan.

I try on one of the purple sweaters. It fits me to a tee, and the color is great with my light red hair or strawberry blonde, as Sandy would say. I hold the white one against me and the pale orange one, too. Eh, not as good. I don't even bother trying them on. I kill a little time, so it looks like I'm busy trying on every single item. When enough time goes by, I slip my jacket over the purple sweater, zip it up to my chin and leave the other three hanging on hooks in the bathroom.

Oh good. The shop is even more crowded than before.

"Thanks," I say as I head to the front door, "but no luck." Both ladies wave at me.

"Come again," says the one in the fancy dress with the mountain of necklaces.

That was a snap! But my heart pounds in my chest, as it did when I dropped packages off to Mr. Conway. I remember to stroll, like I don't have a care in the world, just another shopper taking a stroll down the street. Even so, I'm sweating under these layers of clothes, but more from nerves than anything else. No one is coming after me. Those two salesladies didn't notice a thing. That was a cinch. *I did it!* Adrenalin powers through my veins.

I don't mention it to Sandy. Not yet. I make another plan for the following week. I need to stay calm, to think and act like a pro and see if I can get away with another heist. On a sunny Tuesday morning, I drive to Geiger Springs and head into a store that's only a few years old. It's kind of an updated general store called Solly's Good Stuff. The man, who must be Solly, stands at the back of the store. He has a round face, double chin, and a pot belly. He waves me in and smiles, although, at the same time, he's busy talking on the phone. I can hear every word as he talks way too loud at the person on the other end.

"What?" he says. "What do you think I am, an idiot? I can get better prices than that." I strain to hear more. When he sees me looking his way, he lowers his voice and turns to face the wall. A young woman approaches me. She, too, has a round face and double chin, the spitting image of Solly.

"Are you looking for something special?"

She has a soft voice. Nothing like her father. And a kind face, as if she never says a bad word about anyone. Should I lift something from her store? The smallest guilt sets in, but I'm on a mission to break out of Pinewood, and the guilt fades away.

Solly's Good Stuff has racks and racks of dresses, coats, sweaters, and jackets. An entire wall of shelves is filled with jeans. It even has a few fancy brands like Calvin Klein and Gloria Vanderbilt. As for me—give me good old 501 Levi's any old day of the week. The glass counters are saved for gold and silver jewelry, some with sparkling stones.

"How can I help you?" says Solly's daughter as I scan the room.

"Oh, hmmm, my mother's birthday is coming up. I'd like to get her a pretty necklace."

"Oh, that's nice," says Solly's daughter. "Do you have anything in mind?"

"I don't know. She's not very fancy," I say. "It should be something simple."

This is such a joke. Mama hasn't worn any jewelry for years. Even if I did buy her something, she wouldn't wear it. Besides, she never likes anything I choose. Last thing I remember her wearing, besides her wedding ring, was a bracelet from Miser's Mercantile. She lost it one night when she and Pops were partying at the Inn. No one ever found it. But it doesn't matter. I'm not shopping for her anyway.

"Hmmm," says the salesgirl, "I guess we'll start from scratch. I do want to help you find the right thing."

"Maybe you can show me what *you* like," I say. Not being much of a shopper, I hope I don't sound like a fool. I wait as she gathers six necklaces and spreads them onto the counter. Some are kind of gold or gold-filled. One has a few little blue stones. Some are silver. If I were buying one for my mother, she'd like silver. But that's not the plan. The plan is to leave here with a necklace and not spend a dime. I pretend to be interested, pick them up, check the price tags, and look them over, but I don't say anything.

"What do you think?" she asks, nice as can be, her eyebrows too sharp for her soft round features. "Does a particular necklace speak out to you?"

"Hmm," I say, stalling for time. "I'm not sure."

"There are some others hanging over there on the wall, just beyond the jackets," she says. "Can you see them? They are less expensive."

"That sounds more like it," I say.

"Go ahead and take a look," she tells me. "I'll be right back." She scoops up the six necklaces and puts them back in the case. I head over to the wall and stand quietly for a few minutes. Solly, still on the phone, has his back turned to me. Just as I stash one in my pocket, he passes gas. Loud! And doesn't even turn around or excuse himself. When his daughter returns, she waves her hand around to try to get rid of the stink. She gives her father a dirty look, but he's still facing the other way. I'm in the same spot as before, at the wall, busy looking at the necklaces, as if I'm trying to decide.

"See anything you like?" she asks. She pulls her glasses off her head and perches them on her nose.

"I see a few I like," I say, "but I'm going to sleep on it."

"Okay, I understand," she says. "You want to find the right thing. Thanks for coming in. Once you decide, we'll wrap it up in a nice little gift box for your mother."

"Sure. Thank you," I say. The thrill of it all puts a big smile on my face. She smiles back.

"See you soon," she says. And I walk out of Solly's with a $25 necklace in my pocket. I don't think they'll miss it. They have a business, a store, and a life. They'll be fine. That's all I want—to be fine, to be okay. Is that too much to ask?

CHAPTER 37

Sandy has more problems than ever. She calls me, her voice breaking so much I can barely understand what she says.

"My landlord told me I need to get out. Can you believe it? He has known me all these years since I was a *child*. Where will I go? Said he was sick and tired of me being late on the rent. Said he doesn't need the stress, that he's in his 70s now, and I'm ruining his health. He's given me sixty days. Says he's being generous. Now what am I supposed to do?"

"Oh, Sandy," I say, trying to sound strong. I try to calm her down, but I don't know what to do or say or how to help. Arthur would never let Sandy come and stay with us. He doesn't like her much these days. But then he doesn't like me much either.

"Let me think," I say. "We'll come up with a solution." I hope she believes me. She starts to bawl all over again. She hiccups between sobs. She has always been there for me my entire life.

"What would I do without you, Angel?" It kills me when she says that. It always reminds me that she's alone. She doesn't have anyone else in the world. This is the time to move forward and go for Arthur's bank. I can hear her breathing into the phone. It takes a while, but she quiets down and breathes steadier.

"I'm on my way over, Sandy. Let's put our heads together. You shouldn't be alone right now."

I roar over to her house. The place looks bad, with peeling gray paint and missing shingles. It's a real shack. She's so used to it I don't think she notices it anymore. And you know how landlords are. Seems to me they always do the minimum. Sandy hugs me for a long time once she sees me at her front door. We sit together on the raggedy couch, and I put my hand on her knee.

"Sandy," I say. "I'm not going into a whole song and dance. I'll get straight to it."

"What?" she says.

"I tried a couple of little experiments."

"Oh yeah?" she says. She wipes her nose with a lacy hanky, as her mama used to do.

"What do you mean?"

"I did two small heists. It was a breeze. One was a sweater from Polly Anne's Dress Shoppe. The other was a necklace from Solly's Good Stuff. I know this is small potatoes compared to going after a bank, but I think we can do it. We just need a good plan. I'm stuck in this joke of a marriage . . . and you're running out of time with your landlord. Let's put our heads together. Things couldn't get any worse for us. This would be our chance at real freedom."

Sandy nods at me through her tears. "Okay, Angel, I think you're right." She blows her nose. "I have no more fight in me. We have nothing to lose. You can count me in."

CHAPTER 38

"Sandy, I'm glad you're here," I say. "It has been one long week. Arthur went out a little while ago." We settle down together on the leather couch. "Last night on the phone, you said you had something to show me. What is it?" She lays out a sheet of paper with the floor plan of Soldier's Bank.

"How could you know what it looks like?" I ask. "It does look the way I remember it. Did you go there?" Sandy beams at me and nods.

"I sure did," says Sandy. "I went the day before yesterday."

"Holy moly. Will you look at that," I say. "Good going."

She points out the teller windows, where the desks are for the VPs, even the one that says Manager, who would be Arthur. She explains she couldn't go into the room with the safe deposit boxes but shows the door leading into it.

"You told me you went to his bank one time," says Sandy. "It would look funny if you started showing up. So, I went over at noon when you said Arthur goes to lunch. Of course, I wore sunglasses. I walked around and studied everything. So here it is on paper, right in front of you. Let's find out when the Brinks truck comes."

"Right," I say. "We want to get as much cash as possible. Give me a pen and paper, Sandy. I should take notes."

"Good idea," she says.

One night after three weeks of planning, we sit around at Sue's house, the three of us drunk on too much Bourbon and Coke.

"Remember Mary Louise from high school?" asks Sue, her eyes gleaming with the nugget she's about to share.

"What about her?" asks Sandy. Whip-smart Mary Louise, with her wavy black Italian hair, olive skin, and coal-black eyes, kept to herself and always had a secret smile on her face.

"*Well,*" says Sue, "listen to this: She got married to Cal Davenport, a filthy rich cattle rancher. Our dear Mrs. Davenport lives on a 2,000-acre spread in Texas now."

"I can't picture Mary Louise with that kind of life," says Sandy.

"God bless her," says Sue. "It should happen to all of us." She pours another round. I tilt off the arm of the couch and chug down my drink.

"Wouldn't that be something?" I say. "Who would have guessed quiet little Mary Louise would go and do it. "I'm sure she's adjusting very well," I say, laughing. "And here we've talked about getting rich all these years." A loud burp escapes. I clap my hand over my mouth.

"You know, Angel, once we pull this off . . . " says Sandy. Then she claps her hand over her mouth.

Sue's head swivels back and forth between us, and her eyes go wide with curiosity.

"Pull what off?" she says.

"Oh, nothing," says Sandy.

I put my fingers to my lips. "Shh." The room starts to spin, and I hang onto the chair.

"What do you mean nothing?" says Sue. "And Angel, why are you shushing her? C'mon now, I know you're up to something. What's going on?"

"Would you pour me another drink, Sue?" asks Sandy.

"Hey, I'm no dummy. You're not going to throw me off track," says Sue. "C'mon, tell me what you're doing. If it's a secret, you know you're safe with me. We've kept each other's secrets for years. Angel, remember that party at Dede's house when we were seventeen? I caught you in the backseat with Spencer. I never told a soul."

"Guess what?" I say. "You just did."

"That's true," says Sue, blushing. "Sorry!"

"Really, Sue, it's nothing."

"C'mon, Angel," says Sue. "Please explain what's going on."

Sandy looks at me, helpless, like we have no choice but to explain now that she opened her trap. Sue leans forward in her chair and tugs at her sleeves.

"I'll talk," says Sandy. "Where to start? Here we go. Angel and I are both sick of our lives. We've figured out a way to make a big change." Sue leans even further towards us, eyes aglow.

"I feel so left out! Please share with me," she says. "And you know I'm not living in a bed of roses. I'm sick of my life, too. Dull, dull, and duller."

"Hey, we're up to our armpits now," I say. "Go ahead, Sandy, tell her." She glances at me, stands up, and takes a deep breath.

"You know what, Sandy?" I say, "I'll take it from here." Before I get a word out, my head spins from the Bourbon and Coke. I make a run to the bathroom and heave into the toilet.

"Are you okay?" Sue asks, right outside the door.

"I'll be okay," I say, not sure at all if I will. I throw cold water on my face, rinse my mouth, and open the door.

"What is going on?" asks Sue.

"Hang on. Give me a minute, and I'll explain." We sit in silence in the living room, staring at each other. A question mark plants across Sue's face.

"Sue, you may not be ready for this, but here it is," says Sandy, flipping her hair back and forth. "We're going to pull off a bank heist like no one has ever seen." The color drains from Sue's face.

"What did you say?" Her eyes are wide and unblinking, her mouth hanging open. Sandy and I don't look at each other, don't say a word, and don't make eye contact with Sue. After a few long minutes, Sue squeaks a few words, "Oh my God. You're not joking, are you?"

"Like I said, we're up to our necks," says Sandy. "Me living hand to mouth for years, and now I'm losing the house. My landlord gave me sixty days to get out," she says, suddenly sober. She takes control of herself. "And Angel is suffering in her marriage. Trapped. Arthur turned out to be bad, bad husband material," she adds. "It couldn't be worse."

"Well, knock me down with a feather!" says Sue. "Look what's been going on in quiet little Pinewood." She slams back into the chair and looks up to the ceiling as if she's worried her dead mother can hear us.

"Are you two insane? Aren't you scared?"

"I'm not scared," I say. "I'm not scared at all. I've got nothing to lose."

"But, but . . . " Sue stutters, trying to make sense of it all.

"Listen to me, Sue," I say. "Not one thing has changed since your mother died. No boyfriend, no nothing. Don't be a panty-ass. And you know what? You're the one who should come up with a timeline." She yanks at her sleeves again.

"Really? Why do you say that?" Her face is pale with confusion.

"We need a timeline. Don't you do lesson plans for your students?"

"Yes, but . . ."

"At least you have some kind of experience." Sandy applauds.

"Sue, we could really use your help," she says. "We weren't planning on telling you, but the more I think about it—we need you. The three of us have done everything together since we were little kids. I sure wish Dede was still with us."

"Sue, I know it's a lot to take in," I say. "It's true. We weren't going to tell you. And now you know. Can you just think about it? Okay? And besides, it wouldn't be the same without you."

Her face softens for the first time since we broke the news.

"We could all be tanning ourselves on a white sand beach," I say, "with palm trees, living happy, easy lives."

"Sue, it took me a while," says Sandy. "But the future in this dead-end town looks like a long black tunnel that never ends." Sue's big blue eyes overflow with tears.

"You're so right," she says. "There is no future here for any of us."

"Listen," I say. "Let's meet at my house next Tuesday night. That's five days from now."

"Whoa," says Sue, putting her hand up to block me out, but I keep going.

"Arthur goes out almost every night. Like I said, think about it, Sue. Let it roll around in your head. Living in friggin'

Pinewood the rest of your life. *Ugh*. Come to my house. You don't have to agree to anything. Just come and be with Sandy and me. Okay?"

"Okay," she says, her voice soft as she turns to Sandy. "You don't have to worry about where to live," she says. "I have plenty of room. Come and stay with me."

Sue doesn't show up for the meeting on Tuesday. Sandy throws her coat on the couch, stands at the fireplace, and warms her hands.

"Sue called me a few times this week," she says. "Then she came over to help me move all my stuff to her house. She even let me bring B.C. And she doesn't even like cats. What a sweetheart."

"You've moved already?" I say. "What a surprise! What's the rush, Sandy?"

She brushes her hands down her sweater as if to remove crumbs and settles in the big chair next to the fireplace. She goes back to warming her hands.

"You know how I am. Somebody doesn't want me, then I don't want them. That rotten landlord of mine doesn't care about our history. I've lived in that house my entire life. If he wants me out, then I want out. Anyway," she adds, "Sue needs some handholding right now. So, it all makes sense for me to be there."

I hand her a couple Lorna Doone cookies on a napkin.

"Do you think she's gonna join us?" I ask.

"Tell the truth," Sandy says, blissfully chewing away, "I think she will. "She wants to be with us, whatever we do."

"I get it," I say. "She doesn't want to be left on her own, but she must truly be ready," I say. "You know very well this is a *big deal*."

"I know. I am so ready myself," says Sandy. "You know I am. I'm sure she'll come around. She hates her life."

We sip on our drinks and reminisce about the good times as kids. Huge Fourth of July parties at the river behind Sandy's house. We played horseshoes on the grass, threw Frisbees to the dogs, and ran three-legged races in old flour sacks. Whoever partnered with Dede in any sport always won. Those were the good old days, for sure.

CHAPTER 39

*T*WO MORE WEEKS GO BY, AND SUE SHOWS UP WITH SANDY. Both stand shivering at my front door.

"Hey, Sue, you're here. That's great. Come on in," I say. "I've got a nice warm fire. Help yourself to donuts. Oh, and a bottle of Gallo."

"Thanks, Angel," says Sue, helping herself to two glazed donuts and a chocolate one with sprinkles. "I've been thinking about everything. And what you guys said is true. I am stuck in my life. All I can see ahead is a dead-end street. If I knit one more scarf or sweater, I'm going to go berserk. I'm here to listen, for now, only to listen. I'm scared to death. But I trust the two of you. Like I just said, I'm only here to listen. Okay?"

"Okay. No matter what, I'm glad you're here." I smile at her. She truly is the sweetest thing. "I know it's a lot to bite off," I say. Sandy does a silent whoop behind Sue's back. But she and I act cool. We don't want to make Sue jittery.

"Listen to this," says Sandy. "Two guys pulled off a big bank robbery in California," she says. "They had an account under a fake business name. They asked to open a safe deposit box and put in some papers. Once the manager walked into the safe deposit room, they drew their guns on him. He gave them everything they asked for. A ton of money. What do you think about that?" As the brains of this operation, I better stay calm. I clear my throat.

"That's a good plan," I say, "but I don't think that will work for us. Someone needs to have an account to get into the safe deposit boxes. You know I can't get an account there 'cause of Arthur, and he knows both of you. It would be funny if, suddenly, one of you opened an account there. We'll come up with another plan. Main thing is, no one gets hurt. Understand? No matter what, Arthur is my husband. I can't stand him anymore but don't want him hurt. He goes to the Pigeon Inn for lunch every day from noon to 1:30. When he's out, the Assistant Manager is in charge. That's when we do it. I don't want Arthur involved in any way. We need guns, but we won't use them. We just want to scare people. Alright? Sandy, you're in charge of getting the guns."

"Okay, I can do that," she says. "I'll drive way past Geiger Springs to get them. By the way, do any of us know how to use a gun?" A dead silence hangs in the room, the three of us eyeballing each other. I better speak up.

"When I was twelve, Pops took me to target practice out there in Silt," I say. "He got a bee in his bonnet one Sunday and thought we should go. And that was the only time. I've never touched a gun since then."

"How about you, Sue? Have you ever used a gun?" I ask.

"No, I never even touched one, even though Mama kept a revolver in the house. She said if anyone ever tried to hurt us, she would blow them away. I don't even know where she kept that thing. I haven't looked for it since she died. It might shoot me in the hand."

"Hmm," says Sandy. "I've never handled one either. Well, that's okay. We don't want to use them anyway." She hasn't even removed her scarf or jacket, her hands shoved deep in her pockets.

Sandy catches my eye and sends me a silent message. We need to get some practice handling a gun.

"Shouldn't we cover our faces?" asks Sandy. I give her a thumbs up.

"I saw Mickey Mouse masks last week at the Dollar Store in Copperville. I'll get three of them this week. That is if you're in, Sue. Oh well, no pressure, Sue, but I'll get three anyway."

"Sandy," I say, focusing her. "I'm thinking we can make it happen two weeks from Friday. We should get to the bank just past noon when Arthur is out of the way. What do you think?"

She's doing her hair flip.

"I don't think so," she says. Lulu promised me a free massage every Friday for a month. She's starting this week. My back has been killing me."

"And Sue, what are you thinking. Are you in? We could really use you."

"You know what, Angel, I'm with you. But I can't do two weeks from Friday. That's when I usually tutor Rodney Dunston. He is doing so poorly in English."

My blood heats up to a slow boil. "C'mon guys, three weeks from Thursday, okay? C'mon, you two. This is serious business! Our lives are about to change."

"Okay," says Sue. "Rodney's exam will be over by then." I unroll the diagram of the bank onto our kitchen table. Sue whistles through her teeth.

"Get a load of that," she says. Very professional!" Sandy turns pink from the praise. A small cherubic smile lights up Sue's face.

"I'm feeling better about this all the time," she says, adjusting the aqua knit scarf around her ample neck. I point at the diagram with a random knitting needle Sandy left at my house.

"See over here. That's the back door to the parking lot. Sandy, you stand guard at first. It makes sense with all your experience. The trained eye of the photographer." They both nod.

"Okay, guys," I say, "I'll drive. We better rent a car. I'll take care of that. We'll have the customers face down on the floor, go to the tellers, and get as much as possible. Like we said already, guns are a must, but just to scare people. We won't use them. Right, guys?" They both nod. "Then you'll both run out the back and jump into the back seat with the money. I have a canvas bag we can use. Anyone else have a canvas bag?" Sue raises her hand like she's a kid in school.

"I have one," she says.

"Yay, Sue!" says Sandy.

We meet to develop our plan when Arthur goes out. I'm guessing some kind of men-will be-women club. I am more fired up than ever to dump him.

CHAPTER 40

We leave Pinewood at 10:45 am. It's a cool, clear October Day, a good sign for *The Big Day*. We give ourselves plenty of time so we can roll in soon after 12 pm. Sweat rolls off my underarms and soaks my shirt. Tums did nothing for my roaring gut. Sandy taps on the window, and Sue cracks her knuckles over and over.

In my loudest barroom voice, I break into "99 Bottles of Beer on the Wall", hoping Sue and Sandy will jump in. Everyone goes silent once we're a few blocks from the bank. Sue gulps in air as I do, and Sandy sneezes three times. As we roll into the parking lot, my hands shake on the steering wheel.

"Alright, you two," I say. "Let's put on our masks." I keep my voice strong like a real leader would. "You ready?"

"We're ready."

"It's now or never," I say. "Remember, we're the Pinewood Babes."

We stroll into the bank as casual as can be. Customers smile and point at the silly masks at first. Soon enough, their smiles fade away when they see our guns. Confusion hangs in the air. Big men shaking in their boots sends a jolt of energy through me.

"Okay, no one move," orders Sandy, our own Annie Oakley. "Raise your hands above your heads!"

"That's right," adds Sue, "hands up!" sounding as croaky as ever.

"Wait! I know that voice," chokes a ruddy-faced woman. "That's Sue from Copperville High. She tutored my Rodney."

"Shut up!" I scream, "Nobody say a word. You hear me?" I swivel, pointing my gun at everyone nearby. Sandy waves her gun, too. One old lady in a pink dress drops a load of poop on the floor, and her husband faints in a dead heap.

"Okay, everyone else, face down on the floor," yells Sandy. "That goes for you, too, Mr. Assistant Bank Manager."

I remember meeting him the day I wore my green dress to visit Arthur, looking so important behind his big desk. Now he's on his knees, ready to hit the floor. He looks around helplessly.

"No, stand up! Hands behind your heads," yells Sue.

A tall, gangly kid with pimples laughs like a donkey.

"Heehaw. Heehaw! What a bunch of amateurs."

"Shut up, you little brat," I say. All our weeks of planning went straight out the window. "Everyone on the floor," I order, "and that's final!"

To show them I mean business, I wave my gun around again. Sandy moves to guard the back door for our escape. She holds the 45 like a pro. Sue plants her little body in front of a teller's window with me right behind her.

"Give her all your cash," I yell. "Right now! And hurry it up!"

"Yeah, that's right," Sue adds, "hand it over." Our sweet little Sue rose to the occasion. I'm proud of her.

The young teller's mouth quivers. She can't be more than nineteen years old. As tears stream down her cheeks, she throws packets of bills into a heavy canvas bag. Sue has another bag over her arm that reads *Love Animals? Support the SPCA.*

"Throw some in here, too," she orders. "Keep going, keep going." Women lying on the floor whimper and sob.

"Shut your traps!" I yell. "If you don't, I'll make sure you never cry again. Got it?" Wow, I didn't know I had it in me. This is crazy fun.

"Okay, tellers, down on the floor," I say. "Now! And don't try to pull anything funny." Sandy and Sue race out the parking lot door, moneybags clutched tight against their chests. With all the employees and customers still on the floor, I back out, sweeping my gun in the air back and forth. We jump as fast as jackrabbits into the rented Mustang. I point my pistol out the window but make a point not to use it. Then *bam, bam, bam,* Sandy shoots a round but aims at nothing.

"Are you stone crazy?" I yell. "What are you shooting at?"

"Nothing! I just want to see what it feels like! You know, just for the hell of it!"

"Are you insane?" shouts Sue. "I'm going to make a run for it."

"Sue, no! We need to stay together," yells Sandy.

"Should I throw the money out the window?" Sue, now hysterical, with her voice an octave higher than usual.

"Hell no!" shouts Sandy.

"Let's go!" I scream.

"Don't forget your seatbelts," orders Sue, always one for safety. I put the pedal to the metal and squeal out of the parking lot.

"Hit it harder," says Sandy.

"Once we get to the airport, we'll be free!" I scream with excitement as I swing the rental car off the street and onto the highway. Lucky day, just a few cars on our side of the road. Everything looks good for our getaway. Sandy places her gun on the floor. She wipes her forehead with a hanky, crashes her head on the headrest, and closes her eyes. All quiet in the car until Sue breaks the silence.

"Ah, ah," like someone has their hands around her neck, strangling her.

"Sue, what is it?" I say. "What's going on?" Screaming sirens tell me what's wrong. A highway patrol car, red light on top spinning round and round, pulls up to our left. Another one pulls up to our right. Sandy, too frozen to move, doesn't try to grab her gun on the floor. Sue shrieks in the back seat as a third patrol car pulls in front of us. We're now surrounded, guns pointed at us from every direction. A booming voice blasts from the loudspeaker on the first CHP car.

"Pull off the highway. Don't try anything funny. We're armed, and we'll shoot."

"Oh shit!" I say, as I take Exit 116 and pull over to the side of the road. The three patrol cars hem me in all the way. How could this go so wrong so fast? Was there a secret buzzer on the floor of the bank? And then I get my answer. Arthur steps out of the first patrol car. He was riding with the cops. I don't know how, but he must have figured it out and tipped them off. An ugly smirk crosses his face as they cuff me. Arthur missed lunch at The Pigeon Inn for the first time ever today.

Now I know it's the getting away that's the big challenge, not the bank robbery. We thought we had pulled it off, but they caught us in no time. In two days, my life changed from rotten to rottener. How did we think we could get away with it?

The fun and games, if you want to call it that, lasted about thirty minutes. For that short time, I wasn't Angela O'Reilly, daughter of a teenage shotgun marriage, but ANGEL, the kickass leader of the Pinewood Babes. Like I said, it didn't last long. I walked into that bank like the Jolly Green Giant, but boy, did I quickly shrink down to a tiny green worm. Nothing says you're under arrest more than the squeeze of cold metal handcuffs clamped onto your wrists.

They shove Sue and me into the back seat of one patrol car and take Sandy off in another. Poor Sue is sobbing, wiping snot on her sleeve. As for me, I'm numb, as if someone dropped me into a tub of ice water. The numbness gives way to a pounding headache, my legs wobble like jelly, and my stomach flips. My Hawaiian Island dreams have taken a nosedive into a nightmare in hell.

CHAPTER 41

Stony-faced guards check us into Geiger Springs County Jail. They fingerprint us, take photos, and strip us down to our underwear. They check for warrants and ask if we belong to any gangs. Only the Pinewood Babes, I want to say. Not a good time to be a smart ass. I shiver. I shake. I can hardly speak.

As they lock us in, that first CLANK of the cell door will stay with me for the rest of my life. The cell looks just the way it does in the movies. Narrow little cot, toilet, sink, tiny metal table, and that's about it. Those gray bars lock me in and the rest of the world out. This could be my new life for a long time. How could I ever think robbing Arthur's bank was a good idea. Dinner comes on a tray—a dry chicken sandwich. I can't even look at it, turn my back and face the wall on my hard-ass concrete bed.

After finishing a Danish and a carton of milk for breakfast a few days later, I face the silver-haired Judge in a wood-paneled courtroom. My legs shake in my orange jumpsuit. The Judge blows his nose with a Kleenex and clears his throat.

"Mrs. Turner," he says loud and slow, like you do to a dumb person, "do you know what an arraignment is?"

"No sir, not exactly," I say, a small mouse. "I heard arraignment on Perry Mason a few times."

A young clerk with thick glasses tries to smother her laugh. The Judge, who sounds like he hasn't slept in a week, frowns at the clerk. He clears his throat again and explains "constitutional rights". He says that everyone is entitled to a lawyer. I don't have any money for a lawyer. None of us do. I don't even know how to find one. Our pockets are empty Why else would we rob a bank?

"I will see to it that you have a court-appointed lawyer," he says. Every word from The Judge sinks me deeper and deeper into darkness.

Ready to plead guilty since they caught us red-handed, it turns out that pleading guilty leaves us without bargaining power. At least we found that out in time from a two-time offender who spent a night in our cell. This new world of courtrooms, judges, and lawyers, not to mention jail, has my head spinning. I know so little about the world, a babe in the woods, that's for sure. I need to learn how to play it smart. Too bad I never did before. They cuff us, and The Judge sends us back to the Geiger Springs slammer to wait for the next step.

If Sandy and Sue blame me for this mess, they don't show it. We also don't say much to each other. Truth is, we've run out of things to say, at least for now. We do need each other. I worry about the day they'll hate me for pulling them into my "plan".

"This has to be all over the newspapers," says Sue, between hiccups. "What will my students and their parents think?" She starts to bawl again. Late at night, I also cry for what I've done. We've landed in jail, and all because of me. I shove my face deep into my pillow, so my friends can't hear me cry.

Two days later, the male guard, who must only know eight words—move it, in there, shut up, and you'll see—

opens our cell. His hooded eyes flit around the room like a lizard searching for a bug.

"Move it," he says, rounding us up like cattle. "Someone is here to see you."

We look at each other, having no idea who could have come. Could it be Pops?

He walks the three of us to a concrete room the same size as our cell. There's a small high window. First, he bolts our handcuffs to the floor, like me and my Pinewood girls are dangerous criminals. He opens the door for our visitor, a chunky middle-aged lady.

"Good morning," she says, in a serious-I-mean-business voice, "My name is Melody Hanover. I have been appointed by the court to represent you." She looks to be in her mid-forties, with long brown hair way past her shoulders, and wears a blue tie-dye dress, not a suit like they do on TV. Those suits make them look smart and professional. Why isn't she wearing a suit? Does she know what she's doing? The beefy guard, who looks like he eats nothing but burgers and fries, slams the metal door and locks her in. She has a buzzer near her right hand.

"First and foremost," she says, "I want to put you at ease. I know you must be scared." Sue, as white as a sheet, nods. Sandy starts to say something and snaps her mouth shut. Ms. Hanover removes a large yellow writing pad and a black pen from her briefcase, clicks it shut, and sets it on the metal table. "You know, a defense attorney does not usually represent co-defendants. You are each entitled to have your own lawyer. I want to make that clear." I wait to see what Sandy and Sue will say.

"I want us to stay together," says Sue. "Please, can we all be with you?" The lawyer checks in with Sandy and me, then double and triple-checks.

"I do, yes, for sure," says Sandy.

"Me, too," I say. "I want you to represent all of us," I say, relieved and surprised that maybe Sue and Sandy don't hate me. They could. And maybe they will one of these days.

"Okay, that's settled." When Ms. Hanover smiles, I am surprised to see that her teeth are crooked. Lawyers always look so good on TV with their straight teeth. Even so, her smile helps me unwind the tiniest bit.

"Innocent or not," she says, tapping her ballpoint pen on the pad, "everyone in this country has the right to legal representation. That's the beauty of living in the United States. Isn't that good news?" she asks. I don't think she expects an answer. We sit as quiet as can be with our hands in our laps. She goes on, "*And* we have something called attorney-client privilege. Have you ever heard of it?"

We all shake our heads no.

"Okay," she says, "I'm glad to clarify. Attorney-client privilege means whatever you tell me is strictly between us. No one is entitled to what you tell me, absolutely no one." She scans our faces. "Do you understand?"

I raise my hand. "I think it means you won't tell anyone else what we tell you."

"That's right," she says. "Everything you tell me is confidential. You are protected by law." Her smile warms up the cold cell, but her right eye twitches slightly. "And most important of all, you must be honest with me," she continues. "It is essential that I trust you and that you trust me. I need you to tell me the truth." She waits, hands on her briefcase, for me to say something.

"It's the only way," says Ms. Hanover, scanning the cold small room, "that I can do a good job for you."

"Yes, I will tell you the truth," I say.

Sandy taps her foot from nerves. It takes everything in my power to keep from telling her to STOP IT!

"I promise," she says.

"Me, too," says Sue in a teeny tiny voice.

"Don't worry. You can trust me." Sandy stops tapping her foot, the strain showing on her face.

Melody Hanover sounds like the name of a music teacher, a singer, or someone who always wears yellow and smiles. This lady became a lawyer to help people in big trouble, like me and my Pinewood tribe. She smiles when she wants to make sure we understand all the legal talk. I bet her parents were good people. They must be proud of her being a lawyer and all. She wears a simple gold band on her wedding finger. They took mine away when they booked me, but I don't care. I should have tossed it in the Crystal River a long time ago.

"I want to make sure you understand everything," says our lawyer. "It's okay if you don't. Just let me know." She looks at us like she's reading our faces. "I can always explain in another way." I never heard someone put their words together the way she does. It makes me think of Ace and how he told me to stay in school. I wish I could sound better when I talk instead of sounding like a hick.

"It's very important," continues Ms. Hanover, "that we understand each other. Just remember, I am here to help you." She sneaks a look at her wristwatch.

"Are we going to prison for a long time?" Sandy blurts out.

"There is no way for me to give you a clear answer right now. We have a lot to discover. In fact, what comes next is called the discovery phase. We gather information, learn all about you, and talk to people in your life that can help your case. Like I said, I will do the very best for you I possibly can." Sandy wrings her hands and squeezes her eyes shut.

"I'll need to get contact names from each of you," says Ms. Hanover. I tell her where to find Faye Vespers.

Even though we robbed a bank, she listens to us with respect. We robbed a bank! I still can't believe it. As the clock ticks away, and I hear what Ms. Hanover has to say, the more I like her and trust her. Over a few days, she asks questions, lots of questions.

"How were your grades in high school? Have you ever been arrested before? How many jobs have you held?" And she takes tons of notes on that yellow pad.

She will interview Mama and Pops if she can track him down. Ever since he became Mr. Rhonda Number Five, no one knows where they moved. Faye Vespers will be the most important testimony. She believed in me, got me a job at the Go Get 'Em Café, found me a place to live, and knew all about my loco parents. Ms. Hanover wants to know about Arthur.

"What was it like when you first met him? And what went wrong?" I explain how he put the clamps on me within six months of getting married, made me quit the Double G, and took away my small life and made it even smaller. I even tell her that I saw Arthur prancing around in a negligee and silver high heels. Her eyes go wide on that one. She always says the same thing when she leaves. "See you soon and keep the faith."

Confined to a cell, got to say, one day runs into another. The boredom is impossible to explain. And I thought my life was small before. Hours drag by until you hope you can sleep for as long as possible. Sue cries like clockwork every morning. I learned early on to keep my tears to myself. Sue lost her smother-mother a long time ago. I have run out of any mom-ness for Sue, run out of steam to give her reassuring hugs. I could use some hugs myself. I'm a trainwreck but do my best to keep it under wraps.

"C'mon now, Sue, you need to toughen up," I say. She nods, but tears continue to roll.

When Ace told me he went to prison, I remember the shock of knowing he had been locked up. Now it's me g-o-i-n-g to *federal* p-r-i-s-o-n. Sandy and I try to solider through and do our best to joke around. I don't have to tell you how that goes stale in no time.

CHAPTER 42

*I*N OUR BAGGY ORANGE JUMPSUITS, THE THREE OF US huddle with Melody Hanover while The Judge settles into his throne as the courtroom fills to capacity. I hope our lawyer will do a good job, as good as anybody could do. We were caught red-handed. At least none of us has been in real trouble before.

I hope Ms. Hanover has what it takes to get us a shorter sentence. She pushes her ample body up from the table where we all sit, unsticks her blue tie-dye dress off her big butt, and sits down again. The young prosecuting lawyer, with thick glasses and a slick dark-blue suit, scribbles notes.

The worst busybodies in Pinewood, Leila the Righteous and her Bobbsey Twin, Marvel, sit on Arthur's side of the courtroom. They wouldn't miss this for the world. Leila wants to show off to the Pinewood old-timers that she was there in court and saw everything.

"I know that old bag," I whisper to our lawyer. Leila the Righteous wags her finger at us, drilling an evil eye deep into my forehead. She'll be chewing on this chunky piece of gossip for years. If she could stay at the front lines of this trial, she would hold on to her title of Pinewood Queen Bee of Gossip for years to come. Arthur looks straight ahead, barely turning his neck, sporting a fresh haircut and what looks to be a brand-new suit.

When we walked into the courtroom today, wrists cuffed together, I spied Spencer and other high school friends from Pinewood. They came to see the circus.

I'm guessing people have strong opinions, one way or the other, about me robbing my own husband's bank. Spencer's pregnant new young wife sits glued tight up against him. And good old Faye Vespers sits on the aisle. First time ever I saw her in a dress, her gray hair pinned up nice and neat. I squirm in my seat until Ms. Hanover places a warm hand on my shoulder to relax. And how am I supposed to do that?

I catch Pops out of the corner of my eye. It has been ages since I've seen him. He made it to my wedding, but it's been zip since. And ever since he married Rhonda, I can't remember one time I saw him without that red-headed menace. Today he sits alone. He looks smaller and much older, his face shiny with tears. What could be worse than seeing your own kid headed to prison? He looks up at the ceiling like someone in church asking God for a favor. Then he buries his face in his hands. I ache inside, never so alone as today. I want to connect with Sandy and Sue to keep our sisterhood strong.

At the arraignment, Ms. Hanover advised us to plead not guilty. We didn't understand since we almost got caught with our hands in the cookie jar. She explained that a not guilty plea would buy us time. She could study our cases, learn more about us, and have the leeway to track down important witnesses.

"Once I have all the information that can help you," she said, "I'll approach The Judge with a plea deal. And that's when you can change your plea to guilty."

Now our fate lies in the hands of The Judge. He holds the strings. I hope she could convince him that we three silly girls did not know how to use a gun. We never intended to shoot. In fact, we would never hurt a fly and deserve a break. Maybe he'll see the light. We made a stupid mistake. We're good people. Still, as a church mouse, I mind my manners, my clammy hands quiet in my lap. I'll respect the trial, the courtroom, follow all the rules, and will do anything to help my case.

My hands shake like a ninety-year-old woman, dreading what comes next. How much punishment do I deserve? How many years will I spend behind bars? I lost my appetite weeks ago. The pillow on my bed was like an enemy who fought me when I needed sleep. Last night I stared at the ceiling all night, worried sick for the future. The sun rose as slow as can be. I was dressed and ready at 7 a.m. to hear our fate.

I hope our craggy-faced Judge got a good night's sleep and had some fun with his wife. He studies the paperwork in front of him. I want to jump up from my seat and scream. Instead, I sit tight and wring my hands. Sandy, Sue, and I look at each other without looking at each other. Our lawyer, Melody, told us to call her by her first name. She wears a long fringe vest over A-line pants. I heard she volunteers her time helping foster children and adopted two little black kids from foster care. I know she has worked hard for us. Has done the best she could do. The Judge sits up straight, my life in his hands, to announce my punishment, my prison sentence, for robbing Arthur's bank.

"Seven years," he says, pounding the desk with his gavel to ensure we get the message. Sue falls forward and faints on the table. A uniformed clerk rushes over with smelling salts. Sandy and I hug.

Seven years is a lifetime.

Melody reaches out to shake my hand. Instead, she pulls me in for a hug. "Faye Vespers was a big help," she says. "I hope you understand; you could have easily gotten ten years." Her face is filled with kindness. She shakes my hand, her other hand clasping my wrist.

"Thank you, Melody," I say. "I know how hard you worked hard for us. It could have been worse, much worse." But, damn, seven friggin' years. I hope I make it out alive.

"Take good care of yourself, Angel," says Melody. "You have tremendous inner strength. Remember to put that strength to good use." She shakes both Sandy's and Sue's hands. "Wishing you the best, girls. Stick together in prison. Your friendship will help you through."

She turns on her heel and leaves. Once Pops takes in the news, he gives me what looks like the old familiar Zoltan salute. Without a second glance, he shuffles out of the courtroom and out of my life.

In a few days, they're shipping us off to the Federal Pen in Littleton, Colorado.

CHAPTER 43

I GASP FOR BREATH, JAMMED UP TIGHT WITH SANDY AND Sue in something like an unmarked bakery truck with rank air, no windows, and hard benches.

"Too bad they don't have a cake lying around with a knife baked in it," says Sandy. We try to laugh it off. Downright fear has taken over, knowing we're on our way to Smollett Women's Correction Facility, otherwise known as the Federal Pen. They've bound my legs so tight they're bleeding. We have no food, nothing to drink, nowhere to pee. After the three-hour trip, we struggle to climb out of the truck, not so easy, with shackled legs and cuffed wrists. The guards don't help. All they do is scream at us.

"Move it, you morons," says one. Her fat pink face and squinty eyes make her look like an old hog. She notices Sue doing her best to hold back the tears.

"Well, well, poor little dear," she says, followed by a nasty laugh. "You're gonna grow up fast." Another woman guard (at least I think it's a woman) with bushy brown hair and thick eyebrows pitches in.

"Either grow up fast or end up in deep shit." She slaps the first guard on the arm. They laugh together like they just saw *Mork and Mindy* on TV.

These two mean old hags remind me of bullies from high school. So, this is what bullies do when they grow up. They go to work in a prison. They can push us around, treat us like dirt, and get paid for it. I know we have no choice. We have no choice but take whatever these guards dish out. And keep our mouths shut. Wouldn't be surprised if I saw Lorena McDougal working here. Pretty name and the meanest girl in school. Loved to spin her cat in circles by the tail. After all these hours, we still need to hold it in. I see a stream of yellow surging down Sue's pant leg onto her foot. She keeps her head down, staring at her cuffed hands. They move us to the next cold bare room.

"Strip down! That's right," says Bushy Eyebrows, "get those clothes off!" The guards laugh and elbow each other some more as we stand in front of them naked and shivering. We bend over for the search. There are no words for it. I'll never forget the experience for the rest of my life. I wouldn't even wish it on Lorena McDougal. Well, maybe I would.

Once convinced there's no contraband up our butt or wazoo, they issue us two sets of slime-green pants and shirts, a few pairs of socks, underwear, a plastic cup, toothpaste, a toothbrush, and foul-smelling soap. I've never been a fancy girl, but I cannot believe we only get these few items. That's the truth of my new life. I will flush my dreams of blue skies, white sand beaches, and swimming in the ocean down the toilet.

"What did you expect, Dumb Ass?" says Hog Face, "a cosmetic kit from Revlon? Now move it!"

And don't forget the *Rules and Regulations* book, I remind myself, so torn and dirty it must be a hundred years old. They shuffle us off to take our pictures. We're assigned an ID number and tag. We'll be in big trouble if we don't wear it all the time except when locked down in our cells. Even then, why take it off? So scared, me and my best friends can't make eye contact. The guards watch every move as we drag our feet down the hall. Yells, screams, and curses bounce off the walls. The inmates hang on the prison bars looking us up and down. Some of them lick their lips over the new meat. That's what we are to them. Sue shoots me the saddest look I've ever seen as they lock her up. The three of us won't see anything but the inside of these walls for a long time. I start shivering again as a guard that stinks to high heaven gives me the ice-cold eye. She smells so bad. No way she could know the meaning of a shower.

"Get used to it, girlie!" she says. "This ain't no high school picnic!" The door clangs shut.

I'm in lockup, a jailbird, a prisoner, a criminal. My life reduced to hard edges in a six-by-eight-foot cell. I've made a mess of my nothing life. My cellie lounges on her metal bed, slumped over a comic book. Other than the beds, we have nothing more than a toilet and a sink.

Maybe other prisoners hang pictures on the walls. This one has nothing but four bare walls staring me down. Across from me, a head of frizzy bleached hair with two-inch dark roots doesn't look up, absorbed by a magazine in her lap. Once she lifts her eyes off the page, she runs her hard dark eyes over me. She looks older than me with that mop on her head, but I bet she's young. Tough life is written all over her face. I can see the cover of her *Roller Derby* comic book.

"Here comes The Fish," she says. It's not a greeting but a challenge.

"Is that what I am, a fish?"

"You're a newbie, right?" she says. "It's so obvious." She slaps her folded comic in the palm of her hand. She wears gray pants and a gray sweatshirt with the number 69 in black.

"At least I don't look like a hard ass," I say.

I worry for a minute that she might take me wrong.

"Listen, Fish. Don't trust nobody," she says. I breathe a sigh of relief she's not going to punch me out. Maybe she's trying to help me. "Don't get write-ups and no fights," she says. "They'll put you in the hole."

"Got it," I say. "Thanks." She sits up on her bunk and sets the comic aside.

"What you in for?" she asks.

"Robbing a bank," I say, taking a seat on the hard bed. How am I supposed to sleep on this thing?

"Oh yeah? Robbing a bank? Big-time stuff, huh? I got busted for cashing my dead mama's welfare checks. She died when I was sixteen. Didn't have nobody else."

"That sounds rough," I say.

"I never got caught shoplifting for food. Oh yeah, they did catch me once, but they felt bad for me and let me go. I'm here this time for burglary. I'm Della. What's your name?"

"I'm Angel. You know what? My head's killing me." I climb onto the bunk and lay my head on the rock-hard pillow. First time I could stretch out since we left Geiger Springs this morning. It seems like it's been days. And this cell is where I'll be stuck for years.

"What do I have to do to get some aspirin around here?" I ask.

"You're kidding, right?" says Della.

"No. Why would I be kidding?"

She laughs, a hole where a front tooth should be.

"They don't give a shit about us," she says. "You'll see soon enough."

Lights go out at 10 p.m. My head still pounds from the headache as I wrestle with the pillow. I pull the blanket over me. Maybe I can tune out this nightmare and get some sleep. I toss and turn, this way and that, adjusting the rock that's supposed to be a pillow. Holy moly, are those bugs crawling all over me? I jump out of bed. No, it's the scratchy blanket.

After hours of tossing, I fall asleep.

CHAPTER 44

A FEW MONTHS LATER, I HEAR FROM GOOD OLD FAYE Vespers, the only one who cares enough to send me a letter. I re-read it all the time. Her scraggly handwriting is as sloppy as her clothes.

Dear Angel,

I'll never understand why you made such a bad choice. I know your folks didn't do right by you. They were so young when you were born. I remember the first time they brought you into the Go Get 'Em. They were only kids themselves. And you were the cutest little thing, all dressed up in pink. From that moment on, I fell in love with you. I always hoped I could help make your life better.

Maybe I should have said something when you worked for me and took money from the cash register. I didn't bother since it wasn't much. Truth is, I felt bad for you. Your Pops ran out on you and married that Rhonda. Year after year, your Mama slugged back the booze. Maybe I could have stopped you going down this path. It breaks my heart into little pieces knowing you are behind bars. I pray for you every single night.

Your friend always, Faye

Faye always had my back, more than any other grown-up in Pinewood. I can't believe she always knew I stole money from her cash register. How could I do that to her? She did more for me than my parents ever did. She found me a place to live, loaned me money, and gave me Christmas presents. She knew what I did, and she never said a word. She says she feels bad for *me*! Once I'm out of prison, I'll pay her back double, triple, quadruple the amount I took. She believed in me, and I let her down big time.

I only get one hour a day to see the sky in the exercise yard, where I run the track, clear my thoughts, and unlock my frazzled brain. With so many hours in my cell, I think about Ace again. Last night I dreamt I was straddling him, hanging on to his long mane of hair, screaming out for Jesus.

"Will you shut up?" shouted Della. "You dreamin' about that Ace guy again?"

Ring. Ring. Ring. I shoot straight up in bed when the bell goes off at 5:30 a.m. We shuffle off to the chow room, where they ladle watery cream of wheat into a bowl with a limp piece of toast and coffee that tastes like pee. They assigned me to laundry detail. I always hated washing my own clothes, and wouldn't you know it, that's my job in prison. Could it get any worse? Like a robot, I load, unload, and fold every day until the bell goes off at 11 a.m. for lunch. No one on laundry detail said one word to me when I started. They put me through the new-kid-on-the-block test. It's a little better now, but not much.

As I finish folding a stack of towels, the C.O. takes the mid-morning count. A story makes the rounds that a crafty con escaped in a laundry cart. They never want that to happen again, so they do the count every single morning. I can understand that rule. Others are downright stupid. The boredom could drive anyone stone loco, knowing it will be the same friggin' routine tomorrow, the next day after that, week after week, year after year.

One night, Della tells me a lady she never met, writes to her. "We're pen pals," she says. "She sends me letters and *Roller Derby* comics."

"Oh yeah, *Roller Derby* comics. I always wondered about that. You were reading one the first day they locked me up in here." First time since I've been in this cell with her, Della's face lights up, and her tough girl attitude drops away.

"This lady pen pal," says Della, "knows my big dream. She's gonna help me find out how I can be a Roller Derby Queen. I want to be a jammer like Lucy Lightning. She has this cool black lightning bolt on her sleeve." Della lifts a magazine off a neat stack, opens to page 25, and shows me a photo of Lucy Lightning rounding a curve on the track.

"I maybe saw *Roller Derby* three times in my life," I say. "It sure does look fierce. You must be a good skater."

"I'm real good," says Della. "Yep, that's what I want to do when I get outta here."

"How do you know all this stuff?"

"My mama was in the *Roller Derby*. She hit the ground one night, and two people landed on her hard. It messed her up so bad she was never the same after that. Had to work in the assembly line at a Buster Brown shoe factory. She didn't make much, so we had to go on welfare." Her shoulders slump down, and she turns to face the wall. "Anyways, you know the rest."

"So how does it work with this pen pal lady?" I ask. "Can you say anything you want when you write to her?"

"No way," says Della. "The guards read every word. You've gotta pretend that cops are reading it first. Anyways, you know how C.O.s think they're the police. Power crazy fuckers."

CHAPTER 45

ONLY FIVE MONTHS SERVED. SEEMS LIKE FIVE YEARS. Today, like always, we march in single file to the chow hall. I grab a tray and stand in line, daydreaming of Faye Vesper's fried chicken. I can smell it and taste it. Caught up in my chicken dreams, I bang my lunch tray into Big Martha.

They don't call her that for nothing. She could play pro football with her linebacker body, huge neck, and gigantic biceps. They say she's a lifer for drugging and strangling her skinny little husband in his sleep. When she turns around, the threat in her eyes makes my blood run cold.

"Do that again, and I will eat you for lunch. Get it?" She must be six feet tall and weigh 300 hundred pounds.

"Got it." I back away. "I'm sorry." And it's true. I have never been sorrier in my life. She is one scary beast. I try to make myself invisible by shrinking down, hoping that will be the end of it. I load overcooked carrots and a bowl of brown slop onto my tray. Big Martha turns to me and jabs at the air with a fork.

"You and your cute little friends better stay out of my way," she says. "Ya hear? That's twice now! Two times too many." Everyone slides their trays along, wondering what crap they will force on us to eat today. No choices for food, where to go, or what to do. No decisions to make except to stay out of trouble.

"O-o-o-o-kay, sorry, I get it," I say, keeping my voice soft. My first run-in with Big Martha happened in the movie room. No one warned me that these cons have their own special seats. Big Martha saw me in hers, lifted me by my armpits, and came close to slamming me on the floor. Ever since then, I stand back from her. I've kept my distance all this time, and now this happens. Sue is terrified of Big Martha. She glances at me, her mouth trembling, as we settle in at our usual table with the other white girls. At the end of the table sits the weird albino chick who stabbed her identical twin fifty times.

She doesn't miss a chance to flirt with Sue. This is not the kind of romance Sue had in mind.

"Hey, cutie." Sue pretends not to hear and looks the other way. With nothing but garbage to eat in this place, Sue has dropped a ton of weight. Her round face and soft blubbery arms have gone by the wayside. Good thing her mama lies ten feet beneath the ground. She would go bonkers knowing her baby girl ended up in the slammer. Sue takes a bite of the carrots, a look of disgust, and lays her fork down on the table.

"How's it going in the laundry room?" she asks.

"Every hour feels like three," I say. "You know what I mean? It could drive anyone to drink. At least you got a nice job in the library." She takes a weak stab at the carrots.

"You know, it's not too bad working there," she says. "You might be surprised, but lots of inmates read the Bible."

"No kidding," I say.

She makes another stab at the stew, her face miserable, chewing it slow, like a cow chewing cud. She gives up and lays into the potatoes.

"God, this food is horrible," says Sue. "How can you eat it?" She downs an eight ounce glass of water to get rid of the taste.

"Sue, we all know your mama was a better cook than mine," I say. "This tastes about the same as my mama's cooking." Sue makes a face and pops a stick of Wrigley's gum in her mouth, a rare treat she bought at the prison store. Her aunt in Fruitvale sends her money.

"My Mama's specialty," I say, "was opening cans." Sue laughs and gives me a soft smack on the arm.

"Angel, I was just thinking. You might like a book called, *A Woman Con Tells It Like It Is*. Our time in the chow room is almost up."

"Maybe I would. Ha! I could write a book called *Robbing Your Own Husband's Bank*."

Sue wags her finger at me and laughs. Sue could hate me and never speak to me for the rest of my life. She may be a wuss, but she's the sweetest person I know.

She almost laughs, but not quite. I scan the room, looking for Sandy.

"How come Sandy's not here?" I ask. Big Martha settles down catty-corner from us with her usual crew of ex-military toughies, with crewcuts, swagger, and bodies of steel.

"Sandy came down with the flu," says Sue. "I wish we could bring her some medicine."

"Oh, right. You know we're not allowed. At least it's not worse than the flu. Let's face it, she's not missing a great meal." I force down the last few bites of food.

"Come on," says Sue. "Let's go and get you *Lovers and Gamblers*."

Back in my cell, I read a few chapters. I set it down on the bed and close my eyes. Visions of Pinewood friends whirl around in my head. Faye Vespers wrote to me again. She said Dede's husband, Richard, still runs the B & B. The guy who never held down a job turns out to be a marketing genius. The place has a huge reputation in China. I hear it's a big country, so he always has a full house. He even speaks a little Mandarin now. Arthur, my dear husband, moved away, the chicken-livered creep. Having your wife rob the bank you manage doesn't do much for your reputation. He upped and left town in the middle of the night and took my precious old dog, Ducky, with him. I miss her sweet little body snuggled up close at night.

And I miss my Pops. I can't believe he only called once since I've been locked up. It's like he gave up on me and wiped me clean out of his mind. Sometimes I daydream about the times he took me fishing, even though I hated taking the fish off the line. And now, I'd give anything to unhook a trout off Pops's fishing line. I know he turned his back on Mama and me a long time ago, but I still miss him, but not so much his crazy bad temper. Truth is, I never expected much from Mama. Sometimes I wonder if she liked me at all. She didn't even show up for me in court. I don't think of her too often, but I twist up inside when I realize Pops has bailed on me. Funny thing, he had strong ideas about Arthur early on.

"Arthur thinks he's too high falutin' for us," he said, waving his finger at me. "Even his name sounds like he's got a stick up his ass." I wish Pops had said it stronger at the time. I wouldn't have listened, but I still wish he would have told me.

I hope you can handle it in prison, he wrote. It was right after I was sentenced. In that short letter, he only mentioned one other thing. *Take good care of yourself, Angel. Keep your nose clean. Stay out of trouble.*

Faye wrote me that Mama doesn't leave the house much, with Four Roses and Johnny Walker her best buddies these days. Not one person from Pinewood has come to visit.

Sandy, Sue, and I spent most of our free time together as kids. We would see each other a couple times a month when we got older. Now with the three of us in prison, we get together daily. Don't think I'm saying it's good in here, but we all plow through books like nobody's business. I never read a thing before. Maybe just a magazine, here and there. Now I love to read. People used to tell me I was smart. How smart could I be if I ended up in this hellhole? Time to get a lot smarter.

You could go stone loco the way the hours drag by. Breakfast, work in the morning, lunch, work until 3 p.m. It's boring as hell for the rest of the day. Some people play Checkers, and others play Scrabble. I'm guessing they're all good spellers. I can't imagine anything worse than people watching me try to spell. It's my idea of a living hell, even worse than knitting. When I get blank paper, I sit in a corner and draw. That can take my mind off things. Every once in a while, I knock off a picture of Ducky by heart, but it makes me miss her.

Sometimes a few of the old-timers smuggle in loose tobacco. The best they can do is roll it in toilet paper and spark a power outlet to light up. I don't touch it since it's contraband. Anything that keeps me here for one day longer than seven years will not happen. I keep learning how inmates figure out all kinds of things to make life a teeny bit better. I learned one important lesson from a tough black woman named Sharnice. She landed here for smuggling heroin into the country.

"Girl," she said, "don't forget to shower at rapid-fire speed. Some of these sex-hungry maniacs have roving hands. Soaped up, they can slide most anywhere." You can bet I'm out of the shower in no time flat.

With no men around, except a few C.O.s, it can mess with your mind.

"I made it with my celly a few times," Sandy whispers as we eat baked hamburgers and baked fries. "I just kept my eyes shut and pretended it was a man."

"What else are we supposed to do," I say. "Part-time lesbos, right?"

"Yep. *Gay for the Stay*, that's what they call it," says Sandy. "I don't want to make a habit of it. It's probably a good thing they switched my celly out yesterday." I roll my eyes.

"What a friggin' education," I say and pop a fry in my mouth. Sandy chuckles.

"You'll never guess what I just found out," she says. I look at her, waiting for more. "Why the chow hall," she goes on, "cuts up hot dogs in little pieces. They don't give us the whole hotdog in a bun. Have you noticed?"

"Here we go," I say, wanting to be the good friend. "Why do they cut them in stupid little pieces?"

"Get this," Sandy laughs into her hands, "some inmates have been caught hiding a hot dog in a glove under their mattress. Guess who won't feel so lonesome anymore when lights go out?"

"C'mon!" I say. "They don't even want us to have a hot dog boyfriend." I wipe my eyes, pretending like I'm crying. "Sad that I can't date my boyfriend, Frank Furter." Sandy points her finger up, her blue eyes crinkling at the corners.

"Mademoiselle," she says, "le hot dog takes on a HOLE new meaning." I crack up.

"That's a good one," I say. "Reminds me of a true story. This old gal worked at the Double G. She would talk about her vibrator, especially after the weekend. She called him Victor—Victor the Vibrator. I would hear about Victor every Monday, like a weekend update."

One day Sally said she was invited to a fiftieth birthday party. Then she said, "But I don't have anyone to bring."

So, I told her, "Then, why don't you bring Victor?" Sandy doubles up in laughter. I join in. "I forgot he wasn't a real person!" It sure does feel good to laugh in this rotten place.

"Hmm. What would be a good hot dog name?" asks Sandy.

"For sure, not Harry," I say. "Harry Hot Dog?"

She grins.

"Okay, let's think of a sexy hot dog name." My belly hurts from laughing like I've done a bunch of push-ups.

"What's so friggin' funny?" yells Big Martha. "Shut your fat traps."

Sandy and I scurry away whenever B.M. gets mad. Free time is up anyway.

CHAPTER 46

BACK ON MY BUNK, I RE-READ FAYE'S LETTERS FOR THE zillionth time. The first one rips as I tuck it into my shirt pocket. I lay back and close my eyes, fly over the sparkling Crystal River on a summer day, and land on a puffy white cloud where I can look over the entire Roaring Fork Valley.

Edith, one of the nicer C.O.s, taps me on the shoulder, shaking me out of my daydream. Her mousy-brown hair in tight little curls you get from those old-fashioned pink curlers. I'm no fashion queen, but that hairdo looks like the ones in old Bette Davis and Joan Crawford movies.

"You have a visitor," says Edith. She has a lisp, so it comes out as vith-itor.

"After two years?" I say. "Who is it?"

"Just come with me."

"Can I wash my face first? You know, clean up a little bit?"

"No, you can't," says Edith. "Leth go." She pushes me ahead of her to the visitor's room. It looks just the way you see it in the movies. The prisoners sit behind a wall of shatterproof glass with little slits in the bottom and a hole to talk through. Guards stand nearby, watching our every move.

Edith points to a chair. When I look through the window, he looks as good as ever.

"Hey baby," he says.

"Ace, what in God's name are you doing here?" A sadness I've never seen before pulls at his eyes.

"I went looking for you," he says. "I couldn't get you out of my mind. I figured someone in Pinewood would know where to find you." He fidgets with his hands and cracks his knuckles. I never saw him nervous before. "I remembered you worked at the Go Get 'Em Café." His hair is still long, he has a slight beard, wears a blue plaid flannel shirt but no black leather jacket. "Your old boss, Faye Vespers, told me where to find you. She cried when she said you were locked up." He looks around at the puke-colored walls.

"How you managing in here?"

I swallow hard. "It's the worst. I stick with Sandy and Sue. That's about it." I want to leap through the barrier and wrap myself around him. "So, I guess you got married, right?"

"The biggest mistake of my life." He jams his hands in his pockets and looks over my head.

"I don't know what I was thinking," he says. "I didn't realize it at first, but I didn't love her. She sprang me out of jail, so I was grateful. Besides, I'm not cut out for that straight-arrow life." His sadness reaches through the glass partition and grabs me.

"What do you mean?" I ask. My words come out calm, as if it's the most natural thing in the world for Ace to visit me here, in prison, after all this time. No matter what, I have mastered the calm face. He reaches his hands out to the partition. I warm up, knowing he wants to lace his fingers in mine. "Can you explain what you mean by straight-arrow life?" I ask. He goes silent for a while. I don't think he wants to talk about this. But he's here, and I need to understand.

"She wanted me to live the same life my parents lived," he says, "fundraisers, everyone dressed up, showing off what they have."

"But you did get married," I say, "didn't you?" He pulls his hands back and folds them up against his chest.

"Here's the thing," he says. "The day we walked down the aisle, I was sweating like a pig." He shifts around in his chair like it's too hot. "I don't know why I went through with it."

"Are you still with her?" I ask. I need to know why he's here. Why does he reach down into the deepest part of me?

"No, I'm not married anymore," he says. "She filed for divorce after eight months. The whole thing was a giant mistake. I felt like a shit."

"Well, you *were* a shit once again," I say, picturing the last time we met up at the motel, how he broke the news, how I hitchhiked back to Copperville. His deep-set eyes laser on me.

"Angel, I never stopped thinking about you." He drinks me in.

"But you've burned me twice," I say. He doesn't say the word, yet apology is written all over his face.

"My weird friggin' husband took off and divorced me," I say, swallowing hard. "That's the good news. But he took my dog, Ducky, with him. She's been with me since I was fourteen."

It throws me for a loop when his eyes fill up with tears.

"It kills me to see you locked up in this place," he says. He wipes at his eyes and nose. "You're my crazy, wild Angel." He touches his fingers to the glass, the skull ring still on his pinky after all these years. "I'll wait for you, baby."

"You know what, Ace? You're a lunatic." He grins for the first time.

"I'm a lunatic?" he says. "What about you?" I can't help myself and flash him a huge smile.

"So here we are," I say, "two lunatics."

"Yep, here we are," he says. I still can't believe he's sitting right here in front of me.

"You know, I feel so bad, hurting you the way I did," his face soft and sorrowful. "Once I heard what happened to you, I had to wonder . . . everything that's happened. You in prison, for Christ's sake. Is it all my fault? You were young. Did I take you down the wrong path? But, seriously, baby, who robs their husband's bank?"

"Well, um, I did."

"My crazy, crazy girl." He smiles at me, his fingers still on the glass. I match up my fingers to his like we're playing itsy bitsy spider.

"I want to believe you, Ace. I do. But it's not so easy. You let me down hard. How can I trust anything you say?" Damn, he looks good.

"You'll have to wait and see that I mean every word. I feel different, I act different, I'm who I was always meant to be." He even sounds different.

"I want you with me," he says. "We're supposed to be together. I know it. You're not saying a word, but you know it, too." I almost gasp for breath. To hear this after loving him all these years. "And I promise you one thing," he says, "you can finally make your breakout from Pinewood. You never have to live there again."

I hope he means what he says. He drove three hours to come see me locked up in prison. I want to believe him.

"You look good, baby," he says, taking me in. "You've been through a lot, but no one would ever know it by the looks of you."

He drops his hand off the window and stares down at the scratched surface in front of him. I touch my hair, having no idea how it looks. If Ace likes it, that's good enough for me. When a loud bell goes off in the visitor's room, Edith walks over.

"Time ith up." She tugs on my shoulder. Ace presses his fingers to his lips and throws me a kiss. I throw one back. All the others have started the march back to lock-up. I can't believe Ace came for me after all this time. I'll have to wait and see what happens from here. So shaken from his visit, I struggle to stand up from the chair. Edith stands behind me, breathing in little snorts.

"Come on, gorgeouth," she says, "leth move it!" Somehow with that lisp, she never sounds as harsh as the other C.O.s. I try to steady myself on legs as rubbery as Mama's jello.

Edith drums her fingers as she waits for me. Once I have solid footing, she holds my elbow with a vice-like grip. I glance back over my shoulder. Ace has already high-tailed it.

Next day, when the free time bell goes off, Sandy rubs cream from a tiny tube onto her chapped hands. Her dishwashing job, even wearing rubber gloves, takes a toll. She buys the cream at the commissary on her own dime. Prisoners pay out of our own pockets for all kinds of basic stuff: toothpaste, soap, shampoo, and Kotex. It's not the real Kotex, but a big bulky thing that makes me walk like a baby with a diaper full of poop. They have some makeup and snack food at the canteen. It all costs a fortune. Someone said it's like the prices at an airport. What a racket. Sandy takes a bag of Fritos from me and finishes it off. After she crumples the pack in her hands and tosses it in the trash, she studies my face.

"What's going on, Angel? I can always tell when you have something up your sleeve." She flips her hair over her shoulder.

"You won't believe it. I can't believe it," I say, stumbling over my words. "Ace came to see me," I told her way back about us spending the night in the motel when he broke the news he was getting married.

"No way," she says, wiping the last few crumbs of Fritos from her mouth, "after all this time. You were so mad at him."

"I never thought I'd see him again, that's for sure," I say. "He got divorced."

"I told you he loved you," says Sandy. "Remember? I knew it. I just knew it."

"You really think so?" I ask. "You're such a friggin' softy, Sandy."

"I do think so. And why not? Nobody ever loved me like that," she says. She touches up her red lipstick like she has a date for the movies. Her Aunt Marsha sends it to her. They don't have good colors like that at the canteen. Some inmates grind up M&Ms and spread it on their lips for a little color. I still don't care about makeup. A new male C.O., about 6'2" with a strong muscular body, head shaved like Mr. Clean, strides toward us.

"Ladies, and I use the term loosely, get your asses in gear. Free time is up." I raise my arms as if to shield myself.

"Okay, okay."

The keys hanging from his belt clank as he moves us along like cattle. Sandy whispers in my ear.

"Check out the muscles. Never saw him before."

"Yeah, I'm new to this section," he says. "I have supersonic hearing. Keep moving!"

He walks us to Sandy's cell. She waves as he opens the door.

"Home sweet home," she says, "see you at dinner, girlfriend." The C.O. eyes me as we walk further down the hall.

"Never seen hair that color red before."

"It's not out of a bottle," I say, setting him straight. My neck tightens, walking next to him, like his beefy hands are all over me. He licks his lips and looks me up and down.

"Are you Irish?" he asks in the deep voice of a giant.

"Could be."

"Hope you're not here cuz you snuffed your mother or sister." He adds a nasty laugh trying to show me who's boss, as if I don't know.

"Nice. See you around the slammer." The door clangs shut behind me. It still makes me cringe every single day. Della sits up on her bunk and sets aside her magazine.

"Is that a new C.O.?"

"Yeah, like a creepy Mr. Clean."

"Anything is better than that dump truck they just switched out."

CHAPTER 47

WORD GOT OUT LATE LAST YEAR THAT I DRAW. YOU BETTER believe it's not easy getting ahold of paper in this rathole. I drew a picture of Della, my first cellie, sitting on her bunk. She liked what she saw and showed it to some other people. I started getting some respect around here. Edith, the nice guard, slips me some blank paper every couple of days.

She would always ask to see my latest. I drew one of my two Pinewood Babes and put them in jeans, boots, and sweaters like we used to wear back home. Sandy's thick long hair draped over her blue sweater, her arm wrapped around Sue's shoulder. Both smiling like they were visiting a friend's house. Nothing said "prison" in that picture. I never figured they'd fight over it, and never in my life have I seen these two act this way. That's what prison can do to anybody, even sweet Sue or my best friend, Sandy. I made a second drawing and put Sandy in a purple sweater this time. Now they're both happy.

"You wanna do one of me?" asks Edith. She was looking at my latest one of Big Martha, who now likes me a little, and ordered me to draw one.

"Happy to do it," I say.

Edith nods her head and gives me a king-sized smile. "Can you pretty me up?" she asks while smoothing down her hair.

"Sure, I will," I say, "if that's what you want." I study her real hard whenever I see her. It's not like we're pals and have someplace we can sit together. I manage to get ahold of some more colored pencils for this one. I glam her up a little bit. I hand it to her when she comes around for lights out a couple weeks later, feeling shaky about the whole thing. If she doesn't like it, would she turn against me? I'm too nervous to ask what she thinks.

Five whole days pass before she says a single word.

"I love it. My guy Billy loved the picture, too," she says. "He looked at it and looked at it some more. He said we've got to get a nice little frame for it and put it on the wall."

Hearing they loved it made my day, like something good happened in the slammer.

Some weeks later, I lose track of time, I hear that Warden Gerald Stott III wants to see me, which scares the living bejesus out of me. I breathe easier when it's Edith that takes me to his office. We're kind of pals by this time. I don't ask her if she knows why Warden Stott wants to see me. No ma'am! I remember the game *Who Is Who*: Me/prisoner, Edith/guard.

"Have a seat," says Warden Stott with a gruff yet sharp voice. It's a plain room with a big paper calendar from a tire company featured on the wall: *June 1979*. Books and bulging notebooks fill the brown metal bookshelves. His big old wooden desk has stacks of paper, with even more papers packed in open cartons on the concrete floor. Warden Scott never stands up. From behind that desk of his, you can't miss his big broad shoulders, pink face, and Marine buzz cut. A roll of fat circles around his neck and under his chin. His collar might choke him any minute. Come to think of it, just like that guard the first day, he looks like a hog ready to be sent to market. I keep the smile off my face. Edith stands by the door.

"I don't have much time," he says, "this is a busy place, as you know." He clasps his sausage fingers in front of him. "And I'm a very busy man." I show my respect for his busy job by keeping my trap shut. Oh no, am I in trouble now?

"It's rare that I call someone in here for a good reason," he continues. He looks down at his hands and doesn't say a word for a minute.

I'm on pins and needles. *What the hell is this about?*

"I hear that you have been drawing pictures of your fellow inmates," he says. I can't read his voice or the look on his face. My stomach does a loop-de-loop. He looks me square in the eye.

"Is that true Angel, that you've been drawing pictures of the inmates and handing them out?" *Holy God, is this a problem?*

"Um, yessir. I have." My voice sounds squeezed up, not like my own voice at all.

"I hear you're quite good at it," he says. His voice has warmed up a little bit. He even bares his teeth in some kind of smile, his eyes as cold and deadly as a rattlesnake.

"I also hear you have been a model prisoner since you've been here," he says. My shoulders drop and relax a bit. "Do you have anything to say for yourself?" He waits. I squirm. Why doesn't somebody dust that desk of his?

"Thank you, sir. I try to be as good a prisoner as possible." Is this really happening? What is going on?

"I see in your file that you have never been called out for any infraction." Another tight little hog smile. "That is good news," he says. I'm glued to my seat.

"You're here in my office because I want you to teach art to other model prisoners." His fat hands play with a pen, clicking the damn thing on and off, in and out. My nerves are jumping. What did he say? He wants me to teach art to other model prisoners. *He's offering me a job.* My first ever job besides waitressing, and it's a real job teaching art.

"What do you think of that?" says the Warden. I sit numb with disbelief.

"Angel? Don't you have anything to say?" His tone is snappy. Near the door, Edith waves her hand at me as if to say *speak*.

"Sir," I take a big gulp, "I am very grateful. I would love to teach art."

"Alright then. You can start next week. Every Wednesday afternoon from 1–2:30," he says. His voice toughens up again. "We don't have the budget for many supplies, but we will have something for you. Maybe five or six in the class. Not more." He levels his gaze, waiting for me to say something else.

"Thank you, sir. I will do my very best."

"Okay," he says, standing up at around six foot three. "Don't fuck it up, Angel. You can go now."

Edith comes toward me with a prison guard attitude. Once the door closes behind us, she has a nice smile on her face. It lasts the entire time we make our way down the long noisy hall together. Did she already know? It doesn't matter.

She walks me back to my cell and locks me in.

CHAPTER 48

ACE COMES TO VISIT EVERY OTHER WEEK. HE WANTS TO prove to me that he will wait for me. He reminds me that I never have to set foot in Pinewood again.

We sit looking at each other through the protective glass. How I want to touch him, just hold his hand is all I ask. But no contact is allowed. I ache for him. I know I can rely on him to show up and stay in my life. This means the world to me.

Don't laugh, but Big Martha joined my art class. She has toned down her act since I first met her. You wouldn't think such a roughneck would have any talent at all for art, but she does. It's fun teaching. I never thought of myself as good enough or smart enough to be a teacher. But here I am. People sit at attention and listen to what I have to say. When I wake up in the mornings, I no longer dread the long boring day ahead of me. I think about what I want to teach that week. I think about who is listening and who wants to learn. I also think about the ones who push the pencil around and only take the class to kill time.

Sue still works in the library. Not a chance they could ever find someone better than Sue. How many people in this place went to college and majored in English? She might be the only one. They're lucky to have her. And she likes recommending books that this group of cons would never dream of reading. You can bet that includes me. She turned Big Martha on to *Jane Eyre*. It's hard to imagine, but Sue said B.M. loved that book. Sandy has been stuck working in the kitchen washing dishes all this time. I'm not sure why, but she got the rawest deal of the three of us. And then she got into a nasty fight with Millie Bones.

We call her that because she's so skinny and mean. Everyone stays clear of her. Sandy stepped on her foot by mistake in the canteen one day. Millie waited until she thought no one was looking and popped Sandy in her jaw. Sandy went berserk and fought back. The two of them were tangled on the floor, and some of the animals cheered them on. I couldn't believe my eyes. They were throwing punches, ripping at each other's clothes. Bones was pulling Sandy's hair. When the CO pulled them apart, they wrote Sandy up and sent her to solitary. She lost ground with all her good behavior. She might have been done washing dishes by now if it wasn't for that tussle with Bones.

"The guards are treating me worse than ever," she says. I wish I could make it better.

After six months, word gets to me that I'm doing a good job with my class. Warden Stott calls me to his office again. I know I haven't done anything wrong but, still, my hands are clammy. What could it be he's calling me in for?

Like before, Edith walks me down, looking straight ahead, doing her job. When we reach the Warden's office, same as last time, Edith stands guarding the door. Warden Stott sits like a massive mountain of flesh behind that same desk and flaps his hand, a silent order for me to sit.

"So here we are again, Angel. Six months later."

"Yessir," I say.

"You're probably wondering why I called you in." His rattlesnake eyes search my face.

"Well, ye-yes, s-sir, I am."

"I won't waste any time since I am a very busy man."

I sit as quiet as can be. I can hear Edith's little breathing snorts across the room.

"Jesus Christ, Edith, what the fuck is that noise?" he says. "Get yourself some sinus medicine."

Edith blushes. First time I ever saw her look embarrassed. She pulls out a tissue from her pants pocket and blows her nose.

"As I was saying, Angel, you are doing a good job. Your record is clean as a whistle." He pulls out a wooden toothpick from his pocket and jabs at his teeth. "I'm here to tell you that in six months, you will be leaving this place."

"What?" I say. I can't believe my ears. Leaving? They're letting me go early for good behavior? I thought I'd be here seven years at least. I'm going home six months early.

"I know you'll be sad to leave," he says. He claps his hands together and laughs so loud I think he's going to bust a gut. "Just a little joke," he says.

"Yes, that's a good one, sir," I say. "I do like teaching art. But I sure am happy about this amazing news. Thank you, sir."

"You can go back to your cell now." His eyes brighten for a minute. "Okay, Edith, take her back."

He smacks his hand on his desk and stands up to watch Edith walk me out. I wonder what will happen with Sue and Sandy. Will they get out of here early, too? Sandy's fight with Millie Bones won't help her case. No surprise that Sue has been a model prisoner this entire time.

Time always moves slow in a prison. I pour myself into the art classes, planning, thinking. I bury myself in art books so I can keep on learning. Ace won't come for another week, so I'll bite the bullet and wait until then to tell him I'm free in six months.

He started sending me art books once I started teaching classes—beautiful books on Michelangelo, Degas, Picasso. He said they opened a huge bookstore in Geiger Springs. His handsome face was alive with excitement when he told me.

"It's always crowded," he said. "People from Denver and all over Colorado come to see what it's all about. You would never think a big bookstore would cut it in a small town like Geiger Springs, but they're doing well."

CHAPTER 49

WHEN ACE COMES TO VISIT, WITHIN MINUTES I BLURT OUT the good news of my early release. He throws his head back, laughs, and circles his arms as if he is hugging me.

"*That is fantastic*," he says, almost gurgling with joy. Then he goes quiet for a few minutes. I wonder why because we have so little time on these visits. Then he looks up with a big smile across his handsome face.

"Angel, I have some good news, too," he says. If there's anything I like to hear any day of the week, it's good news. Light shines from his turquoise eyes.

"Please, tell me."

"I promised you," he says, "that you would never have to live in Pinewood again, remember?"

"You did," I said. "It would be the worst if I had to face all those folks again. I would love to see Faye Vespers. I owe her so much. I'll figure out a way. But I never want to go back to Pinewood." Doom and gloom sit on my shoulders whenever I think about the stifling smallness of the town, the same old conversations all the time, and the never-ending gossip. No doubt about it, I would be the choice piece of chatter if I ever stepped foot in that town again.

"Here goes," says Ace, snapping me out of my dark thoughts. "I heard about a Harley-Davidson dealership in Lawndale, California."

My fingers twitch with excitement. I wonder what he'll say.

"Make a wild guess who is the new owner?" He goes pink with joy. I want to cry with happiness for him.

"No way, Ace! Are you the new owner?"

"You got that right," he beams. "I've been wanting this my whole life. Never could have done it without inheriting money from my folks. But still, it's a dream come true. And remember Gus?"

"Yeah, I remember Gus." I mainly remember he was my mama's boyfriend for a short while, and he dumped her.

"So, Gus is my partner," he says. "We took ownership a few weeks ago."

"Why didn't you tell me until now?" I ask. I want to be a part of everything he does.

"I wanted to make sure it was a done deal." He can read me like nobody else. "That's why I waited to tell you. And that's what it is, a done deal."

He looks proud like I've never seen before. I wish I could jump through the glass and hug him. And then my stomach squeezes up.

"Wait a minute. Does this mean you're moving to California?" The smile stays planted on his face.

"I *am* moving to California, Angel . . . *but not without you*. You always told me you wanted to escape. So, this is your big chance to break out of Pinewood, Colorado forever."

"*What? Is this for real?*"

"Yes, darlin', this is for real. Gus is moving there in a month. He'll manage the business until we can make the move. And now with your good news it will be sooner than I thought."

I slap my hand over my mouth. Is this really happening? Moving to California with Ace. This is beyond my wildest dreams.

"Holy hell, Ace, are you my Prince Charming on a motorcycle?" I ask. "This might be the happiest day of my life—even sitting here behind glass and locked up, for sure, the happiest day." The bell rings to end our visit. Ace stands up and throws a kiss.

"Angel, I promise you, there are going to be much happier days than today." He runs his hand through his hair and throws me a kiss. Edith nods at me and walks me back to my cell.

I'm afraid to tell Sandy and Sue they're letting me go early. What if they're stuck in here longer than me? That's not right. We were in it together. We should all get out at the same time. I've run these thoughts over and over in my mind. Now that I can leave, I hope they can, too. I'm losing sleep, losing weight, beating myself up. All of it has been my fault.

Sue pulls me aside in the canteen a few days after my visit with the Warden.

"Hey, Angel," she says. "Let's sit in the corner and eat this delightful lunch." Today we carry our trays to the farthest point in the canteen and sit across from each other, the walls the same vomit-green as most of the place. Prison has taken its toll on her. Even though she works in the library, her sweet soft self has had a hard time with the roughnecks, bad language, crappy food, and constant sex propositions. I doubt she ever said yes. And I don't care if she did. But it's tough fighting off some of these sex-crazed inmates.

"What's going on?" I ask. She wears her light-brown hair in a ponytail these days. She pulls at the rubber band before she speaks.

"Did you want to tell me something?" I lean towards her. She scans the room to make sure no one is looking our way. She lowers her voice to a whisper.

"I don't know where to start," she says.

"Go ahead, just tell me." I notice dirt under her fingernails. That's not like her. Must be from shuffling books around every day.

"Okay, Angel. I'll just tell you, nobody else just you." She scans the room.

"C'mon now," I say, "spit it out." She breaks into a wide grin as she flushes with joy.

"They're letting me go," she bubbles. "I'm getting out in seven months!" Big drops of relief roll down her cheeks. She wipes them off right away. We all learned early on, crying in prison is not cool.

"Sue, that is crazy good," I say. "I'm so happy for you." I take a deep breath and keep quiet for a few minutes, not to rain on her parade. We eat our tacos. You never get used to the lousy food. I wipe my mouth with the flimsy paper napkin and place my hand on her arm. I pull it away fast before anyone can see—anyone who might give us a hard time.

"Sue, I'm getting out, too! I think teaching the art class did it!" Our eyes hug each other. "I hope to God Sandy is getting out with us," I say, putting my hands together.

'I hope so," says Sue, "but I'm worried. You know, the brawl . . . it doesn't look good."

"That has me worried, too," I say, "big time worried."

In the canteen that night for dinner, I search Sandy's face. Her eyes don't hold any good news to share. How can I tell her? How can Sue? We got in this mess together. The three of us should leave at the same time. My stomach clenches with guilt. I got my two good friends into this mess in the first place. I'll have to tell Sandy on another day when something has gone right for her. No matter what, she may go into a tailspin. The three of us were all sentenced to seven years. I hope, like crazy, she gets out before then.

It takes a month before I can screw up my courage to tell Sandy. Sue hasn't said a word about her early release either. We're in the exercise yard as Sandy huffs and puffs after a short run. She leans over, hands on her thighs, breathing hard.

"I'm happy for you." Her tone's flat, mouth screwed up tight. I don't blame her. She'll still be stuck in this hellhole after me and Sue have high-tailed it out of here.

"I'm sorry, Sandy," I say. "I feel rotten that you're not getting out early." She steps away from me and yells over her shoulder.

"Seriously, Angel? Knock it off," she says. "I'll survive." It kills me that she's been stuck working in that cruddy old kitchen all these years. Sandy has had more than her share of bad breaks. She spits on the ground and keeps marching forward without saying another word, without looking back at me, her movements rough and angry. What has become of the Pinewood Babes?

Whenever I see Sandy after that, she stops dead in her tracks and walks in the other direction. My best friend has turned against me. I'm getting out and she's not. It's as simple as that. We've been there for each other since we were young girls. And now I'm leaving her behind. Who will she have in this place to help her through? She's okay with Sue leaving. They still talk, but not with me. Why isn't anything ever easy?

Mama's words ring in my ears. *You got into this mess, you'll have to get yourself out.*

Hey Mama, I want to say: *I teach art!* You always said it was a waste of time. Now it's my ticket out of here. But I'll never get to tell her since she's dead and gone. Faye Vespers sent me a short letter six months ago. She said that Mama fell off a barstool at Paddy's Saloon, hit the ground, and never came out of it. She died with a belly full of whiskey, feeling no pain. Funny, but I don't think about her much. Don't miss her. She was always so hard on me. No hugs that I can ever remember. No kisses. Faye wrote that she has no idea where Pops lives now. How can I forget he turned his back on me as soon as I landed in this stinking place? I can only imagine what kind of life he's living with Rhonda, that trampy wife of his.

When I think about the charge I used to get from shoplifting as a kid, it seems a lifetime ago. So much has happened since then. And, of course, the major life-changing heist that landed me in the Federal Pen. Let's just say that locked up in prison has cured me of itchy fingers.

I will make it right for Sandy. Once I'm out of here, I'll write to her all the time. Once *she's* out, I'll help her get her life on track, whatever it takes. I know Ace would be crazy about her. That's if she hasn't changed too much for the worse. I wonder how much I've changed. This place can really take it out of you.

CHAPTER 50

1979

ACE SENT ME SOME CLOTHES TO WEAR ON MY LAST DAY, MY exit from the pen. I have brand new everything: blue jeans, a powder-blue shirt, a black belt, and matching boots. Everything fits like I bought it all myself.

Word spread like wildfire in the Rockies that today is my last day, so all the other inmates know I'm leaving. People I've seen every day for years watch from their cells as I make my way down the hallways through Smollett Women's Correctional Facility for the very last time.

"Whoop, whoop!" say some of my best friends, like Della and inmates that took my art classes. Not everyone is happy for me, especially the long haulers and the lifers. That's how it goes in prison. In the distance, I hear two women in a screaming match that goes on for a few minutes. One last reminder of the brutal life I've been living.

The warden chose Edith, my favorite C.O., to walk me out. We walk side by side, almost like friends, but not quite.

"You know," she says, cracking a half smile. "I still love that picture you drew of me, Angel."

"Thanks for telling me." My voice a notch above a whisper. "That makes me happy."

Sue and Sandy stand side by side as I pass by them. Sue nods as if to say, see you soon on the outside. Sandy gives me a tiny sad wave goodbye. I want to rush over and hug her. I motion to her that I'm writing a letter. And I will. I love that Sandy of mine. I want her to know she's not alone.

"I know we'll never see you here again," says Edith. "You're not like most of 'em that come through here." Even though my stomach flip-flops, I squeeze out a small laugh.

"Well, I'm not planning on it," I say. We walk in silence until we reach the front door. My first chance to see the outside world in six and a half years.

Edith slaps her hands together and shoots her index finger at me. "Have a good life, Angel." She makes a quick about-face and goes back to work.

They escort me out the door of Smollett Pen to Ace as he wrings his hands, waiting for me. It's been fourteen years since we first met—me a sixteen-year-old girl, swept away by this hunk of a man. He has lived by his word since he first came to see me four years ago, standing by me like no man in my life has ever done. He bought me art books. Who would have ever guessed Ace, the motorcycle man, would become interested in art, something we could share? He loved me no matter how low I sank and loved me right through the rest of my time in prison.

Even though he's older than me, I would say we've grown up together.

Ace opens his arms to welcome me in. He squeezes me tight like he never wants to let me go. The mid-day September sun softens as a refreshing breeze sets the aspen leaves to shimmer and sway in a dance of celebration. The sky is clear and full of promise.

Ace and I hold on to each other for a long time.

Unembarrassed and unashamed, tears roll down his cheeks.

He brushes my wild hair off my face and kisses the top of my head. With all he's been through, he looks fantastic with his sun-streaked hair and those piercing turquoise eyes. Ace grabbed my heart on a summer night in Pinewood Park all those years ago. I never stopped loving him. He has proven himself by showing up for me, keeping his word, and planning our future. Without a doubt, I know I can trust him now.

"Look at you, Angel." He stands back and holds onto my hands. "I've been dreaming about this for a long time."

"No kidding," I say. "Me too!" We choke with laughter, just like old times, and we hug again. When he gently kisses me on my lips, I sink into him.

"More of that later," he says. "Let's blow this popsicle stand." He walks me over to a sparkling red Chevy pickup truck. Holy moly, what a beauty. I touch the hood with care like I would an expensive piece of art.

"Is this yours, Ace?"

"Yep. I bought it special for your homecoming." His grin so wide it could reach from Geiger Springs to Denver. "No motorcycle for my Angel," says Ace, "not today. I want you to ride out of here in style and into your new life with me."

Happy tears flood my face.

"It's okay, baby," he says, his voice so gentle and kind. "Let it go. You've had a very tough time. You're safe now."

I pull myself together and can't get enough of the endless blue sky, sweet breeze, and puffy white clouds.

I'm leaving this place forever. The tough part is leaving Sandy. I'll miss her and Della and other friends. We've been in the trenches together. It reminds me of stories I've heard from soldiers once they're home from the Vietnam War, that a special bond forms, a bond that folks on the outside can never understand. It will take time to adjust to my freedom, eat whatever I want, move without being told, and make my own decisions.

"I can't believe this is happening," I say, picking up a shiny penny on the ground and slipping it into my pocket.

"That penny is a good luck sign," says Ace, "but there are signs everywhere. Look at this beautiful day."

The world looks so high and wide and big; it's like I'm seeing it for the first time in my life. A baby chick newly hatched from an egg.

He opens the door for me and guides me into the passenger seat. The scent of the new upholstery is as fresh as a pasture after spring rain. Ace circles around the front of the truck with a reassuring wink through the windshield. He slides behind the wheel, leans over, and kisses me on the cheek.

"Don't want to throw too much at you," he says, "but I think this'll make you happy."

"What is it?" I ask. He hands me a pale blue envelope. I turn it around in my hands.

"Go ahead, darlin', open it."

Once I rip it open, my jaw drops. I have no words. Plane tickets to Hawaii.

"We'll be going in six months or so," he says, a smile lighting up his face. "I'm taking you for a two-week vacation. First, you need some time to adjust to your new life." His voice, his face, so tender, it brings me to tears once again.

Ace starts up the car, sweeps his hand at Smollett Women's Federal Penitentiary as if to wipe it away. He shifts into drive.

"C'mon, Baby," he says, "let's go home."

ACKNOWLEDGMENTS

First, I'd like to thank the witty and talented Tom Toro for planting the seed of this story with his hilarious *New Yorker* cartoon, "And to Think We Started as A Book Group" (July 11, 2016). I am also indebted to the town of Redstone, Colorado, for inspiring the setting.

Many thanks to my warm and wonderful writing group. For Martha Fuller's guidance and critiques—and the valuable feedback from core participants: Susan Brown, Charlotte Lubert, Jackie Nach, Meg Watt, and Alina Zetu, with special thanks to Linda Shaffer for her ongoing encouragement from day one.

Much appreciation to everyone who has heard bits and pieces over time and cheered me on. I'm forever grateful for the discerning eagle eyes of Suzanne Weerts and my editor Martha Fuller. Many thanks to Wendy Hammers and Sheldon Herman for their unwavering support. And a special nod to Jack Grapes for his commitment to deepening the writer's voice.

LINDA K. GOLDMAN

A native born Angeleno, Linda always loves a good story. In her 20s, she was more interested in new adventures than going to college. Instead she moved to New York, then to London. In her 40s, she graduated from UCLA with a B.A. in Sociocultural Anthropology. In 2020, Common Forces Press published her poem, "On Blix Street" in the anthology, *Side-Eye on the Apocalypse*. In 2021, Bambaz Press published her short story, "Moving Mom" in the journal *On the Bus*. In 2023, her short story, "When you Gotta Go" appeared in the anthology, *Rings of Kindness* published by Matthew J. Goldberg. She currently lives in West Los Angeles with her two pugs Ollie and Abby. *Breaking Out of Pinewood* is her first novel.

This book is typeset in Niveau Grotesk designed by Hannes von Döhren of HVD Fonts. Influenced by classic 19th century faces and based on geometric forms, it is a minimalist yet legible sans serif typeface.
Display fonts include Modesto and Cracked.

Printed in the USA
CPSIA information can be obtained
at www.ICGtesting.com
CBHW051649140824
13126CB00056B/1366